IF HE'S TEMPTED

Brant set down his brandy glass, clasped Olympia's hand tightly, and pulled her toward him. He laughed softly when she stumbled somewhat gracelessly into his lap. This was what he needed. Passion eased pain, more so than any drink he had ever imbibed. Olympia stirred his passion in such a way it cleared his head of every thought save ones of her. He wanted that now, wanted his body and mind consumed by her and all that she made him feel.

"I believe we are behaving unwisely again," Olympia said but curled her arms around his neck instead of scrambling out of his reach as a little voice in her mind told her she ought to.

"Are you about to become the wise one and flee the room?"

"I think not."

His kiss quickly cleared her mind of all thought save for how he tasted, how he made her body burn. Olympia knew she would not be pushing him aside this time. . . .

Books by Hannah Howell

THE MURRAYS

Highland Destiny
Highland Honor
Highland Promise
Highland Vow
Highland Knight
Highland Bride
Highland Angel
Highland Groom
Highland Warrior
Highland Conqueror
Highland Champion
Highland Lover
Highland Barbarian
Highland Savage
Highland Wolf
Highland Sinner
Highland Protector
Highland Avenger

THE WHERLOCKES

If He's Wicked
If He's Sinful
If He's Wild
If He's Dangerous
If He's Tempted

VAMPIRE ROMANCE

Highland Vampire
The Eternal Highlander
My Immortal Highlander
Highland Thirst
Nature of the Beast
Yours for Eternity
Highland Hunger
Born to Bite

STAND-ALONE NOVELS

Only for You
My Valiant Knight
Unconquered
Wild Roses
A Taste of Fire
A Stockingful of Joy
Highland Hearts
Reckless
Conqueror's Kiss
Beauty and the Beast
Highland Wedding

Silver Flame
Highland Fire
Highland Captive
My Lady Captor
Wild Conquest
Kentucky Bride
Compromised Hearts
Stolen Ecstasy
Highland Hero
His Bonnie Bride

Published by Kensington Publishing Corporation

HANNAH HOWELL

IF HE'S TEMPTED

ZEBRA BOOKS
KENSINGTON PUBLISHING CORP.
http://www.kensingtonbooks.com

ZEBRA BOOKS are published by

Kensington Publishing Corp.
119 West 40th Street
New York, NY 10018

All Kensington titles, imprints and distributed lines are available at special quantity discounts for bulk purchases for sales promotion, premiums, fund-raising, educational or institutional use.

Special book excerpts or customized printings can also be created to fit specific needs. For details, write or phone the office of the Kensington Special Sales Manager. Attn.: Special Sales Department. Kensington Publishing Corp., 119 West 40th Street, New York, NY 10018. Phone: 1-800-221-2647.

Zebra and the Z logo Reg. U.S. Pat. & TM Off.

ISBN-13: 978-1-4201-1880-3
ISBN-10: 1-4201-1880-3
First Mass-Market Paperback Printing: April 2013

eISBN-13: 978-1-4201-3098-0
eISBN-10: 1-4201-3098-6
First Electronic Edition: April 2013

10 9 8 7 6 5 4 3 2 1

Printed in the United States of America

Chapter 1

Lady Olympia Wherlocke hated crying women. The younger the woman crying the more she hated it. All her mothering instincts leapt to the fore at the sight and she did not wish to feel motherly. She was too young herself to feel that way toward a young woman who looked almost ready to begin the hunt for a husband, at least in a year or two. The huge gray-blue eyes of the young woman standing on her doorstep were so full of tears, however, that Olympia expected the flood to begin at any moment.

When she noticed the girl stood alone on the doorstep, Olympia had to bite back a curse. The expensive gown the girl wore and her gently refined looks spoke of quality. The cape she wore in a vain attempt to disguise herself would fetch enough in the secondhand market to feed a poor family for a year, perhaps even longer. There should be a maid accompanying the girl, even a burly, armed footman or two.

"I need to speak to Ashton, to Lord Radmoor," said the girl.

"He is not here," replied Olympia, glancing up and down the dusk-shadowed street and seeing that this small confrontation was beginning to attract far too much attention. Her family might be slowly buying up all the houses on the street but there were still a good number of strangers living near at hand. People who had no blood loyalty to her or her family would not hesitate to gossip about them.

"Come inside," Olympia demanded even as she grabbed the girl by one slim arm and yanked her into the house. "You do not truly wish to discuss whatever troubles you have out here on the street," she said as she led her uninvited guest into the drawing room.

"Oh, no, of course not," the girl whispered as she hastily sat down in the chair Olympia waved her toward. "Word of our conversation might somehow make its way to Mother's ears."

That the girl was concerned about such a thing did not bode well, Olympia thought. It implied that this young lady might be seeking to drag someone into the midst of a battle between her and her mother. Olympia busicd herself serving her guest tea, briefly regretting the fact that the tea and cakes she had planned to quietly enjoy would now have to be shared. As would the sweetness of some time all alone with her own thoughts and no sign of trouble on the horizon.

"Might you tell me exactly who you are?" she

asked the girl and watched her pale cheeks redden with obvious embarrassment.

"I am Lady Agatha Mallam, sister to Brant Mallam, Earl of Fieldgate," she replied.

It was not easy, but Olympia fought down the urge to snatch back the cup of tea she had served the girl and throw her back out onto the street. It was not because Lord Fieldgate had made himself increasingly notorious over the last few years, either, for her own family had its share of rogues and debauchees. It was because this young lady's mother was a woman Olympia would prefer to avoid at all costs. Brant might well be notorious for his drinking, gambling, and wenching, but his mother was known throughout society for the cold power she wielded without mercy. The shine of perfect manners, style, grace, and excellent bloodlines could never again hide the rotted heart of Lady Letitia Mallam from Olympia, or from the others in her family who knew how the woman had sold an innocent young woman to a brothel to keep her son from marrying the girl. That cruel act had led to the girl's death and, Olympia strongly suspected, Brant Mallam's slow sinking into the murky waters of debauchery.

Olympia nodded in response to the girl's introduction of herself and responded in kind. "I am Lady Olympia Wherlocke, the Baroness of Myrtledowns."

"I know. We have never met, but I have had you pointed out to me. Do you know when Ashton will return?"

"I believe he intends to bring everyone back to the city in the fall, once my niece recovers from delivering their child. The city is not a good place for small children at this time of year."

And now the girl's bottom lip was trembling, Olympia noticed with alarm. She hastily pushed the plate of cakes and biscuits closer to the girl. She was not certain that tea was the wondrous panacea so many claimed it to be, but she hoped crying would prove to be impossible while drinking it, or while eating some cake.

"That will be too late to save me."

The girl looked as if all her hopes had just been thoroughly ground into the mud. Olympia fought down the urge to hug young Agatha, pat her on the back, and tell her that all would be well. Such assurances were not hers to give, especially since she had no idea exactly what was troubling Brant's sister.

And just why did she constantly think of the man as Brant, Olympia wondered. She doubted she had spent more than a few hours in the man's company over the past few years. He should be referred to as my lord, or Fieldgate, or even Lord Fieldgate to her, not just Brant as if they were lifelong friends or close kin. It was odd that she could also see him so clearly in her mind. Even odder, she grew a little warm at the mere thought of his dark, gray eyes and fine physique. That truly puzzled her for, although she did enjoy looking at handsome gentlemen, she had never experienced one tiny flicker of warmth when doing so.

"Too late for what?" she asked, and silently cursed herself for her inability to ignore the girl's distress and send her right home.

"To stop my marriage."

"Marriage? You do not look as if you are old enough to even step out into society yet."

"I am newly turned sixteen, but Mama has decided that it is time I wed. At this very moment, she is in negotiations with a man who very much wishes to marry me." Agatha took a deep, unsteady breath in an obvious, yet not fully successful, attempt to calm herself. "She is negotiating with Lord Sir Horace Minden, the Baron of Minden Grange."

Olympia nearly dropped the cup of tea she had been raising to her lips. She had little to do with society, finding it all tedious and often cruel and mingling with it only if she needed to find out something, but even she recognized that name. The man was notorious and not simply because he was an aging libertine. There were too many titled gentlemen who could be counted amongst the ranks of the dissolute, the Earl of Fieldgate included. What made Minden stand head and shoulders above all the other rogues and lecherous dogs in the aristocracy was that the man was rumored to indulge in sins even the most hardened rake stepped away from. It was also rumored that his other three wives had not died from illness or accident as had been claimed, but nothing could be proven. No one had ever met his children from what little she had heard though it was recorded that he had eight living offspring.

"Are you quite certain of that?" she asked the girl.

"I heard them talking," replied Agatha. "Mama wants a lot of money for me. The baron has not yet stepped away from the table for, as I heard Mama say, he is very eager to have a young, virginal wife." Agatha blinked furiously in a vain attempt to keep back her tears. "I know it is my place to marry as my family wishes me to but I had thought I would have at least one season in which to meet a few worthy gentlemen. I did not even worry overmuch that the man chosen for me might be older than me. That is a common enough situation. But, I cannot bear the thought of being married to Minden. Even I have heard whispers of what sort of man he is, what he does in the stews, and the tales turn my stomach."

"As they should," Olympia murmured and sipped at her tea, idly wondering who was cruel enough or coarse enough to tell a young innocent such tales. "What did you think Ashton could do to help? He is not of your family."

"He would be able to find Brant and tell him of my concerns. I have tried to reach my brother as he is the head of the household but he has proven to be impossible to reach. None of the letters I have sent him have been answered. I cannot even be certain they were actually taken to him although I did my best to try to keep my letters to him from being intercepted. 'Tis just so difficult to know who I can trust at home. The servants are all terrified of Mama."

"Is there no one else in your family whom you can turn to?"

"My two elder sisters are wed and I do not believe they would heed my pleas for help. They are much older than I and have been married for quite a while now. Papa arranged their marriages and I believe both men were chosen more for what Papa could gain from them than any thought of what might suit Mary or Alice, or what might make them happy. I recall a fierce argument between Papa and Brant for the whole business was settled and done whilst Brant was away from home. My brother was not even sent an invite to the weddings. I think Papa knew Brant would not like it.

"My other siblings are younger than I and Brant saw to it that they were sent away to school." Agatha frowned. "I am not certain what happened, but Mama had no more children after Brant for almost seventeen years, and then she had me, Jasper, and Emery."

Olympia could all too easily guess what had occurred. A man too short of funds to afford the mistresses and courtesans he had enjoyed the company of for years suddenly decides to make use of his long-neglected wife. For a moment, Olympia could almost feel sorry for Lady Letitia, thinking how the behavior of her husband could have caused all her bitterness, but then shook the sympathy aside. Lady Letitia's actions concerning Brant, the ones that had caused him to turn his back on the woman, were too dark and evil to be explained away by the neglect of a husband. There had to have been a darkness already seeded deep in the woman's soul.

"Do you know how to reach Ashton or Brant, m'lady?" Agatha asked, cutting into Olympia's thoughts.

"As I said, Ashton awaits the birth of another child so I do not believe you will find much help there, no matter how sincerely he may wish to offer it. He will not wish to leave his wife. Nor does he truly have the power to help you since he is not a member of your family, not even a distant cousin."

"He could shoot Minden," muttered Agatha.

"There is that but I believe Penelope would prefer it if her husband was not hanged or exiled." Olympia bit back a smile when Agatha grimaced. "I could attempt to reach your brother."

Even as she said the words, Olympia wished she could take them back. She had but recently been caught up in her brother Argus's troubles and, before that, those of her niece Penelope, and their cousins Chloe and Alethea. This trouble was not one that affected her family at all. Yet, she knew she would march right into the midst of it. What woman would not wish to help a young innocent girl avoid a forced marriage to a man with as black a reputation as Minden had?

"Would you do that for me?" Agatha asked, clasping her hands together and pressing them against her breasts.

"I will try. That is all I will promise. Now, finish your tea and I will see that you are safely returned home."

"And discreetly, if you please." Agatha blushed. "Mama cannot know that I sought out someone to help me for she will do all she can to stop it. I do not think she will allow anything to stop her plans. I have to move about with the utmost secrecy."

"Trust me in this, m'lady. One thing my family excels in is secrecy." Olympia frowned as it began to sound as if more than an unwanted marriage was entailed here. "Since your brother is the head of the household, however, I do not see how your mother could believe that she could marry you off without him knowing all about it. She would, at the very least, need your brother to sign a few papers before she hands you off to Minden."

"She intends to forge his signature. She has done so many a time. I think she has also convinced some men in power that she must be the one who rules over me because of what my brother has become."

For the next half hour, Olympia gently drew out all the information Agatha had concerning her mother's tricks and schemes. Agatha had learned the art of eavesdropping well and had a lot to tell, even if the girl did not appear to fully understand all she had heard. Brant's sister held no firm proof of anything, was even uncertain about her suspicions at times, but everything she told Olympia was more than enough to reaffirm Olympia's personal opinion that Lady Letitia Mallam was long overdue for a hanging. It would not surprise Olympia in the least to discover that Lady Letitia was joining up with Minden for far more than marrying off the last of her daughters.

The moment she was certain that young Agatha had no more to tell, Olympia called in her footman Pawl. She gave the girl strict instructions on how to secretly get in touch with her if she needed to and then made sure her footman understood the need for discretion in getting the girl back to her home unseen. When the door shut behind Agatha and Pawl, Olympia slumped in her seat and closed her eyes.

She needed to harden her heart, Olympia mused. She truly could not help everyone who asked. If nothing else, the difficulties her family constantly stumbled into all on their own took up enough of her time and strength. While helping Argus she had actually faced physical danger and the fear that had caused still shadowed her mind, stirring up old and ugly memories. Each incident she had involved herself in over the last three years had held many dangers but none of them had actually touched her personally. Now that one had, she realized she was reluctant to charge to the rescue yet again.

"I have become a coward," she muttered, utterly disgusted with herself.

"Nay, m'lady. Cautious, I hope, but ne'er a coward."

Olympia opened her eyes and smiled faintly at her maid Enid Jones. More of a companion than a maid for Enid had been with her since they had both been small children. She knew Enid spoke the truth as she saw it, could see that in the woman's brown eyes, but Olympia was not sure she believed in that truth herself.

"That young lady needs help and I have just offered myself up as her champion." Olympia said.

"I suspected ye would and that is hardly the act of a coward."

"I am too old for this."

"If that were true, then I must have one foot in the grave, for I am two years older." Enid smiled as she sat down next to Olympia. "Now, what must be done to help that lass?"

"It appears that Lady Agatha's mother, a wretched specimen of humanity and a black stain upon womanhood itself, wishes to sell the girl off to Sir Horace

Minden, Baron of Minden Grange." Olympia was not surprised to see Enid pale.

"The man has to be old enough to be that child's grandfather and he is notorious for the depths and variety of his depravities."

"He most certainly is and I fear it is those depths the girl's mother wishes to dip her claws into."

"Why? Why would any woman wish to stain her hands with the sort of filthy business that man deals in?"

"Money. If dear Mama unites Horace to the family through marriage to Agatha, the woman can then seek to gain new ways to nicely fatten her purse."

"How could any woman give her own flesh and blood to such a man?"

"Did you not catch the name of my visitor, Enid?"

"Nay for it was you who greeted her and let her in."

"Ah, aye, so it was. That young girl your adorable husband Pawl is escorting home is the sister of Brant Mallam, Earl of Fieldgate." She nodded as, after frowning in thought for a moment, Enid's eyes began to widen with horror. "Exactly. The very woman who sold off to a brothel the woman her son loved and wished to marry is the one who now threatens that girl. Although 'tis true we cannot prove the woman ordered poor sweet Faith to be killed, her actions were what put the girl into that hell and thus into a grave. That sweet-faced child who just left is Lady Letitia Mallam's daughter, the poor dear."

"Why did she not go to her brother the earl for help?"

"I do not know if she actually tried to visit the

man, but she claims she has been sending him word about this for a fortnight or so. No reply. Not even a little note thanking her for writing to him. She is certain her brother has not seen any of her messages, that despite how careful she has been, someone is stopping her messages before they reach Lord Fieldgate. I suspect she is right. She has probably been writing to him on a regular schedule and gotten some response over the years. There have been rumors that Fieldgate is skipping down the same path Minden did. Well, years ago. When he was still nimble enough to skip. Minden, that is. Last I saw of Fieldgate, he looked very nimble." Olympia grunted when Enid elbowed her in the side.

"You were rambling," said Enid.

"I know. Men like Minden put me in a mood to ramble. The thought of that young girl being handed over to a man like Minden turns my stomach which also causes my thoughts to wander." Olympia shrugged. "What sane person would ever want to think about such things?"

"Not a one, I am certain," agreed Enid. "Why would the girl think you could do anything about it?"

"She was not looking for me, but for Ashton. She was hoping the earl's childhood friend would know how and where to get word to her brother."

Olympia drummed her fingers against the arm of the settee. She supposed she could send word to Ashton but she was very reluctant to do so. It was better for the family to be away from the city. It was certainly best for Penelope, who had conceived again much too quickly after her birthing her twins as far as Olympia was concerned and needed the quiet, clean air, and good food available in the country. And once the child was born Olympia intended to give her niece a very thorough talk on how to avoid getting with child so frequently. Ashton would hear from her, too, if needed.

"I believe we shall try to keep Ashton out of this mess," she murmured.

"Lord Radmoor might not be pleased with that." Enid moved to collect up the tea things.

"Too bad. Penelope needs to stay in the country and, if Radmoor thought to go to Fieldgate, she would insist upon going, too. Unfortunately, as I think on it, most of my family appears to be out of the city and quite busy at the moment."

Enid shook her head. "I doubt that is so, m'lady. If naught else, your family is simply too large. The chances of them all being gone or out of reach at the same time are very, very small."

"Perhaps, but I cannot think of any near at hand at the moment." Olympia stood up and brushed down her skirts. "I must send a message to Fieldgate. We shall see if he ignores only those from his family or if he is ignoring everyone and everything."

"You are intending to deal with this matter by yourself, aye?"

"Was I not the one who was asked for help?"

"Not really. You just happened to be the one who opened the door." Enid ignored Olympia's scowl as she nudged her way past and headed toward the door. "I think you should at least let Lord Radmoor know that trouble is brewing."

"If I can think of a way to do so without having him come racing to aid his friend, I will."

"Fair enough. I have heard that the Earl of Fieldgate has become quite the libertine. While it may be true that he does not carry the taint such men as Minden do, the earl has reached that point where doors are being closed to him. There are some dark rumors about him beginning to make the rounds. That despite the fact that he is a young, somewhat wealthy bachelor, a few families already begin to protect their daughters from him. S'truth, the more I think on this, the more I think you should hand this trouble over to one of the men."

"Nonsense," snapped Olympia as she followed Enid out of the room. "I plan only to make the earl fully aware of the danger his sister is in."

"And what if the earl does not care?"

Olympia did not wish to think on that. She had heard all about how Brant had been bowed from the weight of his grief when the body of his Faith had been found. Heartbreaking though that scene must have been she had seen good things in Mallam since then, things like tenderness and love, although both had begun to fade as time passed. She could not believe that a man who had suffered such a loss would now turn his back on his sister, would just walk away and allow his mother to destroy yet another member of his family as she had destroyed him.

Destroyed his life, she hastily corrected. Olympia refused to believe the man himself had been destroyed despite all the tales of drink and women. It was not unusual for a man who suffered heartbreak to try to bury the hurt beneath the numbing effects of wine and women. For some strange reason men appeared to think that would help. A battle with his mother over his sister's happiness could even be the medicine the earl needed to pull himself free of the ills of a life of dissipation.

"He will help," Olympia said and hurried to the library where she had left her writing materials. "This could be just what he needs to get himself back to what he was before he discovered just how evil his mother is."

Enid put the tray of tea things down on a table in the hall and hurried after Olympia. "I do not like that look in your eye, missy."

"Missy?" Olympia sat down at the desk and set her writing materials in order even as she thought about what to say in the letter she was about to write. "Where, oh where, is the respect I should command as a baroness?"

"It will return when you rid yourself of the thought of riding to this man's rescue. He is a rogue, a libertine, a man who spends more time in the shadows of brothels and gambling dens than he does in the clean air of the country."

"I believe he is, at this very moment, in the country," Olympia said as she dipped her quill in the inkpot and began to write. "Breathing all that clear, country air."

Olympia peeked at her companion and nearly grinned. Enid had her arms crossed over her chest and a scowl on her pretty round face. That disapproval could have something to do with the condition the earl had been in the last time they had glimpsed him. The man had tried to be all that was gentlemanly, bowing, and then helping her into her carriage outside the Benson home where she had attended a musicale. Unfortunately Fieldgate had been so drunk he had nearly fallen on his face while bowing to her and helping her into her carriage had been more akin to throwing her into her carriage where she had landed with her face in Enid's lap.

Enid's distaste for men who drank too much was fully understandable. The woman had grown up beneath the brutal hand of a father who had too often been drunk. But, at times, Enid could be a little too firm in her stance, a little too unforgiving. Olympia was not sure Fieldgate could be saved from his own follies with drink and women, but there was no harm in at least trying to drag him out of that pit.

"And I suspect he has just taken all the women and drink to a different place to enjoy them," snapped Enid. "He is no longer the sort of man you should be acknowledging."

"He is my nephew's friend. Ashton's oldest, closest friend. Fieldgate is almost family." She held up her hand when Enid opened her mouth to say something. "No. I will contact him. I will be ready to help his sister. Alone if he chooses to turn his back on the girl, or at his side if he decides to do something himself. The important person in all of this is young Agatha, is it not?"

Enid sighed and nodded. "That it is, m'lady. I just do not like the thought of you getting all mixed up with a man who is so fond of the bottle."

"If he is so fond of it that he is no help, or refuses to put the bottle down for a moment to help his sister, then I will look for someone else to help me in some way. But first, we try to find out if he is ignoring all messages or just those of his sister."

"What if he is ignoring all messages?"

"We shall give him a fortnight to reply to the messages I intend to rain o'er his home, and, if he does not answer, I shall write one more and then we shall travel to Fieldgate to read it to him."

Chapter 2

"This is a bachelor's residence and no place for a young lady of quality."

Olympia looked at the tall, thin butler blocking her way into Fieldgate Manor. She did not think she had ever seen a butler appear so stiff and outraged. When one considered Lord Mallam's growing reputation for debauchery, she could understand the man's reluctance to allow in a woman who probably looked far more respectable than most of Brant's companions, but she had no time to cater to such delicate sensibilities.

A fortnight of ignored letters and messengers had passed since she had told young Agatha that she would help her. If Mallam lived in Yorkshire, she might have waited longer for a reply before acting, but Fieldgate was only a half day's ride from London, even less if the journey was made on a fast horse or in a swift carriage. Olympia had fully adhered to her decision of one fortnight of waiting that she had made before sending out the first letter, but she had become more and more anxious as each missive remained unanswered. Agatha did not have the luxury of waiting any longer for her brother to pull himself out of the bottle or whatever woman he was currently entertaining to heed her cries for help.

"This is a family matter, my good man," she said.

"You are not one of his family."

"I come here as a chosen messenger from his sister as she is far too young to travel here herself."

"Then you may tell me her message and I shall deliver it to his lordship."

"I have wasted a fortnight trying to get a message to the man. He is either not getting any message sent here or he is disinclined to reply no matter who sends word."

Something in the way the man's eyes narrowed told Olympia she was facing the reason Brant continued to receive no word of his sister's dilemma. As she calmly closed her parasol, she wondered what inspired this man to betray his lord. Money, most likely, she decided and then hit the man over the head with her parasol. He cursed, stumbled back a few steps clearing the doorway, and Olympia stepped forward to hit him again. The second blow sent the butler to the floor. She winced at the sound of the man's head hitting the marble floor, but could not help but be pleased that he was now unconscious.

"Pawl," she called, certain her footman and Enid were only steps away, and was not surprised when he immediately appeared at her side.

"Aye, m'lady?" He grinned when he got a good look at the felled butler.

"Do not allow that man to come after me."

"Want I should knock him down again if he tries?"

"If you must. I believe he may be long overdue for such punishment for I begin to suspect he is the one who has been working against his lordship's best interests."

"Tsk. What is the world coming to, eh?"

She ignored Pawl's nonsense as she tried to decide where to look for Brant first. She had not realized that Fieldgate was so large. The man could be in one of any of the dozens of rooms in the place. The longer it took her to find him, the more chance there was that there could be more interference from the servants. The butler might not be the only traitor at Fieldgate. She briefly considered standing there and yelling his name. Indelicate but usually quite effective.

"His lordship be in the library, m'lady."

Olympia looked at the boy who spoke to her. He was a bit dirty and thinner than she thought he ought to be, but she saw no guile in his wide blue eyes. Instead, each glance the boy took at the fallen butler was filled with glee and satisfaction. The butler could be guilty of more than just being a traitor to his lordship.

"And you are?" she asked the boy.

"Thomas Pepper, m'lady," he replied. "I be the boot boy." He grimaced. "And sometimes I be the pot boy, sometimes the slops boy, sometimes . . ."

"A lad of all work," Olympia hastily interrupted. "Aye, I understand."

All too well, she thought. It was not just his family that Brant was paying little heed to. There was obviously trouble brewing within his own household. Since she had met him shortly after her niece Penelope had met his friend Ashton, she had noticed his slow descent into drink and debauchery each time she had seen him since, although those meetings had all been short and few, the awkward time when he had helped her into the carriage being the most memorable. She had the feeling the man had reached the point where he now only cared about his drink being close at hand and a woman in his bed. Olympia prayed she would be able to pull him out of that dark hole. The more she thought on young Agatha being forced to marry Minden, the more she needed to save the girl.

"Lead on then, Thomas," Olympia said.

"This way, m'lady."

Following the boy, Olympia decided it could not hurt to gather a little information about his lordship and how matters stood at Fieldgate. "The butler is not completely loyal to Lord Fieldgate, is he?"

"No, m'lady. He gets paid by that old besom to spy on his lordship. Aye, and does it while taking money from his lordship to work for him. You be the one what's been trying to get a message to his lordship?"

"I have been, aye, although his young sister has tried as well. The butler took the messages, did he?"

"Aye, he did. Hope you told no secrets in them. They will be secrets no more."

"I was most careful in all I said."

"Clever."

"I like to think so. I just wish I could be certain his lordship's young sister was as careful because I suspect all that was said was then reported back to the, er, old besom."

"It was. This here is the library," the boy said as he stopped before a pair of high doors. "His lordship be alone but not feeling too sharp, if you know what I mean."

"I know exactly what you mean. I have many a male relative." She exchanged a brief grin with Thomas. "Could you fetch me some very strong tea? Perhaps some food that is filling but will be gentle on the stomach? 'Tis not just the head which is tender after a bout of drinking."

"Yes, m'lady."

The boy hurried away and Olympia faced the doors to the library. They were very impressive doors, thick oak and adorned with carvings of ancient scholars. The Mallams had obviously been very wealthy once upon a time. She knew Brant successfully invested his money along with Ashton but had to wonder how much of that gain he now wasted in drink, whoring, and gambling. Did the man not see that he was rapidly falling into the same trap his forbearers had?

Shaking that thought away, she entered the room. Requesting permission to enter would have been the polite and well-bred thing to do, but she was not feeling particularly polite at the moment. She also had no wish to be refused entrance and be put into the position of yelling through a closed door trying to convince the man to speak to her.

The Earl of Fieldgate was sprawled on a settee, his eyes closed. The lines on his handsome face were clearer and deeper than they had been before, a result of his increasing dissipation. As Olympia moved closer to the man she caught the faint, sour scent of liquor. Since she could see no sign of spilled liquor or forgotten drinks close at hand, and the earl looked clean in both body and dress, she suspected the smell was a result of a night of heavy drinking. Her father had often smelled that way, as if all the drink he had consumed was leeching out of his body through his skin. Brant Mallam was in a sad state indeed, she decided.

When she reached the foot of the settee, he suddenly opened his eyes and looked at her. Olympia nearly sighed aloud for his fine, dark gray eyes, the one feature she had always sharply recalled about the man, were cloudy with fatigue and the whites of his eyes were well veined with red. He scowled at her for a moment and then hastily, and clumsily, got to his feet.

"What are you doing here, m'lady?" he asked.

"Sit down, Fieldgate, before you fall down," Olympia said, resisting the urge to reach out, grab his arm, and steady him as he swayed before her. "Please. Sit. I have no wish to try and catch you when you fall, as you most certainly shall in but a moment or two."

Brant slowly sat down, taking a few slow, deep breaths through his nose and letting them out slowly in an attempt to quell the dizziness caused by his abrupt rise to his feet. Embarrassment began to creep over him but he beat it down. He had not invited Lady Olympia Wherlocke into his home nor had she announced herself before entering the library. She could just accept him as she found him.

He ignored the part of him that heartily wished she had not found him suffering from too much drink.

He looked into her blue eyes, saw a hint of pity, and bit back a curse. Disgust he could have easily tolerated. Pity from such a strong, beautiful woman made him want to curl up and hide, a weakness that deeply embarrassed him. It was quickly replaced with an urge to throw her out of his house. Curiosity worked to quell both urges. Since meeting her when his friend Ashton and her niece Penelope had gotten together, he had seen very little of Lady Wherlocke, no more than a few brief moments of polite conversation passed during a few social meetings. He could think of no reason for her to be at his home.

"Why are you here?" he asked again, not caring if he sounded somewhat rudely blunt, and then he suddenly recalled how she was now closely related to one of his oldest, dearest friends. "Has something happened to Ashton?"

"Aside from having a very fertile wife who will soon present him with yet another child? No," she replied and moved to answer the soft rap at the library door. "We will talk about my reasons for being here in a moment."

She opened the door to let in a small boy and a nervous maid both carrying trays, one with tea and one with food. Brant fought to recognize his own servants, to thank them by name, and failed. He murmured his appreciation as the boy handed him a tankard filled with Matt the stablemaster's famed cure for the effects of too much drink. Ashamed that his servants were so well aware of the wretched state he was in, Brant concentrated on drinking down the potion. By the time he finished the servants had prepared him a cup of strong tea and filled a plate with food, food clearly selected with care to soothe a drink-battered stomach. Just as he felt he could speak without Matt's potion rushing back out of him, a frowning Olympia stepped up to the boy, gently took the child's slightly pointed chin in her hand, and touched his cheek with her other hand.

"This is new," she murmured and gave the boy a stern look. "Who and why?"

"Cook's helper. Molly," the boy replied without hesitation, responding quickly to the tone of authority in Olympia's voice. "I washed my hands." The boy looked at Brant. "T'ain't supposed to touch the soap since Molly thinks it is all hers, but I knew you have a liking for the ones who bring you your food to be clean and all."

"Wait here, Thomas," said Olympia even as she strode for the door.

A little voice told Olympia that this was none of her business. This was not her home and these were not her servants. That truth did not slow her steps at all, however, as she continued to march toward the kitchens. No child deserved a slap so hard that it marked him just because he tried to wash his hands to please his lordship.

"Which one of you is Molly?" she demanded as she strode into the kitchen and startled the three women working there.

"I be Molly," said the woman by the stove, pausing in the stirring of something that smelled like a lamb dish. "And who be you then?"

Molly looked a little long in the tooth to be no more than an assistant to the cook. She also looked as if she sampled far too much of what she cooked. The insolent tone of the woman's voice was a surprise for any servant would know, with just one look at Olympia, that she was quality. Either Mallam entertained a high quality of mistress or Molly was so certain of her place at Fieldgate that she did not care if or whom she might offend.

"I am Lady Wherlocke, the Baroness of Myrtle-downs, and I wish to speak to you about your treatment of Master Thomas Pepper," Olympia said as she walked over to stand by the woman.

"Filthy little brat," muttered Molly as she wiped her hands on her dirty apron.

"So, you think him filthy yet you deny him, even punish him, when he attempts to clean the dirt away?"

"He touched my soap with them dirty hands."

"I believe most people who touch soap do so because they have dirty hands. 'Tis often why they reach for the soap to begin with." Olympia ignored the badly stifled laughter of the other two maids in the room as she fought to control her rising anger at Molly, but it was a losing battle. "And any soap within this domain is most certainly not yours alone. You had no right to strike the boy."

"I had every right. He be in my charge. And just who be you to be telling me what to do? Just another one of his lordship's trollops, I wager. Aye, 'tis why ye stand here to defend that wee bastard. He be naught but the old lord's by-blow by the stablemaster's daughter. No need for you to be trying to pamper him to win his lordship's wandering eye."

"I believe it would be very wise if you ceased to speak," said Olympia, knowing she was but one more crass word from knocking the woman down.

"Oh, ye believe, do ye? Thomas," she spat. "Such a grand name for a lad what was born in sin. He should have died with his mother and joined her in hell. And I doubt ye are all that much better because no true lady of quality would come to this house. Why not get yourself on back to that whoremonger and do what ye came here for so that ye can get your shameful self gone all the quicker, ere you stink up the house. Aye, and why not take that little bastard Thomas with you if'n you be caring so much about how he is treated?"

Olympia slapped the woman, knocking her back against the ovens. It did not really surprise her when Molly, screaming invective and insults, lunged at her. The woman had made it very clear that she did not see Olympia as her better. This could end up being very embarrassing, she thought as she moved to skillfully defend herself.

Brant frowned and slowly stood as the door shut behind Olympia. "What is she about now?" he muttered.

"I be thinking she is about to have a talk with Molly, the cook's helper," replied the boy.

It was then that Brant noticed the bright red mark of a hand on the boy's cheek. The woman Molly had obviously hit the boy very hard for some small infraction and that was not behavior Brant would allow in his home. He started toward the door, intending to have a word with Molly and thinking that Lady Wherlocke was taking a lot upon herself to meddle in the workings of his household.

Just as he stepped out into the hall he could hear loud female voices drifting up from the kitchens. He hurried down the stairs only to come to an abrupt stop when he saw his butler Wilkins sprawled out on the floor of the foyer. He looked at the burly man who was clearly standing guard over Wilkins.

"What happened to Wilkins?" he asked.

"He would not let Lady Olympia in to speak to you," the man replied.

Before Brant could ask what the man meant by that more screeches echoed up from below stairs. Alarmed, he raced toward the kitchens, not even pausing to tell Thomas and the young maid, both close at his heels, not to follow him. He burst into the kitchen to see one of his servants attacking Olympia. Even as he stepped forward to help Olympia, he realized she did not need any help, and was in truth defending herself with an admirable skill.

It was tempting to stand there and watch Olympia, a baroness, brawl with a kitchen maid, but Brant decided he had best stop it. The only problem was, he was not sure how to break up a fight between two women as it was not something he had ever done before. When he stepped toward the women, a sharp tug on the back of his coat brought him to a halt and he looked down at Thomas.

"I would wait, m'lord," Thomas said.

"But I do not wish for Lady Olympia to be hurt," Brant said.

Thomas snorted. "She is doing right fine, she is. But, not to worry. Old Molly is fair winded and will go down soon."

Brant was just thinking it would be absurd to take advice from a boot boy when Olympia neatly pinned the much bigger Molly against the wall. The look of fury and hate on Molly's florid face made him uneasy. How long had the woman worked for him despite feeling such obvious distaste for the ones she served?

"You may consider me something less than you, my dear woman," said Olympia, "but I am actually a baroness and I might remind you that physically attacking one of the aristocracy carries a very heavy penalty." Olympia nodded when Molly grew pale. "I will, however, forget this undignified tussle if you apologize to young Thomas." She nodded toward where a widely grinning Thomas stood beside Fieldgate. "He is right there so you need not go far to do so."

Molly's eyes widened so much at the sight of Fieldgate that Olympia thought they had to sting. The woman also grew very pale. Since Fieldgate looked more confused than angry, Olympia was not sure where Molly's fear came from. She was just about to ask the woman if she was worried about what Wilkins would do, even assure her that Wilkins would soon be no problem when a sly look came over the woman's face and Olympia tensed.

"I will not apologize to that misbegotten brat,"

Molly said. "I did as I ought when I set the lad straight about touching my things."

Olympia stepped back and frowned at the woman. "You had no call to strike him so hard that the mark still lingers upon his face."

Molly brushed down her skirts. "And I do not need to be lectured by you about how I treat the lad. If anyone thinks I am not treating the boy well, then they should be talking to the only one who has a right to say something."

Suddenly recalling what the woman had said about Thomas being the old lord's by-blow, Olympia had a very bad feeling about what was about to happen. She took a step toward Molly only to have the woman neatly dance out of her reach with a speed and grace that was rather surprising in such a large woman. Olympia felt a brief pang of sympathy for the woman as she recognized what was a skill learned from many years of dodging the fists of the men in one's family.

"The only one that has a right to say what happens to the brat is his brother, m'lord."

All sympathy fled and Olympia glared at the woman, aching to wipe the smug look right off Molly's face. Brant had gone very pale. Young Thomas had obviously known exactly who fathered him as he watched Brant with an odd mix of bravado and sadness. Olympia suspected Thomas waited for Fieldgate to toss him out as many another lord would do.

"What did you say?" he demanded of Molly.

"I said you be the only one who can decide what

to do about your brother." Molly nodded toward Thomas. "That be him right there. Born not long after the old lord died, he was."

Brant stared at Thomas and slowly began to see the familial resemblance. He had the Mallam eyes and looked very close to having the Mallam nose as well. "Is what she says true?" he asked the boy.

"It is," replied Thomas.

"Are there others lurking about my household whom I should know about?"

"Not anymore. Not in the house."

That statement struck Brant as somewhat ominous but he turned his attention to Molly. "And you never saw the need to inform me that my own sibling was the boy cleaning my boots?"

"He be a bastard and we all know how the gentry feel about them," Molly said.

"You may leave now."

"What?'

"I said, Molly the cook's helper, that you will leave now. I do not recall hiring you or even approving of your hire, but I can make you leave. So, go."

"You would toss me out for telling you the truth?"

"No, I am tossing you out for not telling me the truth sooner and, I begin to think, for not actually being in my employ."

Brant turned to walk away but paused to look back at Molly. "You may collect what little is yours, and do not think I will not know if you help yourself to few extra things for I will as I have a very precise accounting of all I own." The fact that he had had to do so to stop his mother from robbing him blind was not something anyone else needed to know. "I would suggest that you wait outside for a while after you pack and leave the house. I believe there will soon be a few more on their way out of Fieldgate soon. Very soon." He looked at Thomas. "Shall we return to the library?"

Olympia watched Brant and young Thomas leave and then looked at Molly. "That was a particularly witless thing to do. Just why has Thomas been kept a secret?"

"Because Lady Mallam told us to keep the secret."

"Lady Mallam does not rule here."

Molly laughed as she tore off her apron and tossed it on the floor. "No? Do you really think that maudlin, drunken fool holds the reins here?"

Olympia watched the woman stride away and shook her head. It appeared Brant had been carefully watched and controlled by his mother. Considering the man supported Lady Mallam far more generously than many another son would, especially one as grievously wronged as he had been, it made no sense that the woman would keep such a close eye on him. There was more to this than a mother who wanted to control her son and whose greed plainly ran so deep she was willing to sell her daughter to a perverted swine of a man. Olympia took a deep breath and started back to the library. She had told Agatha she would help and so she would. She just hoped whatever needed doing did not pull her too deeply into the Mallam family's trouble.

"Still here, m'lady?" Brant asked when Olympia stepped into the library.

"I have yet to actually discuss what I came here for," she replied and could tell by the look he gave her that he was very close to trying to throw her out.

"And what would that be?"

"That your sister has been trying to reach you because she fears your mother is about to sell her in marriage to Lord Horace Minden."

Chapter 3

Brant stared at Olympia, opened his mouth to speak, could think of nothing to say, and closed his mouth. It was rude but, despite the fact that Olympia was still standing, he slumped down on the settee. It was as if all the strength had left his legs. He glanced longingly at the brandy decanter.

"That will be no help at all, m'lord," Olympia said, pausing in her pacing to stand before the large stone fireplace. "You do not need it."

"No?" He sighed. "I barely finished breaking my fast when you arrived. My butler is now laid out cold on the floor in the hall, you have had a fight with the cook's assistant, whom I have just dismissed, and have had it made known to me that the boot boy is actually my half brother." He glanced at Thomas who gave him a big grin. "Now you tell me my mother is trying to sell my sister, a mere child, to the worst, most depraved debauchee in the aristocracy. A drink might be just what I need."

"I doubt that Minden is truly the worst debauchee

in the aristocracy," Olympia murmured and leaned back against the wall next to the fireplace.

She tensed as images flickered through her mind. A blond woman pressed against the wall. Brant rutting fiercely with the woman. His eyes closed. There was another half-naked woman behind him running her hands all over his body. Olympia quickly stepped away from the wall.

"Men," she said, disgust weighing her tone. "The wall? Against the wall, Fieldgate?" She shuddered, silently admitting that part of her disgust came from the sharp stab of furious jealousy that had struck her heart. "And two at a time?"

Brant blinked slowly in confused surprise. Then he recalled what Olympia's gift was. He nearly cursed when the heat of a blush seared his cheeks. Some of the embarrassment he suffered was from the fact that he had only the haziest of memories about what she had seen. If he recalled her particular gift as well as he believed he did, Olympia probably knew more about that incident than he did and that was even more humiliating.

"Shall we return to the subject of my sister?" he asked and waved a hand toward a chair opposite him in a silent invitation for her to sit down.

Olympia eyed the chair a little warily before she sat down. She wanted no more images of Brant's dissolute behavior crossing her mind. Sitting down cautiously, she breathed a sigh of relief when no memory of some past scandalous event entered her head.

"I met your sister Agatha a fortnight ago when she came to the Warren in an attempt to find Radmoor.

Since she arrived alone, I knew there was some trouble brewing. It took awhile to get the whole tale from her." Olympia helped herself to some tea. "As I said, your mother is bargaining with Lord Sir Horace Minden, the Baron of Minden Grange, for young Agatha's hand in marriage. Your sister is utterly terrified that a deal will soon be reached and she will be forced to marry the man. 'Tis quite bad enough that she is being offered to a man old enough to be her grandfather, but he is . . ." Olympia groped for a word that was bad enough to describe Sir Horace yet not completely profane.

"A swine," Brant said and dragged his hands through his hair. "I do not associate with the man but know enough about him to know that no mother should ever wish to give the man her daughter."

"I fear yours does."

"There will be money in it for her. I send her a most generous allowance but she has ever been greedy." Brant made himself more tea but doubted it would do much to ease the rage burning ever hotter inside him. "The need for more has always led her."

"And I believe your dear mother and Minden deal for far more than a simple payment for a sacrificial virgin."

It pained Brant to hear the child he recalled, one who had been all smiles and curls, being named so, but he suspected it was close to the truth. Agatha had barely taken her first steps into womanhood. It was true that many girls had been married at very young ages for centuries, but that practice had begun to fade away. It was also true that marriages amongst those in society had little or nothing to do with love or romance, or even compatibility, but to marry a girl barely out of the schoolroom to an aging roué old enough to be her grandfather would be frowned upon by most all of his contemporaries. It was not even excusable by Minden desperately needing a fertile young wife to breed him an heir for he already had several.

"Mother is evidently not seeking out the approval of society with such a match."

"Nay." Olympia idly finished off a piece of shortcake as she thought over all Agatha had said. "I believe your mother seeks Minden's help in some business venture. Agatha complained that much of what she overheard sounded more like merchants bartering than the settling of a betrothal agreement. 'Tis true that many betrothals are little more than business arrangements, but there had to be something unusual in the discussion she heard to make her think such a thing."

"Whatever business Minden is in can only be a sordid one." He softly cursed when Olympia simply cocked one delicate black eyebrow as she sipped her tea. "But, of course. As I have learned to my cost, the stain on the money does not trouble my mother at all."

The bitterness in his voice coated every word and Olympia had to struggle against the urge to wince. She wondered if he still mourned his lost love, and then immediately doubted it. He had not seen Faith for a year before he had discovered that his own mother had sold the woman to the brothel where she was cruelly murdered. It had been two years since that discovery. A touch of grief for chances lost would be reasonable even after so long but Brant did not strike her as the sort of man to cling to such a loss like some mournful poet. Something else kept him bitter and angry, but she knew now was not the time to try to work out that puzzle. Agatha needed their help and her cause held a great deal more urgency.

"Can you not simply refuse to consent to the arrangement?" she asked and frowned when he looked a little embarrassed. "You are the head of the household, are you not?"

"I am, but, let us just say that my power has been severely reduced, especially as concerns anything that pertains to my sister Agatha."

"How was that done? Law always puts the man in the ruling position."

"Well, I suspect some very attractive bribes were used. Perhaps a little blackmail. And, I also aided in my loss of power with my own less than sterling behavior over the last two or three years. Mother demanded full control over Agatha and got it. I was thinking of how I might get my sister out of Mother's reach, especially since I cannot just send her to school as I did with my brothers, when all chance to do anything was abruptly taken away from me. It was as if Mother had somehow heard of my plans soon enough to ruin them."

"Ah, well, I suspect she did just that. I believe your butler is her man. I began to suspect there was something amiss here when there was no response to any plea Agatha sent you or any of my messages. Debauched though you might be," she said, ignoring his frown, "you never seemed to me to be the sort of man to be so, well, rude. Then when the man so disdainfully dismissed me and refused me entrance . . ."

"You knocked him down."

"I realized my suspicions were right."

"Ah, so that was what happened. Your acknowledging your own suspicions flattened him." He smiled when she scowled at him and he could hear Thomas snickering. "Shall we have a word with Wilkins?"

"I believe that is a splendid idea."

"I can have one now and then," he murmured.

Olympia ignored him. "Shall we speak to him in here or in the hall?"

"I shall have your man bring him in here and help him into a seat."

She watched Brant walk to the door. For one who spent far too much time buried in a bottle or a woman, he was still a fine figure of a man. There was a graceful strength to his walk. Broad shoulders required no padding to make his coat fit superbly. His long legs were shaped perfectly and clearly well muscled. To remain so fit, there had to be times when he was not sunk deep in the damaging ills of debauchery.

Olympia began to feel a little flushed and warm again and scowled. That made no sense to her. She was no schoolroom miss unused to dealing with men, and far past the age where a pair of very fine gray eyes set in a handsome face should be enough to make her heart beat faster. When Pawl dragged in Wilkins, who was very unsteady on his feet, she forced her attention to them. She refused to embarrass herself before the earl with signs of some foolish infatuation.

The moment Wilkins was seated with Pawl standing behind him, the man began to sweat and all the insolence he had shown Olympia rapidly disappeared. She looked at Brant as he stood in front of Wilkins and decided the butler's nervousness was warranted. Brant was every inch the Earl of Fieldgate at the moment and, she sensed, a very angry earl as well. No one liked to be spied upon. To be spied upon by a mother he had disowned yet continued to support most generously had to gall the man.

"I have been told that my young sister Agatha has been attempting to reach me concerning some trouble she is having, yet I have seen not a word from her in weeks," Brant said. "The baroness," he nodded his head in Olympia's direction, "has also sent me messages concerning the very same troubles for nearly a fortnight but, yet again, I have seen nothing, heard nothing."

"M'lord, you have been indisposed," began Wilkins and then he hunched his shoulders in a self-protective gesture as if he could defend himself against the fury darkening Brant's eyes.

"Do not attempt to cast the blame for this upon my shoulders. I may have sunk myself too deeply into a pit of debauchery to still be considered respectable, but I have not done that so deeply that I would miss or forget weeks of desperate messages from my own sister. Most days I am able to tend to the business that keeps us all fed and clothed. I believe I was more than capable of reading a message or two from my sister or the baroness as well. Why did I not see or hear anything, Wilkins?"

Wilkins replied in an unsteady voice. "Her ladyship warned me that your sister was having some childish fit over the marriage being arranged for her and that you should not be troubled by any of it."

"Should not be troubled by the news that my mother means to force my sister, a girl newly turned sixteen, into a marriage with a man more than thrice her age, a man so debauched and reviled that even his great riches can no longer gain him entrance into any of the better homes? So reviled that despite his good birth he is considered by most to be no better than some dockside heathen?"

"Her ladyship warned me that you did not like the man she had chosen for young Lady Agatha."

"Did she? So you not only denied me the right to read my own correspondence but you discussed the matter with my mother. Since you apparently bow to her ladyship's will, and not mine, I believe it is past time you joined her household."

"But, m'lord . . ."

"No, Wilkins, I will heed no more of what you have to say unless it includes other secrets you have kept from me. The ones who work for me owe me their loyalty. You have chosen to give that loyalty to my mother instead. Now, before you leave to join the one you truly work for, I would like the names of any others within my household that she holds in her service." When the butler said nothing, Brant shrugged. "I suspect I can determine who on my staff bows to my mother without your help." He looked at the boot boy, the child that was by blood his own brother. "Perhaps, Thomas, you would be so kind as to accompany Wilkins to his rooms and make certain that he takes only what is truly his when he leaves."

Wilkins leapt to his feet, startling Pawl, who had stepped back to allow the man to leave the room. "You would put that misbegotten brat in charge of me? I am the butler. He . . . he is naught but the boot boy and a by-blow."

Brant crossed his arms over his chest and studied Wilkins. "Might I remind you that you are no longer the butler in this household? Did you just miss the moment when I quite clearly dismissed you? I am curious, however, to know just how long you have known the truth about young Thomas."

"From the beginning, m'lord," Wilkins replied, the regret he felt over being forced to tell the truth clear to hear in his voice. "Her ladyship made it very clear to all of us that no one should speak of the matter. Ever. Especially to you. It was a shame she preferred to keep hidden away."

Shaking his head, Brant asked, "Are there any others?"

"I can tell you about the others, m'lord," said Thomas. "You do not need to talk to this fool about it."

"You watch how you speak to your betters, lad," snapped Wilkins.

"Out," Brant ordered Wilkins, knowing that he was very close to hitting the man and he refused to stoop to such behavior. "Gather up what is yours and leave here now."

It was several moments before Wilkins, still reluctant to be escorted by Thomas, had to accept his fate. Pawl went along with the boy to keep an eye on the butler. Olympia watched as Brant walked to a window and stared at the sadly neglected gardens it overlooked.

"It appears I have paid a gardener to do naught as well," he muttered. "When I discover what the man actually does instead of tending to my gardens, I will send him trotting off to my mother right behind Wilkins."

Olympia knew the words of annoyance about the neglected garden were not the subtle change of subject some might think. Or even just a quiet statement of annoyance over the many machinations his mother was involved in within his own household. Brant was in shock. She could read the echoes of the strong emotions wrenching through him; they marked the air wherever he stood. The man was groping to accept the truth he was far too intelligent to ignore. He may have turned his back on his mother, but she had never taken her claws out of him, had continued to keep a close eye on all he did and said.

Not certain what to do, Olympia moved to stand beside him. It was not a comfortable place to be as it left her sadly torn between the urge to comfort and the urge to demand that he hurry up and do something to help his sister. Accustomed to stubborn, even moody, men, Olympia quietly studied the neglected garden, could see the bones of an elegant design amongst the overgrown flowers and weeds, and decided Lady Mallam cared nothing about Fieldgate. It did not fill her coffers enough to make the woman happy. Olympia also suspected that the blatant neglect of her son's properties probably delighted the woman. Lady Letitia Mallam was not the sort to have even her own blood turn a back to her and ignore what she wanted of him.

"I suspect my family can help you find trustworthy, hardworking people to replace the ones your mother has corrupted," Olympia said.

"And why should your family care to assist me?" he asked as he leaned against the thick wooden frame of the huge window and looked at Olympia.

"You and Ashton are very close and Ashton is now a part of the Wherlocke-Vaughn clan."

Brant knew it was foolish but he was deeply touched by her words. It had been a long time since he had heard anyone say such things. Through his own actions he had lost touch with most of his friends. Ashton was married and his other closest friends did not care to join him once he had begun to sink so deep into debauchery. Cordell, Whitney, and Victor were busy doing the tour of the various estates holding grand house parties, none of which Brant had been invited to.

That good feeling began to fade beneath anger although he was not truly certain exactly what or whom he was angry at. It was just wrong that his only offer of aid and support should come from a young woman he barely knew. The fact that there was no one else close at hand was not fully his fault either, despite his poor behavior of the last two or three years.

"I do thank you, m'lady, but this is my trouble, my family, and I will tend to it."

"I believe you will have more than enough to do,

m'lord, since it is not just a new staff you must needs tend to, is it?"

"The fact that my sister Agatha is in dire need of whatever assistance I can give has not escaped my attention."

Olympia knew she should just step back and say nothing for a while. The man was getting angry. She knew it was not really an anger aimed at her, but whatever he said or did if he let that anger loose would be directed right at her. She was the nearest target, the bearer of the bad news. Backing away from an argument was not in her nature, however.

"If you wish a fight, m'lord, then I am more than ready to give you one. But, if all you are looking for is someone or something to shake a fist at, mayhap you should take a walk until your blood cools."

Brant cursed and began to pace the room. He was being forced to look too closely at the wreck his life had become in the last few years and he did not want to see it. Seeing it made him also see what he could have done differently. For one thing, he would not be wondering what he could do to help Agatha for he would have her in his home, out of reach of their mother's plots and schemes.

"I should have done something about the woman," he muttered.

"Such as what? She is your mother, a countess. You probably cannot even threaten to beggar her to bring her in line. I suspect she has a few holdings of her own as well, does she not?"

"She does, but nothing of any great value. Her lands produce a good income, adequate for a widow. It was her dower property. When she married my father she did appear to gain more and more access to all of his properties, her skill with the finances of them all making him amiable to the arrangement. And, she did keep the lands running efficiently and at an impressive profit for a while despite all his profligate ways. Then shortly after my father died things grew a little less profitable and efficient which is why I entered into some investments with my friends."

"In other words, as soon as your father was no longer watching her so closely or perhaps when all entailed lands went to you at his death, she was not so careful with the money."

"You believe she has been cheating me."

"I do."

He sighed. "That is highly possible. I have been the one dealing in the investments since the beginning so she gets only what I send her from that for maintaining her households. I have consistently had difficulty in getting all the accounts from the other properties but I did get the ones from this one. It being the main seat of the earls of Fieldgate, it was rather difficult for her, or the man of business my father used, to hide them."

Olympia had to bite her tongue to keep from asking him why he had not torn the woman's greedy little hands off everything he owned. It was not her trouble, not her family. She supposed it was a hard thing to face. He would have had to accept that his mother not only sold the woman he loved into death but had been cheating him of his inheritance from the beginning. One crime, no matter how vicious and cold, could be excused, explained, ignored.

Two could not be. What he was being forced to see was that his own mother was not simply cold and heartless to others, able to do things to others he found reprehensible, but she had no real feeling for her own children, either. He had faced that enough to try and get his younger siblings out of the woman's reach but Olympia suspected a lot of the drinking and wenching were done to help him ignore the full, vicious truth.

"There were a lot of inconsistencies," he said quietly. "A lot."

"So she has been bleeding you dry for a long time."

"I suspect she started even before my father died. I was looking into it but now believe the men I had doing the work of unearthing the truth were already her men, never mine."

"Clever," Olympia murmured. "She has probably been turning them to her side for years."

"Do you know, it should have been the first thought I had when I noticed some of the entries in the estate books were incorrect. It was subtle and I could see that subtle bleeding away of funds had been going on for a very long time. Yet, despite what she had done to Faith, I could not completely accept the fact that my own mother would steal from me, from all of her children for she has undoubtedly bled funds from every property my father willed to each one of us.

"There could be excuses made for what she did to Faith. Nothing that would forgive what she had done but ones that could mitigate the horrible results of her actions. There is nothing one can think of to excuse the blatant theft from her own children."

"It all comes back to why she is about to sell Agatha to Minden."

"Money. Lots of it, I suspect. Why trouble yourself with a slow theft when you can get a lot of money quickly by selling your own child. I have the appalling thought that she may have done the same to my two older sisters although that was surely done with my father's full consent, for he too loved money and was always in need of more. Nor did he bow to my mother's wishes very often."

"Your older sisters are unhappy in their unions?"

"Miserably so and have been for a very long time. When young and still idealistic, I did attempt to thrash some faithfulness and caring into their husbands but failed at that. They healed and continued on as they always had. Mary and Alice told me not to trouble myself again. Since then I have noticed that both of them have grown much harder, more bitter."

"You would not have had to trouble yourself for me. I would have killed and buried them before you would have had time to be outraged." She smiled faintly when he laughed. "I do not fully jest, you realize."

"Oh, I do indeed realize that."

"There has to be some way to get your sister Agatha clear of this mess. She is a sweet child and I shudder to think of that filth Minden touching her."

"It is good of you to care so much for what happens to my sister but I know of her troubles and can handle them now." Brant thought that sounded a bit arrogant but could think of no way to soften the words. "It is my place as her brother to do so."

"I am the one who promised her the help she needed and thus I believe I have a place in the solving of this trouble."

"I am certain Agatha knows you have done all you are able to or should be expected to do. The thought that my sister would expect you to actually join in the solving of what is a private family matter is absurd." The moment the words left his mouth, Brant knew he had just made a serious mistake.

Chapter 4

"Did you just call me absurd?"

Brant almost took a step back from the feminine fury before him, but was proud of how he stood firm. He doubted there were many men who could do so before the look in Lady Olympia's eyes. Although the woman had done a great deal to warn him about the danger Agatha was in as well as help his sister finally reach him, he could not allow her to get any more involved than she already was. His mother was a dangerous woman.

"I did not call you absurd," he said firmly. "I meant no more than the fact that you intend to ride to Agatha's rescue at my side was somewhat absurd." The way her full lips firmed as her frown became more of a scowl told Brant that he was not explaining himself well at all, was quite possibly just making matters worse.

"Was *I* not the one who brought you the news about your sister?"

"You were indeed, m'lady, but now it is *my* place, *my* duty, to help Agatha."

"All on your own."

"As you told me earlier, I *am* the head of the Mallam household."

"Whose mother wielded enough power to grab hold of the guardianship of Agatha. Do you even know who to speak with to try and regain that power? Will they even speak to you? I am certain that, when your mother got their agreement to give her full sway over Agatha's life and future, she made very certain that they understood, and possibly believed, every nasty thing she said about you."

He crossed his arms over his chest. What he really wanted to do was hit something, hit something hard enough to make his knuckles bleed. Everything Olympia said was true. He was an earl, but Brant knew his mother had been undermining his power for years, from the very minute his father had died in fact. The woman had always done her best to undermine his father's power as well. Letitia Mallam had always resented the fact that men she did not consider worthy, starting with her own father, held all the power in the world. It had taken her years but she had finally gathered some formidable power of her own and it would not be easy to take any of it away from her.

Brant had no difficulty in accepting powerful women. He knew he was looking at one right now and he found her not only acceptable but alluring. Olympia was strong because of her intelligence, confidence, and that big heart he knew she fought very hard to hide. His mother was powerful because of guile, because she knew secrets and used them to get what she wanted, and because she had a cold-blooded ruthlessness that would give anyone the chills. The fact that he had known that about his mother yet had never seen the danger she presented to Faith left him suffering the constant gnawing of a guilt he could not banish no matter how much he drowned himself in drink and the pleasures of the flesh.

Shaking aside the unsettling emotions any thoughts of his mother always stirred within him, Brant fixed his attention back on Olympia. She was a stunningly beautiful woman; all the more so because she showed no real awareness of the fact. Her hair was a glorious black, a deep, rich color and shining with health. It was a dark frame for the fairness of her skin, which was a soft cream with hints of rose and invited a man to stroke it. Her face was faintly heart-shaped, the bones finely cut in a way any sculptor would envy. Eyes so blue he suspected you could see the color of them from a goodly distance were wide, heavily lashed, and set beneath eyebrows naturally thin and arched. There was the faintest hint of a point to her chin, her neck was long and slender, her body strong yet intensely feminine with curves that made a man think of long nights spent savoring each rise and hollow. Even her hands were beautiful with the graceful way she moved them and long, slender fingers.

He was not at all surprised by the pinch of a growing desire for her. It was a bad time for such a thing, however. It was not simply that it was a complication he did not need, but Lady Olympia was far too aware of the sort of life he had been living of late.

"My lady," he began, groping in his mind for the correct words.

"Oh, please, let us end this weighty formality, at least when we are not performing before society. I am Olympia. Call me Olympia."

"I am not sure that is wise. I have not known you for very long."

"Longer than most. Only in private, m'lord. I know better than most how petty-minded society can be and neither of us needs the trouble gossip can bring."

"Fair enough." He nodded and held out his hand for her to shake. "Then you must please call me Brant."

Olympia shook his hand and immediately wished she had not. Warmth spread up her arm from the point where their hands met, something that had never happened to her before. She could believe it more readily if she had removed her gloves. Touching anyone bare skin to bare skin was so rare even in the most innocent of circumstances that some response to such a touch was to be expected. But this was no more than a short impersonal shaking of hands while she wore gloves.

Perhaps, she mused, it would be wise to step back from the difficulty young Agatha was mired in. Olympia barely allowed that thought to pass through her mind before she shook it away. She was the one who had told Agatha that she would get help; the promises made to the girl had come from her heart and her lips. There would be no turning back on this now, even if it would be wise to keep her distance from the Earl of Fieldgate.

She cautiously withdrew her hand from his, needing to escape that warmth yet not wishing to yank her hand free of his light grasp as if she feared he would give her the plague. It all made Olympia experience an awkwardness she detested. She was pleased when young Thomas strode into the room and interrupted the tense silence that had developed between her and Brant.

"I think you may have a problem, m'lord," said Thomas, studying Olympia and Brant with narrowed eyes.

"What problem do I have now?" asked Brant, taking a subtle step away from Olympia only to see by the way Thomas's gaze followed his move that it had not been done subtly enough.

"No one left to tend your needs save for me, Merry, and near everyone in the stables."

"All my servants have left?"

Thomas nodded. "Ran like rats deserting a sinking ship, if you will pardon me saying so. Merry is making a meal for you and her ladyship with her ladyship's maid's help. It will be a cold one. Merry was only just learning her way about the kitchens and the other lady said there was not enough time for much else. I think Missus Hodges will be back in a few days and I swear she is your servant and none other's. She never much liked the countess. Half the stable be the old earl's by-blows and the rest just never liked the countess."

Brant dragged his hands through his hair as he struggled to understand what was happening. "So I have lost all of my household servants?"

"Save me and Merry."

"And Merry is?"

"My aunt. She be but a few years older than me but has had most of the raising of me. Me mother died when I was born. The countess let Merry join the household when I was but five or six." Thomas shrugged. "I think the countess wanted Merry to help her keep a watch on you."

"Why did Merry not do so? It appears that near everyone else within my household did so readily enough."

"Merry is my aunt as I said. That makes her on my side. Ye and me are kin of a sort so that makes her on your side."

"And she does not much like the countess either, I would wager," said Olympia.

Thomas grinned. "Fair hates her." He glanced at Brant. "Beggin' your pardon for saying so, m'lord."

"Pardon granted."

Olympia stood beside Thomas and they both watched Brant walk over to the window that overlooked the garden. It was difficult to know what to say to the man. Her family had long suffered within the confines of shattered families but she did not think they had suffered anything akin to what Brant was suffering now. The ones who had turned their backs on her and others of her clan were the family members not of their blood. They were the ones born with no gift and no true understanding of the gifts even their own children were born with. Usually the rejection was brutal, but swift and clean. Olympia had no idea how to help a man whose own mother continually rejected him, undermined him, and disliked him. Since she suspected the woman did so mostly because she deeply resented Brant being the earl, perhaps even being his father's son, there had to be the added frustration of knowing he could do nothing about it.

"I believe I shall go and see if young Merry needs help," Olympia said after several moments of heavy silence and was not surprised when both Thomas and Brant turned to stare at her in shock.

"I thought you were a baroness," said Thomas, ignoring Brant's murmured disapproval of his outburst. "A baroness got no place in the kitchens."

"She does if she wants to eat. Not everyone who carries about a title always has a full purse as well. Some have to learn to do the things others hire servants for. I will leave you two to see what else needs doing to sort this mess out or can be discovered about Lady Mallam's many little intrusive machinations."

Brant watched her stride out of the room and frowned when he heard her call for Pawl to come and help her and Enid. He had seen her large handsome footman Pawl but had no idea who Enid was. Just how many servants had she brought with her, he wondered. A not so gentle nudge of a small sharp elbow in his side pulled his attention back to young Thomas.

And there, standing at his side, was yet another problem Brant had to think about, although he hated to consider the boy in that way. Now that he took the time to closely study the boy he could see the familial resemblance. Their mutual father had clearly been a careless rogue who had left a strong mark on his offspring from both sides of the blanket.

"I have other relations to greet, do I?" he finally asked the boy.

"Aye, m'lord, you most certainly do," Thomas replied. "Stables were their choice to work in."

"How many are there?"

"Four. Used to be six up until a fortnight past."

"What happened a fortnight ago?"

"Ted and Peter went away and the rest of us are fair certain they did not do so willingly." Thomas started out of the room, waving for Brant to follow him. "It happens now and then, folk disappearing from the Mallam properties, but we never thought it would happen to any of us since we share Mallam blood."

Brant grabbed the boy by one thin arm and yanked him to a halt. The brief look of fear on Thomas's face stung him to the heart, but he ignored that pain. He also beat down the flare of angry insult that look stirred within him. Thomas would soon know that Brant was not the type to abuse a child in any way.

"What do you mean by folk disappearing?" he demanded and found that just asking the question was enough to make his stomach roll with dread.

"That they be here and then they be gone. Like Ted and Peter. Right here and hard at work one day with nary a word said about leaving, and then gone. Been a few gone missing from the village too, like my other aunt. S'truth, some thought it was your fault, m'lord. Thought you had taken the lads and lasses, but no more."

His mother was selling people again. For all Brant knew, she had never stopped doing so. Fresh young men and women, girls and boys, from the country would bring a nice price in the flesh markets of the city. She had been using his estates to pick and choose her victims. While he had been so obsessed with drowning his anger and guilt in drink and women, he had not noticed how his own people were suffering. The guilt that assailed him over that nearly brought him to his knees.

"Are ye feeling ill, m'lord?" asked Thomas. "We can go to see the lads in the stables later if ye like. May be that her ladyship has a cure you can take for what ails you."

"No. We shall go and meet the lads now."

"If ye be sure . . ."

"I am very sure. It is something I should have done a long time ago."

Within moments after entering the stables, Brant decided he may have overestimated his strength. There were four young men in the stables who claimed Mallam blood ranging from a year older than Thomas's eight years to six and twenty. It was not hard to see once they let him know that his father had also been their sire. Eyes or hair, the shape of the nose, even height and build were all clues to their parentage that he should have noticed time and time again as he came and went from the stables. Knowing there were two more out there only added to his shock.

Brant was not sure how he got back to the drawing room, but he roused from his distress and self-castigation when a worried Thomas pushed him into a chair and asked if he wanted something to drink. He did but he knew it would be the first step on a road to complete obliteration if he had a drink now. The urge to drink away all knowledge of the secrets that had been kept from him for so long, of how he had failed to know his own half brothers worked for him, served him, was too strong.

He briefly wished his father was still alive so that he could beat the man for his callous treatment of his own blood. There had been no mention of the men and boys in his father's will and Brant had no idea how to settle them all as he should have done years ago. He wondered if that was what had made his mother what she was, and immediately doubted it. It may have helped, may have stirred to life something inside of her, but Letitia Mallam had a deep streak of cruelty and a large dose of pure, hard self-ishness that could not have come to life within her without the seeds having been already there. His father's faithlessness and roguish life had simply watered those seeds until they grew into full life.

"That was the dinner bell, m'lord," said Thomas.

"Then we had best go and eat after all the trouble Lady Wherlocke has taken to feed us properly."

"Mayhap I should just go and eat with the others," Thomas said even as he followed Brant toward the dining room.

"Is that what you wish? To continue as a servant?"

"No, m'lord, but it is a better life than many an-other bastard gets. I at least have food and a roof o'er my head. Most of the time. Lady Mallam fair hates us, and that is one thing I do not blame her for, but at least we eat and have shelter. Get enough coin that we can e'en put a little aside."

"And that is all you want? All the others want?"

"Aye, more or less. Merry got the vicar to give us all lessons so we can all read and write, even cipher some." He grinned. "Merry is young and little but she has a lot of spine, she does."

"It sounds so." Brant paused outside the doors to the dining room. "But you should all have more. You are the sons of an earl. All of you should be more than servants. You can never be heirs to anything but you could be most anything else you wanted to be. There is no need for any of you to spend your lives mucking out the stables."

"Not certain there is much else for us to do."

"There is a lot. You could become teachers, tutors, secretaries or men of business, solicitors . . ."

"A solicitor? I saw one of them once. Might be a good thing to be."

"Well, we can discuss it whenever you wish. Now," he opened the door to the dining room, "we go and eat. It would be very ungentlemanly of us to leave a woman to eat alone, especially one who has helped in the fixing of our meal."

Olympia silently waved Enid and Merry away when Brant and Thomas walked in. She waited until the pair reached the table before taking her seat. Brant looked less shocked than he had, as if he was beginning to accept the harsh truths he had had to face in such a short time. The fact that he was treating young Thomas as the brother he was made her believe he could accept the ones his parents had so obviously tried to forget and wanted to deny.

"We shall have to leave for London soon if we are to make it before dark," she said after several moments of silent eating had passed.

Brant sighed. "I know. I just am not sure where I shall stay while I am in the city. All my friends are away at the moment or I would impose myself upon them."

"You have no house in the city?"

"I do but Mother holds it. It was in Father's will that she would be able to use it as her own until she died. I cannot stay with her even though it might be best to do so, for Agatha's sake if naught else."

"No little house for the mistresses?"

"You are far too knowledgeable concerning the ways of men," he drawled. "A small house but I cannot stay there as I have let it to someone else. I had planned on staying in the country for a while and saw no need to leave it empty when it could bring me some profit. Still, there are others I could stay with although I could find myself being pushed to wed a daughter, niece, cousin, or the like."

"You could stay at the Warren. It is empty save for me at the moment and is quite large enough, plus you have no servants so it would save you the time and expense of getting some."

"You know I cannot do that, Olympia. It would destroy your reputation."

"I am a Wherlocke, Brant. My reputation, if I even have one, is shaky at best."

"It would be far more than shaky if I took up residence with you."

Olympia could tell by the hard tone of his voice that there would be no arguing with him on the matter. She would continue to work on some solution to where he could stay, however, as she had the feeling that he would find many a door closed to him. It was going to be another blow for him but there was nothing she could do to shield him from it. He had been sunk in debauchery for so long he had obviously not kept an ear to the gossip about him. She did not believe he had done any more than many another unwed man of the aristocracy, certainly not the things she had occasionally heard whispered about him, but others believed it all.

He left to pack as soon as he finished his meal and she found herself alone with young Thomas. "Do you not have anything to pack?" she asked.

"Wearing near all I own and Merry is packing for both of us. His lordship said he will have need of a maid and me in the city. He is thinking he will be able to find his own lodgings after a few days."

"Merry may stay with me until he does then."

"Thank you, m'lady. He be right, you know."

"About what?" she asked as she helped herself to the last of the tea.

"That it would be bad for your good name if he stayed with you. Not good for a single lady to have a man what's not her kin staying in her home."

"This is true but I am six and twenty—quite past the age of worrying about my dainty reputation. I am also a widow and such women are allowed more freedom. It is also why I need not suffer that foolish nonsense about being on the shelf and all."

Thomas frowned. "Was your man sickly? You are a bit young to be a widow."

"Married very, very young. My husband did not live long after the wedding. Not many recall but I remind them when they begin to act as if I am some poor, on the shelf lass who needs guidance." She winked at the boy. "Not that many try such a thing with me."

Thomas laughed but then grew serious. "You should still have some man to make sure no rogue takes advantage of you."

"Oh, I have more male relatives than most women want and can call on them whenever I wish. You will undoubtedly meet some as I think we will need some help before this is all through. There is far more to all this than Lady Letitia thinking to sell off her daughter for a tidy profit."

"I think so, too, m'lady. There be all the missing, aye? I also think this is going to be hard on the earl. Very hard. He knows his mother is a bad woman but I think he doesn't know just how bad she is."

"No, he does not. I heartily wish it otherwise but I fear he is about to suffer a lot of hard blows as this problem is sorted out."

"I will take care of him, m'lady. So will the others. He is our brother even if he was never told so. He was still good to us and brothers have to watch out for each other."

Olympia nodded and hoped Brant had plans to help young Thomas become more than a servant for the rest of his life. There was such strength and heart in the boy it would be wasted if all he did was tend horses in some lordling's stables for the rest of his life. It was a strong point in the boy's favor that there was no hint of anger or resentment in him toward the man who got all the benefits of being the son of an earl while he and the others got so little. For that alone, he deserved far better than he had been given so far.

It was two hours before they set out for London. Olympia sighed as she settled herself comfortably in her carriage seat, ignoring the stern look of her maid. Brant and Thomas had set off in a separate carriage, leaving young Merry to ride with her and Enid. The man was determined to protect her reputation, Olympia thought with a smile. It was something she was well accustomed to. The men in her family had been doing so for years, ever since that horrible night thirteen years ago. She had long ago given up trying to make them see that it was no fault of theirs.

"He does not know what is said about him, does he?" asked Enid.

"No," replied Olympia, glancing at young Merry and knowing, by the sad look upon the girl's face, that she knew at least some of the rumors about the earl. "Do you think I should have told him?"

"No, he had had enough shocks, I am thinking. Needs a rest from it for a bit. He will find out soon enough. But, you cannot be letting him stay at the Warren with you."

"Enid, who is the baroness here?"

"Do not get all up in the boughs with me. You know I am right. If he moved into the Warren when you are there alone, there would be nothing left of your reputation by week's end, if not sooner."

"I still do not believe I have a reputation of any sort. I just am. And part of what I am is a Wherlocke and our reputations are not so grand."

"Good enough that you get invited to a lot of things and are welcome in most of the better houses. That would soon come to an end." Enid held up her hand when Olympia started to speak. "And do not say that would not bother you. It might not do so as much as it would some other lady of breeding but it would hurt and I will not believe it if ye tell me otherwise."

"No, you are right. Depending on who did the shunning it could hurt a great deal. More importantly, it could hurt others in the family. Howbeit, the man is about to discover that he is not welcome anywhere. What is one to do? He can hardly stay out on the street or even in some inn for all the time it might take to save poor Agatha."

"Then we shall just have to think of some solution as we make our way home. There is an answer to it all. We just have to find it."

"You have changed your opinion of him."

"Some. Merry tells me there is no meanness in the man, even when he is deep in his cups. There is a sadness in him though. A deep hurt. He is trying to drown it in women and drink. Fool man." Enid shook her head. "I have never understood why they think that will work."

"It clouds the memory and dulls the pain for a while and sometimes that is good enough. If all Penelope told me is true, I think there is also a lot of guilt in the man. I could feel it at times. I fear the trouble with Agatha and the discovery that his father has filled the staff at his homes with his illegitimate offspring has only added to that. Now he will be facing the consequences of trying to dull that pain."

"So you think he will be drinking again."

"No, because he has the wit to know he needs his head clear to help his sister and his need to help

Agatha is strong. Very strong. But as soon as he begins his search for a place to stay in London and the doors are shut on him again and again, he will need to be watched."

"But you just said you did not think he would be drinking like a sot again."

"And I am sure of that, but he will be angry and we both know who that anger will be aimed at. We will have to make certain he does not do anything particularly foolish until he gets that anger under control."

Neither of the other women argued her opinion and Olympia sighed, closing her eyes against the looks of understanding on their faces. Brant was about to walk into a dark truth that had been hidden from him for too long. He might know that he had been behaving badly for two years but he had obviously been kept utterly ignorant of how his mother had used his behavior to further destroy him in the eyes of society. His pride was about to be eviscerated.

Chapter 5

Humiliation was no stranger to Brant. It was not usually delivered at the hands of a sneering butler, however. He was, after all, the Earl of Fieldgate, a man with centuries of history and breeding behind him and, due to some clever investments, quite a lot of money. Not long ago many a mother would have plotted long and hard in an attempt to get him to marry her daughter. Now no one wanted him within a mile of their women.

He stared down at the shreds of his calling card the butler had torn up in his face and thrown at his feet, all the while reciting Lady Anabelle Tottenham's sincere wish that Lord Fieldgate curl up and die. There had been a reference to an overdue journey to the fires of hell as well. Brant could not recall insulting the woman at any time but then there was a lot he could not recall from the last few years. Nor could he recall insulting her somewhat oafish son who had been side by side with Brant in many a round of dissipation. He would be extremely surprised, however, to discover he had attempted or succeeded in seducing the lady as she was sixty if she was a day and she had not aged well.

Idly straightening his coat, he went back down the steps and began to stroll down the street to where he had left the carriage. He had no idea where he was going now. Every door he had knocked upon had been firmly shut in his face. Every person he had tried to speak to had refused to see him and sent him on his way with cold precision or outright rudeness.

He shook aside his confusion over the why of that for he had a more important problem to sort out. Where should he go? He had hoped to find some old acquaintance to stay with but the women of the aristocracy were blocking him from that goal at every turn. The Mallam town house, owned for many years by the Earls of Fieldgate, could never be denied him but the very thought of sleeping under the same roof as his mother turned his stomach. He was not sure he could restrain himself from acting upon his anger with her. He glanced over at Thomas, clean and dressed fine, walking at his side.

"It appears that I have no place to stay," he said.

"Foolish women." Thomas shook his head as they reached the carriage. "You may be a rutting swine, m'lord . . ."

"Thank you, Thomas," Brant murmured. "How kind of you to say so."

Thomas ignored Brant's interruption and continued, "But you would never, ever hurt any woman, not even the most evil-tempered besom."

"Thank you. 'Tis a shame none of my friends are

in the city right now. If they were, I would have been saved from this rather humiliating exercise."

"Then we had best take ourselves back to the Warren. There is a lot of room there."

"I cannot stay there, Thomas." Brant fought to ignore how much the idea of doing so tempted him. "Lady Olympia is unwed and none of her male relations are staying at the Warren to act as chaperone. To share a house with her under those conditions would damage her reputation beyond repair."

Thomas made a sound that was rife with disgust and mockery. "Society is full of fools. She is no tender young lass but a widow. And good thing she is a widow, too, or she would be taunted sorely for being on the shelf and all."

"She would?" Brant blinked as all Thomas had just said finally settled in his mind and grabbed the boy by the arm. "Wait! Lady Olympia is a widow?"

"You did not know?" Thomas finally pulled his arm free and started to climb into the carriage. "She was wed while little more than a babe and the fool then died. She says there are a lot of privileges to being a widow and one is that she does not have to be beholding to anyone."

Since he had no idea where else to go, Brant told the driver to take them to the Wherlocke Warren and climbed into the carriage. "That may be true but she must still take great care with her reputation, especially since I doubt many recall what must have been a very brief marriage. Even if we had a few of her close kinsmen there to chaperone us, it could still stir up some damaging whispers if I stayed at the

Warren whilst in the city. We have just seen, most clearly, that I am a pariah."

Thomas frowned for a moment. "That means a bad person?"

"Very bad."

"What? Because you drank too much and bedded a lot of doxies? Pah! That be what most of the toffs do."

"Perhaps, but I think not with the vigor I have over the last two years." He sighed and looked out of the carriage window, fleetingly wishing he had not sent his own carriage back to Fieldgate. "I cannot think that I did anything worthy of this amount of scorn, however."

Brant wished his friends were in town. Somewhat estranged from him though they were, he knew without a doubt that not one of them would have denied him a place to stay. He had only briefly thought of going to their town houses anyway, hoping the invitation to use such places whenever he pleased had remained open, but decided it was wrong to put the onus of granting him or denying him entrance upon some hireling or relative.

"There is, of course, nothing to stop us from going to the Warren to enjoy a little tea and company as I plan my next step," he said after a moment of regret for allowing friendships to lag.

Brant was pleased that Thomas simply nodded. The boy's expression implied that he thought Brant had no idea of what needed to be done, but at least he did not voice his doubts about Brant's intelligence aloud. For someone who had been no more than a boot boy a very short time ago, young Thomas had become quite confident of his place at Brant's side. Under better circumstances, Brant knew he would have found great amusement in the way Thomas was striding out of servitude into the world of being an openly acknowledged bastard brother of an earl. It was not a particularly kind world for one born on the wrong side of the blanket, but, with every passing moment spent in the boy's company, Brant suspected young Thomas would do just fine.

As the carriage wound its way through the streets to the Warren, Brant thought about the new half brothers he had met as well as the ones who had gone missing. He had always known that his father had been consistently unfaithful to his mother yet had never considered the possibility that the man had bred a small army on the women in the countryside. That had been surprisingly naïve of him. He now wondered what he would find in the city as his father had been just as great a rogue when in London as he had been everywhere else.

Upon meeting what appeared to be a stable staffed mostly by his father's offspring, only Thomas had really cared to attempt to step away from the life of a simple country lad. Brant was determined to make life better for the others as well, appalled that his father had left nothing for the children he had bred so carelessly. There was a lot he could do to help the others step up from the rather lowly place of being no more than stable hands yet allow them to remain in the simple country life that they so obviously preferred. According to Thomas, Ned and Peter would also be wanting to better themselves. Brant just hoped the boys truly understood what they would face as children born on the wrong side of the blanket, even if that sire had been an earl.

"This be where her ladyship lives, m'lord," said Thomas, breaking into Brant's thoughts as the carriage rolled to a stop.

The Warren was looking much better than it had the last time he had visited it, Brant decided as he paid off the carriage driver. He had paid little attention to the place when he had stopped to ensure Olympia was settled and sent his carriage home before hurrying off to find a place to stay in a rented carriage. Penelope and Ashton had brought the house back to all its former glory. Looking up and down the street, he could see that many of the other homes were also looking much better than they had been when he had been here two years ago, the air of slow decay almost completely banished. A few more acquisitions and repairs and the little street would no longer be the less respectable neighborhood it had become.

He suddenly smiled. Of course it would also be packed with Wherlockes and Vaughns. As he rapped on the door, he decided it might be wise to look into other areas that sat unobtrusively on the edges of society's chosen neighborhoods to see if they, too, could be brought back to the higher standards that society had. It could be a very profitable venture. He was startled out of his thoughts when Olympia herself opened the door.

"So, do you stay or do you go?" Olympia asked as she waved both Brant and Thomas inside and closed the door behind them.

"I cannot stay and well you know it," Brant said as Pawl arrived to take his coat, hat, and cane.

"But you have no place else to stay, either, I wager." Before Brant could reply, she said, "Come into the drawing room. Enid will soon bring us some tea and cakes and then we can talk."

It was going to be embarrassing to have to tell her what had happened to him, but Brant followed her, sensing that she would not be too surprised by it all. He felt a brief flash of anger that she had obviously kept secrets from him but easily banished it. Whatever had turned him into a person no respectable citizen wanted in their home was probably not something she would have been comfortable telling him. He was not sure he would have fully believed her anyway.

Out of the corner of his eye he watched Thomas disappear down the hall toward the kitchen. Enid would spoil the boy with treats just as she was thoroughly spoiling young Merry. Brant could only pray that he would be able to find the girl's sister, Thomas's other aunt, who had disappeared about the same time as Ned and Peter.

By the time the tea and cakes were served, and he and Olympia were alone again, Brant was prepared to discuss the humiliating fact that he had nowhere to stay. He now believed he could do so without complaining, something he felt he had no right to do. It was by his own actions that he was no longer accepted anywhere. If he had paused to consider the consequences of his deep plunge into debauchery at all, it had not really included the possibility of being utterly banished from the society he had been born into. He was, after all, that most cherished of English gentlemen. He was unwed, titled, without debt, and with a very respectable income. Even more in his favor, he was young, modestly handsome, in good health, and had all his teeth.

"Something amuses you?" asked Olympia.

Brant had not even realized that his last thought had made him grin but he quickly grew serious again. "I was just thinking on how I should be all any mother would want as a husband for her daughter."

"Ah, well, yes, you are." And the fact that she absolutely loathed the thought of him with any other woman alarmed Olympia a bit.

"But, I have seriously blotted my copybook with my behavior in the last few years as no one wished to even let me step inside their home."

Olympia set down her tea, folded her hands in her lap to subdue the urge to go to him and stroke his hair, and studied him for a moment. "You have rather thrown yourself headlong into a pit of debauchery and done so somewhat publicly, but so has many another gentleman. I do not believe, and never have, that you have done anything more than many another has, and they were not banished from society."

"Yet all doors are now closed against me."

"Perhaps," she began, but then hesitated as she tried to think of how to express her thoughts on the matter in a way that would be the least painful for him to bear.

"Perhaps my behavior has been made to sound a great deal worse than it was by someone so close to me no one would ever question the truth of such tales."

Olympia grimaced. "Yes, that was my thought when the first whispers about you began to slip through a drawing room or two."

"Whispers about what?"

"That is not truly important." She really did not wish to repeat any of them.

"It could be important to me since I am the one who must try to repudiate them."

"You have been made to sound as if you are of the same ilk as men like Minden," she finally confessed and saw him pale a little.

"My mother has been a very busy woman, it seems." He noticed she did not dispute his choice of enemy. "Not only was I not welcomed inside a single home I went to but no one would even discuss the letting of a room or house with me. I wonder what variety of evils she has accused me of. Minden has so many, if she chose his way of living as the one to blacken my name, she had a great many sins to lay at my feet. I shudder to think what they might be."

"I suspect you will soon discover that. If it is bad enough there will be many people willing to whisper the rumors in your ears or mine. After the first few I caught wind of, I ceased to listen."

"But did you cease to believe them?"

"Of course. I know all your true friends, Brant. They would never have anything to do with a man of Minden's sort, therefore you were being slandered. Now, as for where you may stay while you are in the city, you need not worry about that."

"I am not sure it would be wise for me to stay here

and not just because my name has been so tarnished even a slight connection to me could be the ruin of you."

Brant knew it would be very unwise and not only because of the damage that would be done to her good name. He wanted her too badly to be within reach of her day and night. Just sitting there watching her sip her tea and nibble on a cake had him taut with lust. Despite how often he had spent himself in the arms of a woman over the past few years, he realized it had been a very long time since he had felt such a swiftly stirred lust, one brought on by merely watching a woman do the simplest of things.

"True. Unfair but true," Olympia agreed.

"It would not even help save you if you reminded people that you are a widow."

She caught the glint of annoyance in his dark gray eyes and winced. He obviously thought she had been keeping secrets. In some ways she had been for she did not like to remember her short marriage. She certainly did not like to talk about it. Olympia refused to be embarrassed by her reticence about her past, however.

"I know, but you could stay in the house next door and that would cause no gossip. It is empty at the moment because it is being redecorated for Argus and his new wife, but it is still quite livable. They will not be occupying it for months yet, either, so there will be no rush for you to find another place to stay."

"That would suit me but are you certain your brother will not mind?"

"Not at all. There may be some work done in the

kitchens while you are there but you will be little inconvenienced by that as you can share meals with us here."

"Olympia, that is most kind of you, but I do not believe my coming and going from here constantly would be a very good idea, either."

"Then it is a very good thing that you can do so without being seen."

She stood up and motioned him to follow her. Brant did so, trying very hard not to watch the sway of her hips too openly. Olympia led him toward the back of the house and into a small conservatory. It was not until he reached the door at the end of it that he saw how he could slip from house to house unseen. A long archway covered in ivy ran from the door he stood in front of to the door of a matching conservatory on the other house. No one would see anyone slipping back and forth along that covered path.

"Ingenious but have to ask why it was done," he said as he watched her unlock the door.

"Argus liked the idea of being able to come and go as he pleased and not even having to worry much about the weather," replied Olympia. "He is trying to convince our cousin Quentin to do the same to the house he recently bought on the other side of Argus's. You see, at the time Argus began the work, he had not had any intention of being married and he rather liked the idea that he might be able to come here for meals rather than just sit in his own dining room alone. The children are often here as well and he would come over when they were and share meals with us."

"And I will do the same," he said as he accepted

the key she held out to him. "Thank you, m'lady. This is the perfect solution." He grinned briefly. "Not only to my current servant problem but to the fact that we are to be working together to keep Minden from getting his filthy hands on my sister."

"Shall I have Thomas called?"

"Yes, please. We shall get ourselves settled in the house now. Later we can discuss what needs to be done. Apparently I will not be able to find out things by attending any events and asking around."

There was a brief look of anger and hurt on his face and she reached out to touch his arm in a gesture of sympathy. "We will sort this out, Brant, and you will be vindicated."

"I doubt I shall be thoroughly cleansed of the stain of rumor. I have been no angel these last two years."

"What you did was no more than others have done and they have not been banished from society. You know that. No, I fear your mother has done this to keep you out of society so that she might not be bothered by any interference from you."

"And hobbled me quite thoroughly in the matter of gaining any information on what she might be involved in. I fear that I will have to call upon you to gather information for me."

"Something I am very good at, if you will pardon my boasting."

He reached out to run the back of his fingers over her cheek, finding it just as soft and warm as it looked. "I suspect you have an envious skill at digging out the truth. Because of what my mother has done, I shall have to travel a darker road to try and find out anything useful that will help us end her games."

Olympia placed her hand over his even though she knew she ought to move away from him, end what was a caress, but she was enjoying his touch too much to end it so soon. She also wanted to comfort him. Brant knew what his mother was because of what she had done to Faith, the girl he had thought to marry, but she doubted he knew the true depths of her cruelty and evil. That she would so completely destroy him in the eyes of society hurt him. She could see it in his eyes. He had protected her name by simply turning his back on her and remaining silent about what she had done. In thanks for that, his mother had stuck a knife deep into his back and twisted it.

"Brant, you will not be able to protect her in any way this time," she said quietly.

"I know." He rested his forehead against hers, needing the sympathy she offered. "I banished her from my life and even tried to take the youngsters away from her, but I could not bring myself to totally destroy her. I felt that would hurt the whole family too much. That everyone would be made to suffer if the full truth about her came out. She obviously felt no gratitude for that kindness. Worse, I indulged myself in ways that allowed her to regain her footing and get the upper hand again."

"You were grieving."

"I was but I was also trying to drown my guilt."

"What guilt did you have? You did nothing."

"I know. I did nothing. And Faith died in fear and pain."

Olympia kissed him. She was not sure why except that she could not stand to hear the pain in his voice. She was startled when he wrapped his arms around her and pulled her close against him. For a moment, she was unsure when he pressed his tongue against her lips but when she parted them and he thrust his tongue into her mouth, she quickly clung to him. Heat flowed through her body and she actually grew a little weak, as if all the blood had flowed out of her head. The thought that she might actually swoon in his arms like some foolish schoolroom girl restored her sense enough that she placed her hands against his chest and lightly pushed.

Brant realized he was kissing Olympia in a way that revealed all the hunger he felt for her and stepped back. His lack of control embarrassed him. He saw no condemnation on her face, however, and relaxed a little. His body was taut with need but he was certain he did not have to apologize for what he had just done and dearly wished to do again.

"And there is the reason it is best that we will not be sharing a roof," he murmured as he fought for the strength to release his hold on her.

"Hah, so there you are!"

Glancing over her shoulder, Olympia saw Thomas walking toward them. He had a look on his face that told her he knew exactly what she and Brant had just been doing. Refusing to be embarrassed about being caught in a man's arms, she slowly stepped back from Brant and smiled at Thomas.

"Yes, here we are," she said. "I was about to call for you."

Before Thomas could express his opinion of that

claim, Brant grabbed the boy by the arm and pointed out the door. "We have a place to stay."

"Oh. So we will not be here to eat what Enid and Merry cook then. Are we to get our own cook?" Thomas asked with little enthusiasm.

"We will eventually, when we finally settle in our own home. For now we will slip in and out of the Warren to get our meals."

"That will be good. I will also be able to see Merry whenever I wish."

"Then let us go and collect our things so that we can get settled in."

"I will send Merry and Enid over to be certain the beds are made and you have all you need," said Olympia even as she started out of the room.

The moment the door shut behind Olympia, Brant found himself faced with a scowling Thomas. "Is the house not to your liking? Would you rather stay here?"

"I would rather you do not play any rogue's games with her ladyship," said Thomas. "I may be but a small lad but I can see when a fellow is being a mite forward with a lass."

"Ah, well, yes I was being a bit forward. It is why we will not stay here. I fear Olympia is a woman I feel a strong inclination to get, er, forward with. I did nothing she did not accept willingly though," he added quietly.

Thomas nodded. "That be all right then. Best we go and get settled. I have a feeling we will be doing a lot of running about soon."

* * *

Olympia sipped a glass of wine and stared into the dying fire. Thomas and Brant had joined them for the evening meal and then hurried back to Argus's house. Although Brant had not been cool toward her, he had not acted much like a man who had melted her bones with a kiss only a few hours ago, either. Olympia did not want to be just another plaything for him but she did not particularly like how he could blow hot and cold. She was still struggling to regain her senses after that kiss, her mind filled with thoughts about what she should or should not do next.

"The man is a rogue," said Enid as she entered the room to bank the fire. "But a day in his presence and he is already kissing you."

She looked at Enid. "What makes you think he kissed me?"

"The way your lips were all swollen and red after he trotted away to your brother's home."

Olympia touched her mouth. "Swollen and red?"

"Not grotesquely so, so do not look so worried. But, you should have enough sense to know when a man is a rogue. You have a lot of them in your family."

"Enid, I know Brant is a rogue and has wallowed in being one for two years. He was no angel before that, either. Howbeit, I am also a woman of six and twenty, not some virginal, innocent child. It was but a kiss." She sighed. "He looked so hurt about how his mother has so thoroughly destroyed his good name, that I felt compelled to try and comfort him. In all fairness to that rogue, I kissed him first. He but responded with enthusiasm."

"You want him."

"Aye, I do and that both alarms and pleases me. I fear I may not be able to, well, enjoy a man and yet am pleased that I would even consider doing so."

"It has been thirteen years, Ollie," Enid said quietly. "It was horrible what you suffered but most of the fear and hurt must have eased by now."

"I think so yet I worry that, at some point, I might find that it has not."

"Do you think the earl is the man you want, the man you could love?"

"I do not know about loving the man, but I do want him. The very fact that he makes my blood heat makes me want to both run away and throw him to the floor so I can ravish him." She grinned when Enid laughed. "I do not know yet what I plan to do with the man."

"If he makes you feel an attraction, makes your blood heat when it never has before, then I say you should see how it goes. You do not have to worry about losing your virginity and then trying to explain it to whatever man you might wish to marry. You are a widow. Maybe it is past time you found out just how broken or healed you are."

"Just what I was thinking." Olympia finished off her wine and then started out of the room. "And, when one considers the matter, who better to help me find that out than a man who has had so much practice in the art of loving?" She closed the door on Enid's giggles.

Chapter 6

Olympia decided that sharing a morning meal with a man she was strongly attracted to was a dangerous business. Brant had slipped in, unseen as planned, to join her for the breaking of their fast. Yet, even though her two young nephews and Thomas were with them, there was an intimacy to it all that she could not shake. He sat across the table from her dressed as many a man would be to enjoy his first meal of the day, but Brant in his shirtsleeves was a sight she found far too tempting. The fact that he kept looking at her hair, which was only lightly tethered back just as it always was so early in the morning, and his gaze warmed each time he did so, only added to that temptation.

She had seen little of him in the past two days and realized she had sorely missed him. It was strange that she would feel so when they had kissed little and been in each other's company so rarely after that day she had gone to warn him of the threat to his sister. He had come round for tea and cakes each day so that they could exchange the information each of them was so busy gathering but it was as if he was trying to put, and keep, a distance between them. It would be a wise thing to do but she knew she could not hold to it. It made her heart ache.

She forced her attention to her nephews Artemis and Stefan in the hope of pushing aside her hurt and confusion. At nineteen and seventeen, respectively, they were more men than boys, but she was still very wary of involving them in what could prove to be a very dangerous situation. It had surprised her when the call for help she had sent out the moment she had returned to London had brought them to her door with Penelope's full approval. They had been a part of the group that had first uncovered the ugly truth about Faith's disappearance and Lady Mallam's part in it. Penelope was well aware of how dangerous this new trouble with the woman could be.

"Ashton also wished us to come," said Artemis, smiling faintly when Olympia scowled at him for using his gift to guess at how she felt, and then he looked at Brant. "Ashton wanted to come but Pen is drawing close to her time and, he worries. This babe appeared too quickly after the twins and he does not want to leave her alone."

"Understandable," said Brant, pleased that Ashton still stood by him and feeling a pang of envy over all his friend now had, but he hastily smothered it before any of the gifted people he sat with could sense it. "I am not quite sure how you can help me, however."

"We lived here for years when it was not such a respectable place and we learned a great deal about even less respectable places when we were sorting out all of Pen's troubles."

"Made a few less than respectable friends who could help us now as well," added Stefan. "Know who to talk to and all."

"Ah, of course." Olympia nodded as she spooned some clotted cream onto the sweet buns Enid had made. "I, too, had thought of making use of the boys."

"What boys?" asked Brant.

"The boys who have just arrived," Artemis said and then frowned. "Something is not right."

Brant was just wiping crumbs from his mouth when Enid opened the door to the breakfast room and four ragged boys hurried in. It amused him a little when he was introduced to each one with all the formal courtesy that would have been used had he been meeting fellow members of the aristocracy. The Wherlockes and Vaughns obviously did not stand high and aloof on some pedestal of good breeding but treated all people with dignity until, he suspected, they lost the right to such respect. He supposed he should not be so surprised as the families had some of the most loyal servants he had ever known, ones who acted more like family than servants.

He took a good hard look at each boy as he shook their hands. Beneath the dirt and poor clothing were the signs of bloodlines that might not be completely common. The biggest of the boys, Abel Piggitt, looked to be on the cusp of puberty. He was tall with blond hair and green eyes as well as fine-boned features that made him almost pretty. Daniel Ashburner was ten, information the boy felt compelled to share as he was introduced, with dark red hair and brown eyes that gave him a look of sweetness Brant was certain the boy knew how to use to his advantage. Smaller than Daniel, yet undoubtedly close in age, David Ewen had black hair and gray eyes as well as a somber mien that made Brant want to make the boy smile at least once. Giles Green, clearly the youngest of the four, had black hair and eyes nearly as blue as Olympia's, making Brant wonder if this was yet another Wherlocke or Vaughn by-blow. Each boy acted and spoke in a way that told Brant someone had seen to some schooling for the boys.

"Enid, I believe we shall need some more food," said Olympia as she waved the boys toward the table.

"We already washed our hands," announced Giles and all four boys held up very clean hands for Olympia to inspect.

Despite the obvious hunger the boys revealed, their manners had only the slightest of rough edges as they helped themselves to what food remained on the table. Brant became even more certain that the boys were being taught by someone and suspected that Olympia was the one seeing that they were trained in ways that could help them better their lot in life. It revealed a generosity of spirit he knew few would ever guess she had.

He sipped at what he considered was the best coffee he had ever tasted and waited as more food was brought in. It was awhile before the boys slowed in their eating enough to explain why they had come to the Warren. Knowing that whatever information the boys had would soon be revealed robbed Brant of the calm and contentment a good breakfast and good company had given him. The hairs on the back of his neck bristled and he could not shake the feeling that he was about to be dealt yet another blow.

"Pardon, m'lady," said Abel as he wiped his mouth with a finely embroidered napkin. "We was sore hungry and that made us forget why we hurried here to speak to you."

"Quite understandable, Abel," said Olympia. "You may tell me your news now."

"The most important news is that Lady Aggie's maid has done lost her brother. Lady Aggie was right upset o'er that and made us swear to tell you as soon as could be done."

"What do you mean by *lost her brother*?"

"The lad disappeared yestereve, he did. He is but eight years, same as Giles here, and the maid has had the care of the boy since he was born and all. Soon as he could he helped some in the kitchens or the stables to earn his keep. Good lad, he was. Everyone says so. No one thinks he ran off or the like, but he be gone for certain."

"Just like our Ned and Peter and my aunt," said Thomas. "I wager the lad was another by-blow."

"Was he?" Brant asked Abel, dreading the answer.

"Well, the maid did say her brother was," Abel paused and frowned, "his lordship's last frolic."

And there it was, Brant thought, the blow he had been waiting for. "It appears my father frolicked quite a bit before he died," he muttered.

Yet another half brother. Yet another child his father had bred and left to be no more than a servant in his household. One could be left to believe that his father had decided to fill his need for workers by simply breeding them. It also appeared that his mother was finally working to rid herself of all living reminders of her husband's consistent unfaithfulness. The fact that, in doing so, she also punished the child and filled her purse she no doubt saw as an added and pleasant benefit. She cared nothing for the fact that she was destroying an innocent child. Suddenly all the food he had eaten churned in his belly with a vengeance.

Olympia took one look at Brant's pale features and quietly sent everyone else out of the room. There was a great deal that needed to be discussed but Brant was too deeply shocked to participate yet. She moved to the sideboard, poured a small glass of brandy, and went to his side. As she held the drink out to him, she lightly stroked his dark brown hair, which was only lightly tied back in a queue. It was something she did to comfort all the boys when they had need, yet the urge to comfort Brant was only a small part of what she experienced as she touched his thick, silken soft hair.

"Not sure I should drink this," Brant said even as he took the brandy she had poured for him.

"Why not?" Olympia reluctantly removed her hand from his hair, certain he might soon guess the fact that it was no longer a completely innocent caress.

"I have become too fond of drink," Brant murmured as he stared at the amber liquid.

Olympia pulled a chair closer to his and sat down facing him. "You begin to think you have reached that point where you have too much need of it."

"Yes. I have not had any since the night before you came to Fieldgate and I was just wondering if I have gone so long without at any time during the last few years. It has not truly been so very long this time, either, yet I now fear that one drink could well lead to too many others. It is also still morning."

"And you have just had a grave shock."

"I believe I have had quite a few of those since you first appeared at my door," he drawled and smiled faintly.

"If you wish my opinion on it, I do not believe you are a drunkard. That is often a thing I can easily sense about a person, despite how well some can hide it from others. I do not sense that weakness in you. I can, however, get you something else to drink, if you would prefer it."

He shook his head and took a drink. The heat of the brandy quickly spread through his body, pushing aside the numbing effect of shock. By the time he finished the drink, the shock that had held him so tightly was gone but the pain of the knowledge he now had still lingered. He studied the empty glass and was relieved, however, as a certainty gripped him. It told him that he would not be looking for peace through the thick cloud of too much drink this time and he set the glass down on the table.

"I knew my father was a faithless swine," he said quietly, "but I never heard talk of any bastards being bred. Considering the number of beds he played in that was remarkably blind of me. Even blinder of me to live amongst brothers, to allow them to serve me and mine, and not even once recognizing them for who they really were."

"And why should you?"

"Because my father was feckless in all he did. At some time in my life it should have occurred to me that he might carry such feckless behavior into the beds, hedgerows, and taverns he frequented." He grimaced. "He bred six children upon my mother, after all. Three when he was a robust young man and three when he was an aging roué whose every sin was carved into his face and body."

"Most of my kinsmen are clever fellows, cautious in many things, yet most of them can also claim an illegitimate child or two." She placed her hand over his tightly clenched one where it rested against his thigh. "The only sure way to avoid breeding a child is not to bed a woman."

"Ah, but your relations do not hide the fact that they have children, claiming and caring for them as best they can. In fact, no one in your family attempts to hide those children away and they certainly do not put their children into service at their own residences."

Olympia tilted her head, leaning closer so that she could smile directly at him. "You have met the children Penelope cared for. Can you see any of them in service to anyone?"

Brant smiled at the thought. "No. Never. I recall tales of young Hector when he played the page for the Lady Clarissa Hutton-Moore. If not for her physical abuse of the boy, the whole interlude would have been the source for many a hearty laugh."

She laughed and the warmth of her breath caressed his face. Brant was surprised at how swiftly his lust stirred to life. His fingers itched to be buried in her thick, black hair, only lightly confined by a ribbon that matched her beautiful eyes, and tumbling in long, heavy waves to her slender waist. There was the glint of lingering amusement brightening her eyes. Her full lips were parted slightly as she gave in to her amusement, and, suddenly, he just had to kiss her.

When he leaned toward her and put his mouth on hers, Olympia's amusement fled beneath a wave of heat. She knew she should pull away from him. It was too soon to act upon what he made her feel, too soon to be sure in her own mind that she wanted to explore the attraction between them to its fullest. Yet, she could not find the strength to move.

Her whole body softened and she pressed against him as he wrapped his arms around her. She readily opened her mouth in response to the light push of his tongue. The way he stroked the inside of her mouth sent heat flooding throughout her body. His hands threaded through her hair only added to that hot need that swept over her.

Olympia had enough sense left to realize that she felt no fear. She felt only want and need. A greedy desire to take even more pleasure from this man. It was not until he moved, his elbow knocking over the glass on the table, that she gained enough strength to retreat from the heady desire he had filled her with. She placed a hand on his chest and gently pushed. The fact that he immediately eased his hold on her only added to her belief that she could trust this man to treat her with care and respect.

She stared into his eyes, the gray darkened almost to black by his desire. It was heady to have such a man show such passion for her. Olympia liked the way it made her feel to have such a man want her. She now knew why she had felt the pinch of envy when she saw how Ashton looked at Penelope.

Brant looked at the woman that he now held lightly in his arms. Her lips were still wet and reddened from his kiss, tempting him as he had never been tempted before. He knew he should fight his desire for her. Not only was she a baroness with a very large family, most of it male, but there was an innocence about her that told him her short marriage had not taught her much nor had she indulged herself with any man since then. He was a man with a mother who thought nothing of selling innocent children into the flesh trade, a lot of dependents including what could be a vast horde of illegitimate siblings, and a reputation as a drinker, gambler, and womanizer.

Before he could think of what to say, or give in to temptation and try to kiss her again, the boys returned. Each one eyed him with blatant suspicion but Olympia soon diverted their attention from him and how close he was to the woman they felt a need to protect. Brant hastily poured himself more coffee as everyone retook their seats.

"I think we need to get out there and hunt for the maid's brother and my brothers," said Thomas. "We have been looking," he hastily added with a glance at Brant, "but mostly for information on what Lady Mallam is about."

"Well, to be fair," said Olympia, "we are now quite certain that Lady Mallam is behind the matter of the children going missing. Finding out who she is dealing with could lead us to the children."

"I know, but I am thinking we need to do both so as to hurry things along. Bad things could be happening to the ones taken away."

Brant had no doubt that very bad things were happening to the ones his mother had spirited away. "Perhaps I should go and talk with my mother," he said even as he realized it would be a waste of his time.

"I think you know that will do no good," said Olympia, sympathy softening her tone. "She will do her best to either not speak to you at all or lie. We only know of her part in the last incident because a ghost spoke to Penelope."

"I pray we do not find any ghosts this time."

"As do we all. Howbeit, I think Thomas is right. We all need to push harder and look in more directions. Now the most important thing is to find those children."

Brant nodded. "You are right. Whatever we discover about my mother or Minden will just be an added benefit to finally putting an end to her crimes."

"You also need to speak to a solicitor. My cousin Andras Vaughn could help there and there will be no need to fear he might be compromised by whatever power your mother might bring to bear against him. Doubt there is anything she could use to bring Andras to heel as he is a surprisingly well-behaved man." She was pleased to see the brief smile on Brant's face. "He could begin to look into how you might regain full control of your own household."

"And how would he do that?"

"By finding out how your mother got the power to

push you aside as head of the household. That is very unusual. In truth, considering the sort of men who retain complete control of their households despite their various deprivations, I would say it is a near miracle."

Artemis nodded. "To give power to a woman when there is a man holding the title is unheard of."

"She got it and I know it is because she found men she could force to do her bidding," Brant said. "Mother always did like to ferret out people's darkest secrets. I have no doubt that blackmail and, perhaps, some bribery was used. I need to find out who she holds in her power."

"Then that is what we will do," said Olympia. "Look for signs of the lost children, find out who was bent to your mother's will and why, and get Andras to talk to you and start to use his magic to dig up all the ugly truth. And, of course, keep Minden from getting his filthy hands on young Agatha."

It was only a short time before everyone but her was gone. Olympia slumped back in her chair as she tried to put her thoughts into order. Brant and Thomas were off to meet with Andras. Her young boys, carefully culled from all the poor boys on the street, were off to try and find out where the missing children may have been taken, and her nephews were off to see what they could discover about Minden. Now all she had to do was decide what society event she could attend that would give her the best chance of getting some information.

"I would rather be out on the streets with the boys," she grumbled as she looked through the scattered remains of breakfast to see if there was anything left to eat.

"Do not even think of joining them on that quest," said Enid as she walked up to the table and began to collect up the dishes.

Olympia stood up to help her only to be waved back into her seat. "Do you lurk outside the door waiting for me to talk to myself so that you can leap in with an answer?"

"But of course. It is my favorite game. Either that or you talk to yourself far too much."

"I suspect it is the latter. And roaming the streets with the boys would be far, far preferable to dragging myself to some boring society event just so I can wade through bushels of useless gossip in the hope of finding some useful snippet."

"True, but the boys cannot do it nor, it appears, can the earl."

"How can a mother destroy the reputation of her own child?"

"How can a woman sell children into a life of pure hell?"

"There is that. We should have done something about her after finding out about her part in selling poor Faith to that madam."

"That was the earl's right and he chose to simply cut her out of his life. I think he had that arrogance men often do concerning women and thought she might not have fully understood what she had condemned Faith to or that she would dare to continue in her evil ways after he had confronted her with his knowledge of her crimes. I think the woman counts very heavily on that arrogance in men."

"Quite possibly. This could all end very badly. He is appalled by what she has done but she is still the woman who gave him life. How harsh a punishment can he make himself dole out to her? Could he hand her over to the authorities for imprisonment or hanging? Could he do her harm himself? It is such a dark, troubling business."

Enid stroked Olympia's hair. "I believe he will make certain she cannot do harm again. I also believe he will lose all softness, if he has any left in him even now, for the woman as he finds out more and more about just what she has done. He treats his wee half brother well and I know he offered a living or schooling to the others so he cares for ones of his own blood as a man should. Think how he will feel when he discovers just what she has done to those children."

"But he already knows."

"He thinks he does but he has not yet actually seen it with his own eyes."

"Ah, no, he has not. One can think one knows something but actually seeing it always makes a far stronger impression. He is still due a great many hard blows."

"And you mean to try and help soften the pain of it, aye?"

"I think I do." Olympia stood up and brushed off the skirts of her morning gown. "I best go and prepare myself for a day of weak tea and stale cakes. I have several little gatherings I can go to. Let us pray I get what I need from the first one or I shall come home in an evil mood." She shared a grin with Enid and then hurried to her room to ready herself.

* * *

Olympia watched Lady Nickerson waddle away and forced herself not to rub at the ache that was torturing her temples. The woman did love to talk and most of it was simply a repeating of nasty gossip. It was no more than she had gotten at the last three houses she had been to but this time was one time too many. It was time to give up, go home, and find out what clever Enid might be able to give her for the headache now pounding away behind her eyes.

Just as she began to make her way to Lady Brindle to take her leave, more guests arrived. Olympia almost groaned in dismay for it was none other than Lady Mallam and young Agatha. She was proud of Agatha, however, when the young woman glanced her way but acted as if she had not seen anyone she knew. Agatha might be young but she had wit enough to know how to play the game they needed to play to free her from her mother.

It was almost an hour before she was introduced to Lady Mallam by their hostess. Olympia had been ready to just give up and go home when the young, sweet, but a bit silly Lady Brindle brought Lady Mallam and Agatha over and introduced them. Although they had never been formally introduced before, it was clear from the look in Lady Mallam's eyes that she knew exactly who Olympia was and that her opinion of her was not a favorable one.

"Your family rarely attends such events, Lady Wherlocke," said Lady Mallam.

"I happened to be in the city to do some shopping and felt I should make the rounds," replied Olympia.

"I believe you have met my son, however. The Earl of Fieldgate?"

"Yes, at the wedding of Radmoor and my niece. And again when my brother wed the Duke of Sundunmoor's daughter." She could tell by the flicker of irritation in the woman's eyes that she did not like to be reminded of the many connections the Wherlockes had.

"I was surprised that the duke allowed my son to attend the event as I fear he has fallen far from grace in society."

"Really? I did not think the duke had much to do with society." The way Agatha suddenly found an intense interest in the drapes on the windows told Olympia that the girl was fighting the urge to laugh but, again, revealed she had wit enough to know that would be a mistake.

"I referred to my son. I heard that you and he arrived in town at the same time. It behooves me to warn you about him. He is not the sort a young woman of your stature should associate with, not if you wish to keep your place in society."

Olympia supposed she ought to be pleased that she now had proof that it was Lady Mallam herself who was blackening Brant's name but all she wanted to do was punch the woman in the mouth. It was odd that such a woman could be so evil. Lady Mallam was attractive, age having done little to dim her classic beauty. Yet there was a coldness in her eyes, eyes exactly like Brant's. Olympia knew that coldness went right to the woman's soul. She also sensed that Lady Mallam hated her own son. She doubted she could ever understand that.

"Fieldgate is the good friend of my nephew by marriage."

"Of course, familial ties and all. Yet, even those should be reconsidered when dealing with a man of my son's ilk." She reached out and patted Olympia on the arm. "You are still young enough to make a good match, m'dear. It would not be wise to allow even that close connection dim your hopes because your good name has been sullied by acknowledging a man like my son has become. It breaks my mother's heart to say such things, but I felt you should know the truth."

Olympia was so angry she barely heard anything else the woman had to say as she took her leave, ushering a silent Agatha toward Lady Nickerson. That Lady Mallam acted as if that woman was her dearest friend told Olympia that Brant's mother knew exactly how to spread her poison about him. There was a good chance she was now spreading a little poison about Olympia as well. The way Agatha tensed ever so slightly told Olympia that.

Quickly taking her leave of her hostess, Olympia stepped outside and took a deep breath. London's air was not sweet but it was far better than what she had been breathing in that little nest of vipers. She had forgotten how vicious the ladies of society could be. Olympia had the sneaking suspicion, however, that she was about to be strongly reminded. Lady Mallam knew she and Brant had arrived in town together. Whether that meant they were allies or not would not be something her ladyship would worry about. All she would want to do is make sure that no one would heed anything anyone might say in defense of her son and, if that meant destroying the reputation of someone connected to Brant through the thinnest of ties, she would do it without hesitation. Lady Mallam obviously held to the tactic of strike first and worry about the need to do so later.

As she told Pawl to take her home and then climbed into the carriage, Olympia tried to decide if she should tell Brant that she had absolute proof that it was his own mother destroying him in society. He had guessed that it was but it would still be a blow. She sighed and closed her eyes.

For now she would say nothing. It aided nothing for him to know and she just did not wish to give him even more bad news. He had had enough since she had dragged him away from Fieldgate and he was facing far more in the days ahead. She just hoped that he did not get proof of it on his own for he might think she was keeping secrets from him and she was certain that trust was something Brant did not give easily. Catching her in what could appear to be a lie could cost her dearly. Then again, she was keeping other secrets from him. What was one more?

Chapter 7

"I do not wish to think of any blood of mine being forced into such a place," Brant said as he stood in the shadows of an alley across the road from Dobbin House.

"No one ever does, especially since the poor lad or lass who is most like to be forced to go to such a place. I doubt anyone goes there willingly." Thomas glared at the dirty, old brick building. "I best not be finding Ned or Peter in there."

There was such cold hatred in the boy's voice, one echoed in the harsh lines of his expression, that Brant actually feared for his mother's life. It was a fear that quickly died away. She might be the woman who had borne him but she was no mother of his, not any longer. It was not because she had sold the woman he had loved and wanted to marry to a brutal killer, either, although he had turned his back on her after that. The woman sold children, was no better than some slaver. He would never again acknowledge her as any relation of his and it was far past time that he removed all sign of her from his life, his siblings' lives, and every single one of his properties.

Little by little, each tiny piece of information they had gathered had led them to this place. Each piece had also let them know who would have sold children into this sordid life. His mother was rather well known amongst the urchins of the street, too many of them knowing someone she had sold into a form of slavery. He had not missed the fear in their eyes when her name was mentioned. From what they had been told, there had been girls of marrying age forcibly placed on ships to plantations in the colonies and the profit pocketed by his mother and her compatriots, one of which was Lord Minden. Brant did not know if he could ever rescue all the ones she had wronged.

"'Tis not your fault, m'lord," said Thomas.

"She is my mother."

"True and that is a sad thing to have to admit to, but she is also a grown lady and must know what she is doing is wrong. Merry always says that it is a choice to do right or wrong and it is only the person hisself who can make that choice."

"How old is your aunt who has gone missing?"

"She was sixteen, m'lord."

Brant cursed. "From what we have learned, I am not sure I can ever get her back for Merry."

"I know. So does Merry. You will give it your best try and that is all you can do."

"Not all, Thomas. I can also make certain that my mother can never do this again. I cannot see my own mother hanged but I can do many other things that will declaw her, steal all power and ability to continue her crimes."

"No sight or word of them, m'lord," said Abel as he and the other three boys joined them, "and we have been looking and listening round here for quite a while."

For three whole days, Brant thought. They had discussed plans to search for Peter, Ned, Merry's sister, and the maid's brother Noah right after he had last kissed Olympia. Three days, fourteen hours, and ten minutes ago. Brant woke several times a night tasting the sweetness of her mouth on his, his body on fire with need. He wanted another kiss; he wanted far more than that.

"I could go inside there and have a look," said Giles, cutting off Brant's thoughts much to his relief.

"No," Brant said sharply, the other boys echoing his command.

"Then how will we ever know for certain if Ned, Peter, or Noah are in there?" asked Thomas. "It is where all those who would talk to us think they are."

"We will need someone to go in, someone who can pretend to be after some of the wares this place offers." The very idea of stepping into such a place turned Brant's stomach but he was certain it was the only way. "Then, once we are certain, if that person cannot free the boys, the fellows at Bow Street need to be called."

"Bow Street," muttered Abel. "Naught but a pack of brawn and no brain, always looking to grab some coin."

"I met a man from there who is a clever, honest man," said Brant. "A man named Obadiah Dobson.

I met him two years ago and he was a good man then, helping us a lot, and doing nothing I found wrong or foolish. I have friends who have turned to him for help since then and they were impressed by him. I think he would find great joy in closing this place down."

"I have heard of Dobson."

"Oh? Because you had need of him or because you had to run from him?"

"A bit of both," said Abel and all five boys grinned. "He does not beat a lad just to hear him squeal when he catches one doing a touch of thieving. He does not let them hang for it neither. I am done with all that though. Lady O thinks I will make a fine solicitor."

"That be what I think I would like to be," said Thomas.

"I think you would both do very well at it." Brant took one long, last look at Dobbin House. "There must be a careful look around done first. I hate the thought of leaving any child in there for even one more minute but, if we are not very careful, and the ones running that foul place catch wind of our plans, the children could be hidden away or worse. That much I am certain of."

"We best get back to Lady O to do some planning then," said Abel.

Brant grimaced as he slipped through the shadowy back alleys of the city with the boys. The idea of even mentioning a place like Dobbin House to Olympia was enough to appall any gentleman. It was the dark side of men that no man wanted women to know about. She would not allow him to protect her from such ugliness, however. He both admired that and was dismayed by it. All he could do was hope that she would be so repulsed by the mere mention of such a house that she would leave all planning to him, but he suspected that was a very foolish hope indeed.

"Dobbin House should be burned to the very ground, preferably with every man and woman who profited from such evil tied securely to a bed as the flames consumed them. And then the ashes of them and that horrid place should be scattered to the four winds," Olympia said, fury making her voice low and husky. "I do not understand how our officials can allow such a place to exist."

"Olympia, you know full well that sympathy for the plight of poor children is lacking in London, in this whole country. Although, I believe poor children fare better in the countryside. But they also hang a starving child of ten for stealing a loaf of bread," said Brant as he watched her angrily pace the parlor. "And, sad to say, some of those officials might not be doing anything simply because they avail themselves of the services offered there."

She smothered the urge to scream and sat down beside him on the settee facing the fireplace. Staring into the flames slowly calmed her, her fury ebbing away, although her outrage remained. Olympia was not so naïve that she did not know such places existed, that such perverse hungers were felt by some men and catered to by others. She was just so very weary of the venality of men, the evil that appeared to know no bounds. When such things reached out to hurt innocent children she was torn between wanting to weep and wanting to become some warrior woman who wielded her sword like a scythe, cutting all such vile people down.

"I am certain they are doing things inside that house that are against our laws," she finally said.

"Which is why we will watch them and then have Dobson and his men storm the place," said Brant. "I just need to find a way to know what is inside there. And who is."

Her anger was weighted with a sadness he could almost taste. Brant could not ignore it any longer. Nor could he resist the urge, the deep need, to try and ease it. He put his arm around her shoulders and tugged her up against his side. The way she settled against him, welcoming the light embrace, was far too tempting. He knew it was a mistake to stay so close to her but he did not have the strength to pull away from her when she was so in need of comfort.

"This is not wise," Olympia said even as she savored the warm strength of him, for her mind quickly filled with the memory of the kisses they had shared.

"No, probably not," he agreed. "Not when we are . . ." He stuttered to a halt as he searched for the right words, ones that would be neither suggestive nor presumptive.

"Attracted to each other. Such proximity only adds to that temptation."

Olympia Wherlocke was not a shy, reticent miss, he thought with an inner grin. He could attribute that to the fact that she had been directly involved in the solving of several dark crimes in the past few years but he suspected it was far more than that. Olympia was also in her late twenties, considered thoroughly on the shelf by most of society who had forgotten her brief marriage, and had a vast array of male relatives.

"Quite so," he agreed, noting that she made no move to push him away. "We are also both adult enough and strong-willed enough for that not to matter." He grinned when she made a soft noise that revealed her utter scorn for his remark. "You do not think us adults or strong-willed?"

"I know you are jesting. Of course we are both. And, of course we both know that that makes little difference. Children running freely through the house does make a difference, however."

"Very true." He gave in to the urge to nuzzle her thick hair, breathing in the scent of her and grimacing when his groin tightened with need.

The warmth of his breath against the side of her neck made Olympia shiver with pleasure, but she struggled to hide her reaction. Brant was the first man she had ever felt any desire for but she was still not sure it would be wise to test her own strength with him. The only other time she had been with a man it had been a horrific experience, a tearing away of her childhood and ability to trust. It had left scars upon her very soul. If she reached out for what her body wanted only to find that fear and the pain of the past held her back, she would be humiliated. Yet, a large part of her wanted to reach out, wanted to grab on tightly and experience that pleasure so many of her family indulged in with reckless abandon. She just wished she was not taking so long to make up her mind.

Another thing that held her back was not something she could change to her advantage even if she wished to. Lovemaking required that one remove one's clothes. Since Brant was obviously a very observant man, she feared he would see the signs on her body that would tell him she had held fast to yet another secret about herself, a very big secret. Olympia did not think she was ready to share that secret with him.

"We must set about making plans for spying on Dobbin House," she said, praying that talking might take her mind off how good it felt to be held in his arms as he nuzzled her hair.

"We?" Brant moved away enough so that he could meet her gaze. "There is no *we* in this particular venture."

"Of course there is. We cannot send the boys to watch that house. They could all too easily be taken up by that scum and I cannot abide even the thought of that happening. You do not have anyone to send in there to look around for you, do you? And you cannot go in as you do not wish to be recognized, which could happen if your mother is known to the ones running the house."

He cursed softly for she was right in all she said. There was no one he knew to send into Dobbin House, his friends all away from the city and the boys too young, and he could not risk word of his being there getting back to his mother. They had to keep her as ignorant as possible of how closely they were watching her and looking into her affairs or she could easily elude punishment for her crimes.

"I will do the spying myself," he said after a moment.

"With no one to watch your back?"

"Olympia, this is no place for a woman. You should not even know such a place exists, should have been thoroughly protected from such knowledge. It . . ." He stopped speaking when she pressed her finger over his lips.

"I know ugliness, Brant. Do not forget who I am and what I can do. Even when I would very much prefer to remain ignorant, I stumble upon the ugliness of what man is capable of all the time. Whatever I might learn from spying on Dobbin House matters less than nothing against the need to help those children. Whatever shock or distress I might suffer will be easily soothed by the fact that I will have helped to free them from that hell."

"You will not go inside and you will not touch anything," he said, thinking of the horror and deprivations a gift such as hers could reveal. "I want to hear you agree."

The words he spoke were a harsh command that would usually cause Olympia to immediately bristle with rebellion but she felt none. Instead, she wanted to smile for his words also told her that he believed in her gift, in what she could do. Olympia began to think that he always had, for that first day at Fieldgate, he had never questioned what she had seen when she had leaned against the wall or that she could see anything at all. She doubted he would ever understand just how much that meant to her.

Unable to resist, she brushed her lips over his and whispered, "I agree."

Light though the touch of her mouth was against his, it sent a wave of heat straight to his groin and Brant nearly groaned aloud. He ignored the stern voice in his head that told him to move away. He pulled Olympia fully into his embrace and kissed her, not even trying to hide the need clawing at his insides. Her mouth was soft and warm beneath his, opening willingly beneath the soft prodding of his tongue. The taste of her banished all caution from his mind.

When she stroked his tongue with her own he lost what little restraint he had managed to hold onto. He ran his hands down her slim back and back up again, savoring the way she shivered beneath his touch. When he pressed a kiss to the side of her throat she tilted her head back to allow him more access. Everything about the way she responded to him made him ache for her. He kissed her again and gently moved his hand up her rib cage until he covered her breast, the ripe fullness of her filling his hand and making him want to scc and kiss the treasure hc now caressed.

Olympia began to feel too much, the fever he created within her too strong. The way he stroked her breast even as his tongue stroked the inside of her mouth had her trembling like a sapling in a strong wind. She liked to be in control of herself and what he made her feel stole that control. It was wonderful yet terrifying. The moment his mouth left hers and moved to her throat, she placed her hands on his chest and pushed ever so gently. For one moment his hold on her tightened but before the flicker of fear that caused her could come into full life, he moved back a little.

"It has been a very long time for you?" he asked as he fought to rein in his desire to make her want him as he did her.

"I was with a man once," she said as she fought to gain control of her breathing. "When I was but thirteen. The man became my husband. He died shortly after."

Shock held him silent for a moment. He knew there was far, far more to the tale than she was telling him. Before he could think of the right questions to ask, the sound of the boys returning caught his attention. He moved away from her and watched as she hastily straightened her gown and attempted to smooth out her tousled hair.

"We have come to say good night, m'lady," announced Abel as he strode into the room followed closely by the other four boys.

Every single one of the boys eyed him closely and Brant just smiled. He refused to feel guilty about what had just happened between him and Olympia. He had taken nothing she had not willingly given him and he had stopped the moment she had indicated that she wanted no more. A quick study of her as the boys gathered around her told him that she had regained her calm, and he felt a little insulted about how quickly she had shrugged off the passion they had tasted. Then he noticed her hands, which were clasped together in her lap far too tightly. She was not as unmoved as she tried to appear.

"Are all of you staying here?" she asked the boys.

"Thomas will be returning to the other house with his lordship."

His lordship was not ready to retire to his house but Brant said nothing. It was probably best if he did just that. Olympia had confessed a secret about her past and he needed to consider the ramifications of it all before he acted on his desire for her again. He no longer wished to be gallant and leave her alone. Such passion as he had tasted in her kiss was the sort a man would be a fool to run away from.

"But do we not need to discuss spying on Dobbin House?" she asked, turning to him.

Brant really did not want her anywhere near the place but she had made sense in all her arguments against leaving her safely tucked away at the Warren. He could not use the boys and he had no one he could call on to go to the House as if he was a customer.

"We will go tomorrow night. That will give me and the boys a bit more time to thoroughly search the area and the outside of the House. We need to fully know the lay of the land before we creep up to do our spying. Easy routes of escape are most important."

"Fair enough. I will make a few plans myself."

As Brant left with Thomas he wondered just what plans she believed she needed to make. Somehow he knew that she would surprise him.

"Do you like the gent?" asked Abel as Olympia led the boys up to the rooms they would use.

"I do," she replied. "Why do you ask?"

"He has a bad reputation, y'know. I have heard some bad things about him."

"Ah, yes. I fear most of those bad things are from rumors spread by his mother."

"His mam said such things about him? And you are certain they are not true?"

"Very certain. The woman did what she had to to make very sure that the earl would be accepted nowhere, thus he would be hard-pressed to find the proof he needs concerning her many crimes."

"That is the woman who has taken the boys, aye?" asked Giles as he skipped past Olympia and entered the bedchamber he shared with David whenever the boys stayed the night at the Warren.

"Aye, it is. I believe she has been doing such things for a long time."

"So why has he not stopped her?"

"She is his mother."

All four boys nodded solemnly and she had to fight the urge to hug them all. They were still wary of too much affection. Olympia especially wanted to hug young Giles. She was certain he was related to her in some way. The mark of the Wherlocke clan was strong in his young face. Unfortunately, he had no idea who his parents were, having been tossed away by his mother while still a babe and raised mostly by Abel. He was also too young to reveal what gift he may have gotten from his Wherlocke blood, something that could have helped in discovering which of the many rogues in her family his father was.

"Get some rest, lads. I feel the earl will be keeping you very busy on the morrow."

The three younger boys quickly ducked into the two bedchambers, set side by side and connected by a door she could hear them open the moment they got inside the room. Abel remained by her side, studying her in a way that made her uneasy. He was far older in spirit than his twelve years and she was saddened by that. He had never had a childhood.

"Where are Artemis and Stefan?" Abel asked.

"Out trying to find out things just as you were," she replied and gave in to the urge to smooth down a few wayward curls in his thick, bright hair. The way he hunched his shoulders yet did not back away from the touch both amused her and made her happy. "They will return soon and will be sleeping in the room across the hall from this one."

"Good. I could help you if there was trouble but they are men and that would be better."

He left her then and softly closed the door behind him. Shaking her head, Olympia went to her own bedchamber knowing her nephews would let her know when they returned no matter how late that was. She was just slipping on her robe and thinking about reading for a while when a soft rap came at her door.

"Ah, good, I was just starting to worry," she said as she let her nephews into the room. "Discover anything of worth?"

"I think young Merry's sister may have been sent away," said Artemis as he sprawled in a chair by her fireplace.

"I feared that might be so," she said and sighed as she sat down on the edge of her bed. "That means she is lost to us."

"Maybe. Maybe not," said Stefan as he moved to sit on the arm of the chair his brother sat in. "We know the name of the ship she was probably sent out on and it was headed up the coast to Scotland first and then out to one of those plantation colonies. It might be possible to catch her in Scotland if we can get word to someone there in time."

"Talk to Pawl. He will know if there is anyone and if there is a chance to reach the person in time. I fear it would take me awhile to think through all of our kinsmen and where they may or may not be at this time of the year. Pawl has the sort of keen memory that keeps all that sort of information right at his fingertips."

"Will do." Artemis stood up and started for the door, pausing to kiss her on the cheek, Stefan doing the same, but Artemis paused in the doorway to look back at her.

"Something troubling you?" she asked.

"The earl," he replied.

Olympia sighed. "I am a widow of six and twenty years, Artemis."

"I know and I was not intending to try and tell you what to do." He abruptly grinned. "I will leave that to Uncle Argus. No, I just wanted to say that the earl is a man who needs to know that people are being completely honest with him. Right now he believes you are. So, I just thought that you might wish to tell him about Ilar."

She cursed as he walked out, shutting the door quietly behind him. Argus could prove to be a problem but she easily shrugged aside that part of what Artemis had said. He was right about Brant and she had seen that truth about Brant almost from the beginning. Brant had good reason to mistrust anyone who kept secrets. He even had good reason to be wary about trusting women since the most important woman in his life had betrayed his trust time and time again. That mistrust had grown in him with every new half-sibling he met. Now he had to think that most of his life had been filled with lies. She was giving him the truth but was doing so in small doses and that was wrong.

Olympia moved to pour herself some wine. She then stood before her window and stared out at the small moonlit garden below. Her secrets had been her own, shared only with her family, for so long it was almost painful to reveal them to anyone else. The things she had told him already had been hard enough. To try and tell him her greatest secret of all could easily choke her.

Ilar, she thought and her heart hurt. She missed him. He was her greatest treasure and her biggest secret. Even her family never mentioned Ilar, just as they rarely spoke of her marriage. Yet Ilar was listed as the Baron of Myrtledowns if anyone cared to look and they would only need a tiny more research to know that the baron listed in the records could not be her husband. In thirteen years no one had bothered to sort out the truth and she had decided to just leave the subject alone, to remain silent and even secretive by keeping Ilar in the country.

"Where he must stay until he is older," she said aloud as if hearing the words would help remind her of the need for that secrecy, that isolation of her own son.

Thinking of Ilar took her mind back to that horrible night thirteen years ago, the night Ilar had been conceived, and she shuddered, quickly drinking deep of her wine to still a rising fear. Her cousin Maynard had always come round the house, been their playmate for years. Yet that night he had looked at her in a way that had chilled her to the bone. Before she could escape him, however, he had used his gift on her, a gift very similar to Argus's. Too young to protect herself from his skill, Maynard had bent her to his will. Olympia could recall very little of what had happened next. She had woken up with her skirts around her waist and a pain between her legs. While staggering to her feet, she had placed her hands on the ground and read in the remaining emotions staining the grass just what her cousin had done to her.

Cousin Maynard had paid dearly for his brutal act. Still in shock she had found herself married and, within a very short time, a widow. She knew her brothers had killed her cousin, had perhaps been aided by others in her far too large family, but she had never asked them for the details of it all. When she had found herself with child, she had been stunned, for she was little more than a child herself. Once or twice she had wondered if she could rid herself of the permanent memory of Maynard's abuse, but each time her child had moved in her womb and she had been unable to even try to be rid of the baby. And thus was Ilar born, the occasional source of memories she would much prefer to forget, yet her joy as well.

Artemis was right. Brant needed to know before

he discovered it for himself. And he would. She knew she would not be able to resist the need to become his lover for much longer. The marks left from Ilar's birth were faint and small but they were there and there was a very good chance Brant would see them. Her reticence about becoming Brant's lover was almost gone and with it would go her ability to tell him to stop.

Just a little longer, she thought, as she shed her robe and crawled into bed. It was nice to be desired by a man like Brant and she wished to revel in the simple joy of that for a while longer. Men did not often react well to discovering the woman they desired had a child. She wanted nothing to disturb the rapidly growing passion she and Brant shared so effortlessly. It was selfish and she knew it, just as she knew she could be risking his trust, but for a while she wanted what was happening between her and Brant to be hers and hers alone.

Chapter 8

Brant stared up at Olympia as she climbed up the strange trellis-style ladder that ran up one side of Dobbin House. He had no doubt that it was but one of many routes of escape for the owners and patrons if there was ever a need to run. What held his complete attention, however, was the sight of Olympia's beautifully shaped backside shown clearly in the trousers she wore. His hands actually itched to caress her there.

When she had come down the stairs at the Warren to join him on this venture he had nearly swallowed his tongue at his first sight of her. Olympia dressed as a man was a sight to heat up any man's blood and linger in his dreams. He had made her put on a heavy cloak but she had left it in the carriage, which waited around the corner and was guarded by Pawl. It was tempting to run back to the carriage and get it, throwing it around her to hide what he so ached to touch from his sight, and especially from the sight of anyone else.

Olympia Wherlocke had long, beautifully shaped

legs, the tight pants revealing a gap between her strong thighs that called out to a man. She also had the most temptingly shaped backside he had ever been blessed to look upon. He wanted to see it naked, wanted to caress it, kiss it. Despite the fact that they were here to save children from the hell callous adults had put them in, he was going to find it difficult to keep his attention fully on the job they had to do.

Forcing his rising lust into submission, he began to climb up after her. Windows around the lower floors of the house had been heavily draped from the inside and even shuttered on the outside. The only windows they might be able to spy through were on the upper floors of the six-story building. It still bothered him that Olympia would be joining him in peering into the abyss that was Dobbin House.

In all honesty, he did not want to peer into the windows of this place. He knew what was happening to all of the children that had been sentenced to this hell. If the boys he looked for were in there, they would be free, but they would be damaged in heart and soul. It would take a long time to heal those wounds and they would leave deep scars. Brant did not think there was a punishment severe enough for people who mistreated children in such a way but, saddened by the truth of it, he knew he was one of few who actually cared what happened to them. Most people barely saw all the poor children, and while some bastards of good blood were supported by their parent, most were discarded with the ease so many others discarded the children of the poor.

A small, soft hand wrapped itself around his wrist and tugged. Brant realized they had reached a narrow landing as he stepped off the trellis. A wooden ledge wide enough to walk on encircled the house, interrupted here and there by other small landings. It looked sturdy enough to hold them. It also looked like yet another way to ensure the patrons and owners would never be caught so long as they had some warning.

"The man who runs this place now has obviously thought of all the ways that might be needed to allow the swine within these walls to escape any attempt to bring them to justice," he said, his voice barely above a whisper. "It explains why there are still so many fine windows in the place when others sealed up theirs to avoid the window tax."

"I am surprised they do not worry about the ones they sell here escaping from them by the same routes," Olympia said, her voice as soft as his.

"I suspect the ones they sell are secured well."

"Aye, they are."

The tone of her voice drew his full attention and Brant realized she was peering into a window. She stood to the side of the window frame and leaned her head around it just enough to look inside. He did the same on the other side of the window. It took just one look and he was fighting the urge to drag Olympia away from there.

A small boy was relieving himself in a battered chamber pot. He was naked and there was a shackle around his thin ankle. Brant doubted the boy could be much more than five. As he watched the child crawl up onto the bed, every move he made shouting out the despair and pain he was in, Brant swore he would get the child out of there. The boy was not one of the ones they were hunting for, but no child should be treated so.

Before he could stop her, Olympia moved to stand before the window and the child looked up, gaping at the sight of her. Brant softly cursed and waited for the alarm to be sounded. No sound was made, however, and a moment later he heard the strange wooden screech of a window being opened.

"Who are you?" asked Olympia, reaching out to lightly stroke the child's cheek.

"Henry. Are you an angel?"

"Nay, lad. I but come here looking for some boys who were taken from us."

"No one came for me," the boy whispered and his blue eyes glittered with tears.

"I have."

"You will take me if you find the boys you want?"

"I will take you from here even if I do not find them."

"There are a lot of others. Not all of them are children. There are a few girls here, older girls. Ones men like to grab."

"We will see to their freedom as well. Now, I know you have probably seen few people inside these walls . . ." Olympia began.

"I get taken for a bath on the nights when I will have company so I have seen a lot of the other ones here. What do your boys look like?"

Olympia carefully described Ned, Peter, and Noah, naming each boy as she did so on the chance that this child had heard a name if nothing else. She found it hard to speak. Every part of her wanted to grab the boy and run but she knew that would only condemn the boys she hunted for. It cut her heart to shreds to see this small boy chained like an animal, and to know what he meant when he spoke about having company. She prayed that when they did bring this house down, a lot of the evil men who frequented it came down with it. She would attend their hanging in her best gown.

"I saw the woman and her man bring in the boy Noah. Some others brought in your Ned and Peter. They were yelling about that bitch when they were dragged in. I think they fought hard as they had a lot of bruises and so did the skinny man who was collecting the money from Mr. Searle."

"What did the skinny man look like?" asked Brant and felt stabbed to the heart when the boy looked at him with fear. "I am with this angel. Those boys are my brothers."

"But you have her eyes," whispered Henry and he reached out for Olympia who quickly took his hand in hers.

"I fear sometimes evil is born into a family. In my case, my father married it."

Henry nodded. "My mother was bad, too. She sold me to Mister Searle for ten quid."

Olympia felt bile sting the back of her throat but fought down the urge to be sick. "Tell us what the skinny man looked like, Henry." Anger pushed aside the sickness still twisting in her stomach when Henry described the butler of Fieldgate. "It appears Wilkins has always been more than just your mother's spy at Fieldgate, Brant."

"So it does. Henry, can you describe the man that was with my mother?"

"You do not want to know how the men with the skinny one looked?" asked the boy.

"I will find out who they were when I have a stern talk with Wilkins."

Henry nodded and described the man who had come with Lady Mallam and handed young Noah over for what sounded like a sizable amount of money. The look on Brant's face told her he recognized the man but she bit back the urge to demand to know who it was right now.

"Do you know what floor the boys are on?"

"All the boys are on this floor or the one below. The girls are on the upper floors. That is where Mr. Searle lives, too. Are you going to help everyone?"

"That is the plan."

"That would be nice."

Olympia could tell that the boy did not believe them. His brown eyes were dark with resignation and despair. She wanted to take him into her arms and hold him, but he was stretched to the very limit of his chain.

They asked him a few more questions but then the boy tensed. Before Olympia could ask what was wrong, he shut the window, even pulled the old worn drapes over it and she was alone with Brant again. Silently they worked their way around the house. Only once did they stop so that Brant could steal a look into a window but he quickly backed away and ordered her not to look as she passed. Olympia was tempted to disobey him but decided she did not really want to see what had made Brant turn so pale with rage.

They were soon back down on the ground and took up a place in the shadows by the corner of the house so that they could watch the door for a while. It took awhile for Olympia to be able to quell the urge to go straight to Dobson and demand he put an end to this abomination. She knew they needed as much information as possible if they were to be able to convince Dobson to bring his men here and help free the children. Dobson would probably come for no other reason than curiosity, even simply because it was the right thing to do, but he needed his men to end this place and most of them needed far more of an incentive than righteousness.

"Brant," she whispered and tugged on his sleeve to get his attention when she suddenly thought of something concerning Henry, "did you happen to notice the way young Henry talked?"

He frowned at first, wondering why she was talking about such things now, and then he thought back on the boy and all he had told them. "He is no street urchin or servant's child."

"No, he is not. Perhaps we should have asked exactly who he was."

"Do you think the boy is some stolen child, that there may be a reward for Dobson and his men?"

"I do not think he is stolen as he said himself that his mother sold him for ten quid."

"We shall have to sort that out later. Look who comes to play."

Watching the overweight man struggle out of his carriage, Olympia had to slap a hand over her mouth to stop herself from gasping aloud. "That is . . ."

"It is. I always knew he was a bastard but I had never thought he was a pervert as well."

"Perhaps he is here for the women."

"Girls, not women. If he is here when we bring Dobson around then that swift rise in politics he has been enjoying will meet a swift death. I wonder if this is how Mother got so much power."

"She knows who comes here. She knows and she uses it to get what she wants."

"That should help me and Andras get her claws out of my sister. This is not, unfortunately, the proof needed to bring her down. She has made her place in the very highest echelons of society and just because she knows a man who goes to a place like this is not enough to destroy her. In truth, she will probably use it to an advantage, claiming ignorance of his evil behavior, all the while delicately dabbing at the corners of her very dry eyes with a delicate scrap of lace."

"Aye, the poor-foolish-woman-that-I-am-look-who-I-trusted-and-who-abused-that-trust performance, most often done before the largest crowd of gossips ever assembled." Olympia smiled when she felt his soft laughter against the back of her neck. "And look there, it is Minden."

"Yes, the swine. And the man who entered before him would be one of the ones who now slams the door in Minden's face."

"With a grand show of self-righteous outrage, I suspect."

"Of the loudest kind."

"Do you believe we have seen enough now?"

"We have. Let us go and talk to Dobson."

"You are looking most fine, m'lady," said Dobson and grinned at Brant's scowl. "What brings you two to my office at this time of night?" He waved his two guests toward the chairs facing his desk.

"I did not know you worked the night through, Dobson," said Olympia as she sat down, crossing her legs and ignoring the fierce look Brant gave her as well as the sly laughter she could see in Dobson's eyes.

"Night is when most of the bad things happen, m'lady. I will admit, however, that I am not often here at this time of night. Just had a fair piece of work to do."

"We have just come from Dobbin House and believe the owners there have my half-siblings inside," said Brant, pleased to see all the teasing light abruptly fade from Dobson's eyes.

"Tell me you did not go inside that place, m'lady, or touch anything," said Dobson.

"Had to promise the earl the same thing and I kept my promise. All I touched was the hand of a small, desperate boy. I did not like having to leave him there."

"If you are sure that the house holds your three half-siblings, m'lord, then we can soothe m'lady's distress about having to leave a wee lad in that hellhole."

"The boy she spoke to," Brant said, "recognized my brothers when I described them. He actually saw them arrive. The boy is also no street urchin, but his mother sold him into the life. So with the reward I have posted and the one the boy might bring, it could be a profitable job for you and your men."

"Which will suit them well. Me? I would knock that place into a pit and bury it without asking a ha'penny. Just do not have me going in there based on a guess or a lie. I could catch a few very important people bare-arsed in there and I like my work."

"We are certain," Olympia assured him. "You would be as well if you could have spoken to young Henry."

"Then I must ask what you mean to do about your mother this time, m'lord?" Dobson crossed his arms on top of his desk and leaned toward Brant. "You now have a lad who could point a finger at her and might soon have a few men who could do so as well."

"I mean to make her pay for her crimes, Dobson. It will not be easy but I will see it done. The boy is but a piece of it. Alone, his word against hers will carry no weight at all, nor will the testimony of any of the other boys or the ones running that place. As for the ones of better blood that may be caught out tonight, they will be very busy trying to save themselves and I do not believe the fact that my mother may have blackmailed them into getting her something she wanted is anything that will help them. I cherish a hope or two that someone will be willing to drag her down with them, but my mother is cunning and I suspect she has covered her tracks or protected her back very well."

"Even the cunning ones trip over their own feet now and then."

"As I hope she will. Howbeit, I believe my part in all of this must be kept very quiet." He explained about Agatha. "I have to make certain that does not happen. I need to retrieve the power she has stolen from me before I strip all of hers away. I can do the latter much easier if she remains ignorant concerning how much I am doing and how much I know."

"Not sure that is going to work for you for very long."

Brant shrugged. "I will take what time I can gain. If I must, I will storm the town house and take my sister out of there. That will then put my mother in the position of being on the defensive."

Dobson got up and reached for his coat. After shrugging it on, he walked to the door and bellowed for someone named Jack. He told the tall, handsome young man who came running to get together ten of their men and a carriage or two for prisoners before shutting the door and returning his attention to Brant and Olympia.

"One thing you have not mentioned is what you plan to do with the children that will be taken out of there tonight," said Dobson, crossing his arms over his broad chest.

"I will take them with me to start with," said Olympia.

"Could be a fair number of them."

"I have a big house and I doubt most of them will remain for long. Three have homes to go to although I believe young Noah should not return to the family townhome," she added, glancing at Brant.

"No. He will stay with me and Thomas as will Ned and Peter," said Brant.

"There are orphanages, workhouses and the like for the children," began Dobson, his distaste for such places clear to hear in his voice.

"And we both know what they are like most of the time," said Olympia. "No, I will deal with the children."

Dobson shrugged. "I suspect many of them will just run off once we arrive."

"Oh, no, I do not believe so. You see, they are chained to the beds."

Still reeling a little from how quickly Dobson had gotten his men ready and headed to Dobbin House, Olympia stood beside Pawl as she watched the man lead his men into the place. Dobson, with his talk of orphanages, workhouses and the like, had seemed unconcerned about what happened to the children after he got them out of Dobbin House but Olympia had known the pose was a lie. Dobson probably cared too much having suffered in a few of those places as a child.

The smashing of the door was sweet music to her ears. After what she and Brant had told Dobson, he had placed his men in strategic spots all around the house and they were soon catching the escaping patrons. Outraged cries from some of the ones who thought themselves far too important to suffer this sort of treatment soon filled the air. She cared about none of it, her gaze fixed upon the door where the children would soon come out.

"'Tis rather demeaning to be hiding in the carriage this way," said Brant, his words a little muffled by the curtains pulled shut to hide him.

"You are too well known, m'lord," said Olympia. "Someone might recognize you."

"I truly doubt that as I go about very little in the city, attend few societal events, and am dressed like a man. Ah, here come the children."

And it broke her heart to see them. Most of the ones being led out clutched tightly to their blankets, looking dazed and fearful. Most of them were also very young, the boys far outnumbering the girls. A few of the girls looked as if they were past puberty but Olympia doubted it was by much.

She stood up a little straighter when Dobson led four boys over to her. It was not hard to recognize little Henry because he stared at her with wide eyes filled with shock and hope and when she held her hand out, he rushed to her side and grabbed hold of it. The three other boys watched her warily after Dobson left them with her.

"The earl waits for you in the carriage," she said and the recognition in the eyes of all three boys told her they had found the right ones. "Thomas is waiting at my home."

While the other boys attempted to slip into the carriage without exposing Brant to any prying eyes, she reached down and lifted Henry up into her arms. When the boy wrapped his arms around her neck and tucked his face up against her throat she had to swallow hard several times to keep from crying. She would give him awhile to recover before pressing him for more information about his parents.

"Carriages are loaded up with the children," said Dobson, who had willingly lent his men to drive the extra carriages that would be needed. "Near thirty of them although the older lasses are already speaking of going home. Are you certain you want them all at your home?"

"They need a place to sleep for at least tonight, but perhaps more. They need clothing, food, and so forth. It will be fine, Master Dobson. One thing the Warren is accustomed to is being packed full of children. We can sort out who they are and if they have somewhere else to go later." She nodded toward the wagons filled with the men and women from inside Dobbin House. "What happens to them?"

"Aside from filling the pockets of me and my men, I see a few transportations, one or two hangings, and a lot of new residents of Newgate who will get a fine, warm welcome from the inmates once it is known what they did for a living."

"Other criminals will find what these men did wrong?"

"Not all, but enough to make life miserable. A lot of the criminals sitting in Newgate were once poor wee lads who could be bought and sold for a pittance at any time and they all loathe the men who deal in it. Be sure to let me know if the children tell you anything of importance. I will be certain to let you know if we have anyone looking for any children. You take care, m'lady."

"Are you ready to come to my home, Henry?" she asked the boy still clinging to her.

"Yes, m'lady. I would like that."

With Pawl's help, Olympia got into the crowded carriage and settled Henry on her lap. She studied the three boys who were Brant's half brothers and almost smiled. It was as if she was looking at Brant at various stages of his life. Ned actually had gray eyes and she had to think they had come from his mother for Brant's father had had blue eyes, which Peter had. Ned and Peter looked bruised and she suspected they had never ceased to fight. Poor Noah looked absolutely terrified and sat as close to Brant as he could.

"I need to ask this," Brant said, his reluctance clear to hear in his voice. "Who took you there?"

"That bastard Wilkins took us," said Ned and then blushed and looked at Olympia. "Pardon, m'lady."

"Quite all right," she murmured as she stroked Henry's back.

Ned looked back at Brant. "Wilkins found us in the village and he had brought along those two brutes from London. There was not much of a fight, sad to say, and next me and Peter knew we was tossed into that evil place."

Peter was barely at the age of puberty, Olympia guessed, and he was, in a word, very pretty with his soft blond hair an unruly whirl of waves and curls and his big blue eyes. Ned had more of a rough edge and his black hair was straight and a bit too long, but he, too, was not yet of an age to be considered even close to being a man. Little Noah had soft, green eyes and the same color hair as Brant. An angelic-looking little boy, she hoped he had not been at Dobbin House long enough to suffer much.

"Noah?" Brant prodded. "You have not told us how you got there."

"Her ladyship came to me whilst I was pulling weeds in the garden. She had Holt the footman with her and he just reached out and grabbed me, slapping a hand over my mouth so I could not call for help. They brought me to that place and got a lot of money for me. She told me she was cleaning house and I did not understand. I do not go into the main house at all so how could I make it dirty? When I asked she just laughed at me and said I was born dirty and I would die dirty but at least she would not have to feed me anymore."

"You will stay with me and never have to see her again."

"Good but I would like to see my sister."

"I will see what I can do about that."

"Will you be sending us back to Fieldgate, m'lord?" asked Peter.

"I can if that is where you wish to go. Get some rest tonight, soothe Thomas's concerns, and we can talk about it in the morning."

Brant looked at her and there was such fury in his eyes she had to fight down an instinctive flash of fear. He had spoken so calmly to the boys, had stayed calmly within the carriage, that she had not really understood how much this was angering him. Beneath that anger was pain, however. A lot of pain and, she feared, a lot of guilt.

She looked down at Henry, who was watching

Brant with wary eyes. "Henry, can you tell us how you got to that place?"

"I told you my mother took me and they gave her some money," Henry said.

"I know. I was just making certain that I had heard exactly what you had said. What is your mother's name?"

"Polly. That is what Papa called her. His Sweet Polly, he always said."

"Do you know what your father's name is?"

"Gerald."

"I need a little more than that, my darling boy." She brushed the curls back from his face. "Gerald what? Gerald the Baker? Gerald the Butcher?" She was delighted when he grinned and hoped it meant he had not suffered too badly while trapped in Dobbin House.

"Gerald the Marquis." He nodded. "Gerald Humphrey Thomas William Understone the fifth Marquis of Understone Hill." He smiled after the careful recitation of his father's name. "He made me remember that and said he would teach me all his titles when I turned six."

"Your father is the Marquis of Understone Hill?" asked Brant, shock making his voice somewhat hoarse.

"But I call him Papa," said Henry.

"But your mother sold you to Dobbin House?"

"She said she did not like me anymore and that she was mad at Papa. Said this would make him love her again instead of giving me all his love." His bottom lip trembled. "I did not take it all. Just a little."

Olympia held the child close and stroked his hair. "Of course you did not take it all. Papas are supposed to love their little boys. You did no wrong."

"But he did not come to find me."

"That does not mean he is not looking for you. We just found you first." Olympia prayed she was right about that. "Now, one last question. The lady with the eyes like his lordship's? Did she see you?"

"She was my company and why I had to take a bath. It was cold, too. She would pet me and tell me that she had great plans for me and that I was going to make her a very rich woman. She said Searle was a fool and let her buy me from him for pennies when I was worth thousands. I did not understand what she meant. I just wanted Papa to come and find me."

"We will see to that for you, lad."

Olympia looked at Brant and inwardly sighed. He looked ill. It made her want to go and beat Lady Mallam until she lost the last of her cold beauty and then chain her to a bed as she had left this child to be chained. Such thoughts were useless, however. Nor did she have the time to indulge that dream. She had several carriage loads of children who needed to be cared for and a man who needed to be made to see that he was not at fault for the evil his mother did. Olympia had the feeling the former was going to be far easier to accomplish than the latter.

Chapter 9

Olympia was exhausted by the time all the children had been settled down for the night. She could only hope none of them tried to slip away, that she had gained enough trust from them that they would stay long enough for her to help them. Smoothing down the skirts of the gown she had changed into, she made her way to the library to sit quietly for a while and sip some wine before she sought out her own bed.

The first thing she saw when she entered the room was Brant. He sat in a chair facing the low-burning fireplace, leaning forward with his elbows on his knees, and staring intently into a half-filled glass of brandy. Olympia quietly shut the door behind her, got the glass of wine she was thirsting for, and sat down in a chair facing Brant. He still looked pale but no longer as if he was about to empty his belly.

"My mother is truly evil," Brant said quietly, never taking his gaze from the glass of brandy.

"What she does is evil, but I believe she is ill or deranged in some way," said Olympia. "Perhaps she was even born with something missing. There is a cold emptiness in her eyes that I found quite difficult to look at."

"Henry said I have her eyes." Brant finally looked at Olympia and found none of the disgust or fear in her eyes that he had worried about. "You changed your clothes," he murmured, realizing he had enjoyed seeing her dressed as a man a bit too much.

"The men's clothes smelled of the city and I wished to be fresh, to try to remove the stench of that horrible place. Now, about your eyes." She narrowed her eyes at him when he smiled faintly at her abrupt change of subject. "You have the same color of eyes as your mother, which is hardly a surprise, but yours are nothing like hers. When I looked into her eyes I saw no emotion, no depth, just the cold, hard determination to make me believe the lies she was telling about you. There is even a coldness in her voice no matter how hard she tries to behave in a correct, sociable way." Olympia looked straight into his eyes. "You do not have that coldness inside of you."

"How can you be so certain of that?"

"I would know. I may not have the sensitivity of some of my family, like Artemis, as that is not my gift, but I would know something like that. Artemis would most certainly know and he has not seen it in you. He had a small confrontation with your mother about a year ago, in the park where he had taken the children to play. She did not appreciate the presence of so many boisterous children as she was taking her afternoon stroll, with that rather large footman of hers. Artemis said that standing next to her felt much akin to hurling oneself into an icy pond."

"And you do not believe that I possess this coldness; that it does not lurk inside me somewhere?"

"Not at all. In truth, I believe you take things to heart too often, too deeply, and for too long." She smiled faintly and sipped her wine when he scowled at her, obviously trying to decide if her summation of his character was a criticism or not.

"What am I to do about her?" he asked, shrugging aside what Olympia had said. "She needs to be stopped yet how do I do that without destroying my entire family, putting a stain upon the name of Mallam that would remain for a very long time?"

"I am sure we can think of some way to do it."

"There is that *we* again."

"Aye, there it is. Thus far, all we have is her word against the word of children and people found using or running a house that sells children. Evil, certainly something that could possibly destroy her reputation and standing with some members of society, but not enough to end her reign and steal all her power. She has established herself as a well-respected power amongst the members of society."

"And established me as her profligate, evil son who indulges in every sin known to man."

"Well, not every sin. I do not believe she has mentioned sheep yet."

Brant nearly choked on the brandy he had just taken a sip of. Once he calmed the need to cough, he grinned at her. "Scandalous, Olympia."

"I do fear at times that a thought erupts in my mind and immediately flows from my mouth." She smiled and shook her head. "It is one reason why I make few appearances at society's many gatherings. Some of the people I must deal with at such events tempt that unrestrained part of me a little too strongly."

"I can imagine. So, what happens with all of these children you have taken in?"

"Many of them were not sold by their families but taken from them and have already expressed a strong desire to go home. I will send them if that is truly what they want but I will also give them enough coin to return to me if they find that their home is no longer so very welcoming. Wrong though it is, since what happened to them was not their fault, a lot of people can and will judge them harshly for it. The ones sold by their own family have no wish to return, as one would expect. That shall also be dealt with. You have your brothers with you now so that leaves only little Henry to worry about."

"We must tell his father where he is."

"True, we must, but perhaps we should attempt to discover why the boy's mother sold him and why your mother was so very interested in him before we tell the marquis that we have his son. Have you ever met this marquis? The name sounds somewhat familiar to me but I cannot place the man so I must not have met him or met anyone who spoke of him much."

"I do not know the man but I know of him as there was a scandal about him. He married beneath him and stepped away from a heavily disapproving society. The story I have heard is that his family was also outraged and he was nearly disowned, but then his wife gave him a son."

"Henry. And thus all was forgiven because the all-important heir had now been born."

"Not completely, but quite near to that. Rumors began that the wife, a daughter of a butcher in the village close to the estate, was not only utterly common but rather strange. Then the marquis retreated even more from society. The fact that we now know the wife sold the only living heir of the marquis for ten quid rather supports the whispered accusations that she is strange. As for my mother's interest in the boy? She had that heir within her grasp and now knows some very ugly secrets about the marquis's wife and his young son. Or, she intended to *find* the boy once a suitable, and very large, reward was offered for him. There may already be one offered and we were very lucky to find him still there and alive."

"Your mother is a very cunning woman but do you truly believe she would murder a child?"

"Once she returned Henry to his father, the boy could have pointed a finger at her, revealed that she was not as she claimed to be, and, yes, to save herself, I believe my mother would do almost anything. I have finally accepted that hard truth."

"We will send a message to the marquis right away then, but something suitably vague that will allow us to deny all knowledge of the boy if the father should prove to be unsuitable. I do not think he will as Henry shows no fear of the man, no reluctance about being taken to him. In truth, the boy was quite hurt and astonished that his father had not come to find him." She reached over to pat Brant's hand. "We will win this, Brant. It might take longer than we like, but we will win. You should set your mind on exactly how you will declaw that cat."

Brant set down his brandy glass, clasped Olympia's hand tightly, and pulled her toward him. He laughed softly when she stumbled somewhat gracelessly into his lap. This was what he needed. Passion eased pain, more so than any drink he had ever imbibed. Olympia stirred his passion in such a way it cleared his head of every thought save ones of her. He wanted that now, wanted his body and mind consumed by her and all that she made him feel.

"I believe we are behaving unwisely again," she said but curled her arms around his neck instead of scrambling out of his reach as a little voice in her mind told her she ought to.

"Are you about to become the wise one and flee the room?"

"I think not."

His kiss quickly cleared her mind of all thought save for how he tasted, how he made her body burn. Olympia knew she would not be pushing him aside this time. Brant made no secret of his hunger for her and that hunger soon infected her as well. As Olympia met the deep intimacy of his kisses, she helped him shed his coat, waistcoat, and neckcloth. She kissed the hollow at the base of his throat and breathed deeply of his scent, that of a clean man with only a touch of cologne.

"Bedchamber or floor," Brant said, his voice no more than a husky whisper.

Olympia stared into his nearly black eyes and knew

it was time to make a decision although, she thought with a touch of amusement eking in through the passion gripping her, he could have found a more charming way to push her to make it. "Bedchamber," she replied, not surprised to hear that her voice was as husky as his.

Brant set her on her feet, stood up, and grasped her by the hand. Olympia hesitated for only a heartbeat or two before leading him to her bedchamber. Her heart pounded with pure anticipation not fear. She wanted this. Wanted him.

She turned to face him when they entered her room and he shut the door behind them, about to make her confession about her son, only to have him silence her with a kiss. Olympia held onto him as he slowly nudged her along, never ending the kiss until the back of her legs touched the edge of the bed. The warm brush of his long fingers against her skin was the only warning she had that he was removing her gown. She had never been naked in front of a man before and a sudden flush of embarrassment attempted to destroy the pleasure she was caught up in. Brant lightly nipped the side of her neck as he tugged her gown off her body, but the first touch of his lightly calloused hands upon the skin of her upper arms was enough to push aside that newly born unease.

There was a hunger in Brant, in his every touch and his kiss, that rapidly invaded Olympia's body. Soon the fact that he was removing all of her clothing with a swift skill did not trouble her. She began to remove his with an equal speed, if not with the same skill. Even the awkward moment when they had to part, their bodies no longer touching, so that he could tug off his boots did not cool the fever they shared.

When they were both finally naked, Olympia was so fascinated with Brant's tall, lean body, she took little notice of how she ended up sprawled on the bed with him crouched over her. He was all honey-colored skin stretched tautly over hard muscle. His chest was broad and smooth, a small triangle of hair in the middle and a thin line of hair beginning beneath his navel, leading to a tidy nest of hair at his groin. She was pleased when the hard length of him that rose up from that nest did not stir her fear. She was just placing her hands upon his chest, delighting in the heat of his skin and the feel of him beneath her palms, when she became aware of how intently he was staring at her stomach. Then he lightly traced each faint line that bracketed her womb. When he looked up at her it was with a slight frown of confusion. There was no hint of anger or disgust and the fear that had begun to build in her heart rapidly faded away.

"Olympia?" He traced each small line again, certain they were the scars of a woman who had borne a child.

"Could we discuss that later?" She slid one hand down his chest and lightly grasped his erection, pleased to find that the discovery that she had borne a child had not dimmed his hunger for her at all.

Brant nearly gasped aloud at the strength of the pleasure that tore through him when she curled those soft, long fingers around him. "Yes. Later would be fine."

Brant was not sure how long he could wait before burying himself deep inside her. He wanted to go slowly, to touch her soft skin, linger over those beautiful rose-tipped breasts and slowly explore with kisses and caresses every hollow and rise of her exquisite form. His passion was running too hot and he did not know how to cool it, however. The way she had spoken of her marriage at such a young age told him there was a lot more to it than she was telling him, although the little she had said had chilled him. She was a woman who needed to be loved slowly, shown how good true, tender desire could be between a man and a woman. Yet, with each touch of her hands, the feel of her soft curves pressed close to him, he had to struggle hard for control.

Olympia was both astonished and a little afraid of how Brant was making her feel. She was trembling with need for him, her blood running so hot in her veins she was surprised she was not sweating. The way the warmth of his skin seeped into her, the roughness of the hair on his legs as they brushed against hers, and the touch of his lightly calloused hands on her breasts as he stroked them had her nearly panting. When he licked the aching tip of one breast she gasped from the flare of heat that shot through her body. When he took the hard, aching tip of that breast into his mouth and sucked she did cry out and thrust her hands through his hair to hold him close.

The wild desire racing through her was nearly too much for her to bear. There was a loss of control to it all that caused the faintest hint of resistance to bubble up through the passion that had seized her. She was ready to push him away, just enough so that she could calm herself, slow it all down just a little, when he slid his hand down over her stomach and between her legs. The touch of his hand was enough to shred that small resistance.

It was not until he began to push himself inside her that she regained her senses enough to understand what was happening and not just cling to him in blind hunger. A shiver of an old forgotten fear went through her but she fought it to keep it from completely cooling her passion. This was what she wanted, what her whole body was crying out for. It was just her mind that was trying to stop what was happening and she refused to allow it to deny her this chance to find out exactly what a man and woman could share.

Olympia wrapped her legs around his lean hips and gasped as he thrust inside her. She felt so full, so completely joined with him in ways she was too distracted by desire to understand, that she could do no more than hold on as he moved. He was saying something as he kissed her neck but she was so enraptured by the feel of him moving inside of her that she could barely understand him. Then he kissed her and she lost the last thread of coherent thought she had been able to cling to.

It was when her whole body tightened, the ache low in her belly becoming close to pain, that Olympia eased free of the hard grip of passion enough to start thinking again. Thinking was not what she wanted to do, however. She wanted to lose herself in the heat and wildness of the desire they were sharing.

"Hush, Olympia," Brant whispered against her cheek. "Let yourself be free. Fly with me, love. Fly with me now."

"Fly," she whispered back. "Aye, I want to fly."

A moment later she did. The knot in her belly snapped and her whole body was filled with a pleasure that rushed through her veins and made her skin tingle as if touched by tiny sparks from a fire. A soft cry escaped her and she tightened her grip on him as if she feared falling. She clung tightly to Brant as he moved in and out with a force that had her shifting against the sheets and then he tensed. A low, guttural groan escaped him and she felt the warmth of his seed bathe her womb as he jerked a little in her hold and then fell against her.

Still dazed it took several minutes before she became aware of the fact that Brant was heavy. Yet, she hesitated to let go of him. She liked the way he felt in her arms, joined with her in the most intimate of ways. A soft sigh of regret passed her lips when he slid free of her and turned on his side. A little embarrassed, she was slow to turn her head to meet his gaze, but the warmth she saw in his eyes eased that. She could see that she had given him pleasure and that pleased her.

"I meant to go slowly," he said as he lightly trailed his fingers up and down between her full breasts.

"One can do that more slowly?" she asked, shifting so that she was close enough to feel the brush of his skin against hers as he breathed.

"Yes," he replied and kissed the tip of her nose. "I thought that would be best for you. Less frightening."

"Ah. You have an idea of why I would have been married at such a young age."

"Am I wrong?"

"Nay, but I think I do not wish to bring Maynard's ghost into this bed with us."

"I think I would rather you did not as well."

"I will just say that you are most certainly right in what you thought. It was not what I wanted." She kissed his chest. "This I wanted."

He rolled onto his back and pulled her up over him. "This I wanted as well. Too much. I think the need is still very fierce."

She rested her forehead against his. "That does take one back just a little. I do not like to lose control." From beneath her eyelashes she could see him grin. "Arrogant sod."

"Yes. A man likes it when a woman loses control in his arms."

"Hmm, and does the man not do the same?"

"He does." He stroked her back, liking the way she pressed against him, rubbing her body against his ever so slightly in appreciation of his touch. "Thus the inability to go slowly."

"That is somewhat comforting."

"Do you wish to see if we can both maintain some control this time?"

"Can that be tested this way?"

"Allow me to show you."

* * *

Olympia was just catching her breath when Brant gently nudged her to the side and kissed her. She had not realized there was more than one way to make love. Ride me, he had said, and she had. A part of her was a little embarrassed about how enthusiastically she had done so but Olympia was determined to strangle that modest, genteel part of her for as long as she and Brant remained lovers. She would not allow anything to interfere with the pleasure they could find in each other's arms.

"I must leave," he said and brushed a kiss over her mouth.

"Aye, I suppose that would be best."

"I do not wish to. I would much prefer to stay here, curled up with you in the bed." He winked at her. "And within easy reach."

"Rogue."

He laughed softly as he got out of bed and began to get dressed. His body felt fully sated for the first time in years. Brant hated to even think of another woman while in Olympia's company and having enjoyed such a passionate interlude with her, but his mind would not stop the memories. Not once, he realized, had he risen from the arms of the women he had bedded with such reluctance and such complete satisfaction humming in his veins. It was something he really needed to think about. But not now, he decided as he tugged on his boots, pausing to kiss Olympia again when she crouched at his side wrapped in a sheet.

"My son is named Ilar and he is twelve years old."

"It is all right, Olympia. I was but surprised. That was foolish of me for I knew you were a widow. We can talk of it some other time. You need not speak on it all right now."

It was cowardly of her but she nodded, accepting the reprieve.

"Tomorrow night?" he asked.

"If it is possible."

Considering how full the house was he knew that was all she could promise. The last thing he wanted was all the children in the house thinking badly of their saviors. They needed to see well-behaved people, ones with kindness and genteel behavior after all they had been through. Brant admitted he also did not wish to deal with Olympia's nephews, Thomas, or her four very protective street urchins, either.

After several more kisses, Olympia watched him leave. The moment the door shut behind him, she fell back onto the bed and sighed. The fact that he had to slip away in the night, to avoid being seen by the others in the house, added the smallest of taints to what they had shared. She would not let that prey on her enjoyment, however, she told herself firmly, and quickly rose to wash up and don her nightgown.

Just as she was about to return to her bed, she thought of little Henry and went to her desk. The decision had been made to contact the boy's father and she saw no reason to wait. It took awhile to compose the note to the marquis, however, as she needed to be very careful in her wording, careful enough that he could not know for certain that she had the boy just in case he was not a man she wished to give the child up to. She then found her book on the peerage and addressed it to his London house.

Throwing on her robe she took it down to the small table in the hall knowing that Pawl would see to it the note was sent on its way before everyone woke.

Now that the chore was done, she realized it was why she had not immediately gone to bed and to sleep. Simply placing the message on the table to be delivered eased that nudge of conscience that had kept her from immediately returning to bed. Now her body was demanding she return to her bed, aches from all she had indulged in tonight beginning to make themselves known. Who knew lovemaking could be such a strenuous activity, she thought and smiled as she made her way back to her bed.

Even after she was snuggled beneath her covers, however, her eyes refused to close and she realized there was one more thing that preyed upon her mind, denying her the rest she needed. Her house was full of children who had suffered. There were so many she had to find a place for. It would not be easy. And then she thought of her very large family and smiled. It might not be so hard a problem to solve after all, she decided, and finally closed her eyes.

Brant lay on his back in his bed and stared up at the ceiling. His bed had never felt so empty. He wanted Olympia's lush body curled up at his side but knew that was impossible at the moment. Her house was so crowded he could never be able to slip away in the morning unseen. Nor did he want to have to face all those boys as he stepped out of Olympia's bedchamber. None of them were so blissfully innocent that they would not guess exactly what he had been up to.

He could still taste her on his mouth; still smell her on his skin. Their lovemaking had been swift and fierce, the desire that sparked between them a greedy thing. All the skill he should have gained over the last few years had disappeared the moment he had gotten her naked and in his arms.

The question that nagged at him, keeping him from immediately falling asleep, was why Olympia had taken him to her bed. She was a widow and those women were given some leeway. Many took a lover now and then. He had certainly enjoyed a few in his time.

Yet, Olympia had not done so, not once in all the years since she had become a widow. It puzzled him that she would suddenly become such a fiery lover in his arms. It also flattered him but he knew it would not be wise to revel in that too much. Her kisses told him she did desire him but he found himself wondering if it was the sort of desire that led to more.

He immediately shook aside that thought. He was not a good choice for any woman. He had a mother that would send any woman screaming from his side, a large contingent of half-siblings he now had to help support, three younger siblings he meant to free of his mother's hold, and a reputation that was so black no decent member of society wanted any-thing to do with him. And then there was his proven inability to protect those he cared for. He may have saved his two young brothers from his mother's machinations but that was his only claim to being the sort of man who could protect anyone.

There were so many failures in his past it hurt to think of them. There was Faith, the sweet innocent daughter of a vicar whom he had thought to marry. His mother had destroyed the girl and he had blindly believed that she had fled him, betrayed him with another man. Not once had he questioned that or looked for her. For that he believed he was as guilty of Faith's death as his mother was. Now there was poor little Agatha, trapped with their mother and facing a horrible marriage to a man most of society would like to see hanged. He had never even thought of his father breeding bastards, which was the height of ignorance, but there appeared to be a lot of them and he had failed them all as well.

If he was a good man, a strong man, he would walk away from Olympia as fast as he could. She deserved so much better than him even as a lover. Yet, he knew he would stay with her for as long as she would allow. If nothing else, she could make him smile and he had not done that for a very long time. All he could do was pray that he had no chance to fail her, too.

Chapter 10

The coffee tasted as good as always. Enid had a true skill with the brewing, so much so that Brant had been a little impatient for the horde of children to finish their morning meal so that he and Olympia could enjoy theirs. He looked at her, her calm beauty stirring him as always, but his mind fixed itself upon the one new fact he knew about this woman who was now his lover. Olympia was the mother of a twelve-year-old boy.

Brant tried to see Olympia as a girl of just thirteen, probably taking her very first steps into womanhood. It was not easy. She was such a strong, confident woman, secure in who she was even with all her eccentricities, that one could only catch the barest hint of the child she might have been when she grew playful with the children. And she had been no more than a child, one who had been cruelly violated by a man who, if the name she carried was any indication, had been a member of her own very large family.

"Good God, you were no more than a child when

you bore your son," he said and then grimaced. "Sorry."

"You seem to have become infected with my disease of straight from the mind to the tongue and out." She smiled at him as she stirred her tea. "No need to apologize. I was indeed a child when I bore my son Ilar. There were times when I think Ilar and I were as much playmates as mother and son."

"Why is he not here with you?"

"Because I came here to shop, to buy a few frivolous things, a few gowns, and perhaps attend a few events. Not anything a boy would enjoy. He is also not really prepared enough to be within the confines of a crowded city. His gifts still need some tempering."

"He has gifts as well?" Brant had to wonder at all the difficulties that must arise when raising a child with such gifts but bit his tongue, not wanting to divert her from telling more about her son.

"He is the son of two Wherlockes."

"Ah, of course. It would be most unusual if he did not have one."

"Quite. And a strong one which is why we discourage the marriage of cousins but," she shrugged, "it is not completely forbidden for the family is quite large and there have been many generations of outside blood mixed in. Ilar can move things with his mind. At times, when his emotions are running hot and wild, he can lose control and things begin to fly about the room. He is much better than he was as a child, when he often did it in play as well, but the boy is starting his way through that tumultuous path that leads to manhood so what control he had learned had suffered some."

"I am not surprised. It can be a very difficult time for a boy."

She nodded. "I found the change from girl to woman not so pleasant myself. His voice changed just before I traveled here. I keep thinking that I am losing my baby." She shook her head and swallowed the sudden surge of emotion the thought always brought with it. "Foolish."

He reached across the table and clasped her hand in his. "A little, yes. He cannot stop the change but he is your son. The very fact that you have kept him with you, raised him as your son, despite the brutal way he was conceived, tells me how well loved he is." He fought the urge to hurry to her side so that he could kiss the blush that colored her cheeks. "I am a bit envious," he murmured, and silently admitted that it was more than a bit.

"True, he will always be my son, my child, even when I need to step up on a stool to box his ears." She smiled when he laughed. "Ilar is also very, well, receptive to how the people around him feel. He has great empathy. Perhaps too much."

"Another gift?"

"Yes, although not as strong as the first one. That is often the case when one of us has two gifts. It is still strong enough, however, to make coming to the city too difficult for him, especially at this time in his life."

"Is that why you have kept him a secret?"

"I have not truly tried to hide him away. I was married after all so he would carry no taint of being a bastard and my reputation would not be hurt by his presence. Yet, I was so young when he was born that my family kept us both tucked away at Myrtledowns, watched over by my aunt Antigone as well as my cousin Tessa." She blushed. "My milk did not come in and Tessa arrived with her five children, one still a babe in arms, to be Ilar's wet nurse. She was with us for three years until her husband left the military and they bought a little farm not far from us. Aunt Antigone is still there, as she was a widow when she came and has stayed because she is very good at teaching Ilar control.

"By the time I was of an age to step out into society, and actually had an urge to go out in it from time to time, my marriage was forgotten by most people and no one appeared to know that I had had a child. We decided to leave it that way. No one in the family mentions my marriage or Ilar before anyone who is not family. I myself only mention my marriage when I feel that the information is needed to stop someone from pushing me to marry." She grimaced. "I believe some people now hold the foolishly romantic idea that I buried my heart with my husband, Maynard. The only thing I buried with that man was my innocence and my wedding ring."

"You have not forgiven him for what he did." Brant was not surprised, would actually be surprised if she had done so.

"And I never will. I know people say one should, but I cannot, not even though I see my Ilar as my treasure, my heart. Maynard broke faith with us all, and used his gift to do so. You see, he did not merely help himself to my innocent body, he forced himself into my mind, ripping away all control I had. Worse, it nearly destroyed my trust in Argus for he has the same gift. I knew in my heart that Argus would never use his gift in that way but it took a long time before I could stop fearing my own brother. A long time. Even now, although I would trust Argus with my life, I often feel a little uncomfortable when he uses his gift."

Brant patted her hand and then returned to sipping his coffee. "But what Maynard did has kept you from men, has it not?"

"I thought it had but"—she inwardly cursed when another blush heated her cheeks—"I now believe it was simply that no man truly roused my interest."

"Until me."

He looked so pleased with himself that Olympia briefly considered throwing a scone at his handsome head. Then she recalled how he had looked last night before they had made love. The look of teasing confidence that was now on his face, the glint of laughter in his eyes, was such a wonderful change from the hurt and despair that had been there, that she could not bring herself to dim it.

"Yes, until you." Then again, she thought, no one would blame her for finding that confident male grin irritating enough to want to slap it right off his face. "Even then I feared that I might be so badly damaged that I would balk at that last hurdle. I have come to believe that the scars from that day were not as deep as I feared because Maynard had taken such firm hold of my will that I was actually unaware of what had happened until many moments after I awoke." She shuddered. "I cannot understand, and probably never will, why he did it then for I was no better than a corpse, just a little warmer."

Brant silently echoed her revulsion. "But, he *is* dead now, correct?"

"Oh, yes, quite dead. He was killed not long after we were married. He lived just long enough for all of the paperwork to be signed and verified protecting all that is rightfully Ilar's. And to ensure that no one could ever question the legitimacy of that claim. I can see by the way you are nodding that you find such an action completely acceptable."

"I do. Any man would. I think it was especially important for the men in your family to act so in your case. Your family is different. From what I have learned, there are many in your family who have gifts that could easily be used in immoral ways. This Maynard fellow used his to steal something you had no wish to give him, were too young to give, and betrayed your entire family with that one brutal act. He revealed that he had no qualms about using his powerful gift for getting what he wanted with no thought to the right or wrong of what he was doing. Your family could not allow him to live and not simply because of the crime he had committed against you. He was a danger to you all."

Olympia badly wanted to kiss him but fought down the urge to rush to his side and do so. He understood. It had not been a revenge killing, although she knew there had been a lot of that behind the act. It had been a necessary execution of a man who had revealed that he was not only a danger to her, but a clear threat to the entire Wherlocke-Vaughn clan. The way he had used his gift to tear from her what

she would never had given him willingly was the very
thing that could cause a return of the dangerous,
and sometimes deadly, superstitious fears that had
plagued the family for most of its history. The killing
of Maynard had been, in many ways, an act of self-
defense.

"Nay, he could not be allowed to continue. He was
of an age to have had full control of his gift for several years so what he did revealed a darkness of the
soul, or mind, that would have been a threat to us
all, to anyone he met, for as long as he lived. Sad,
but it does happen now and then. The family has
rules and all know it. You use your gifts to do harm
in any way, even through deceit and theft, and you
will pay. The court was convened on him and judgment was passed. That allowed my family to take the
revenge they were all bellowing for."

"You have a court?"

"Aye. We have to. Can hardly take such a matter
before the King's Bench, now can we?"

"Ah, no, of course not. So a private familial court
is easy to understand. It must require a great
strength of character not to use some of the skills
you are born with for one's own benefit."

"Well, I would never claim that some of us do not
do that anyway, if only in small ways."

"But never to harm."

"Nay, never to harm. We are all taught the danger
of such temptation and the penalty for giving into
it from the cradle. We watch everyone in the family
and, believe me, that grows more difficult every year
as we are a fertile lot and no longer have people
aching to hang or drown us as witches."

"M'lady," said Pawl as he abruptly appeared in the doorway, "there is a man asking to speak with you. He says he is the Marquis of Understone Hill."

"Good Lord, the message I sent him could only have gone out a few hours ago," Olympia said and hastily turned in her seat to check her appearance in the mirror over the sideboard.

"I saw to it the moment I rose this morning."

"I shall need to change. I cannot meet a marquis dressed in my morning attire."

"I am not sure he will wait for you to do that. The man is very agitated."

"You look perfectly presentable," said Brant. "The man has arrived at your home at a time when none but family or the closest of friends would admit him. He can take us as we are," he added, waving his hand over his own attire of shirtsleeves, riding pants, and riding boots.

"Then show him in, Pawl, and bring us some fresh tea and coffee." The moment Pawl left, she looked at Brant and cocked one eyebrow. "You realize what he shall think when he sees us sharing a morning meal and dressed in this manner."

"I believe his mind will be too full of the need to find his son to care what we are about."

She was just nodding in agreement when a tall, fair-haired young man strode into the room. He walked right past Pawl, who was still announcing him, and then stumbled to a halt when he saw that Olympia was not alone. Brant stood to introduce himself and Olympia before showing the man to a chair. Olympia almost smiled at the man's look of frustration when he began to speak only to have

Pawl enter with more coffee and tea, instigating the formality of ensuring that a guest had all that he might want.

"Please," the marquis said once Pawl had left again, "you said you might have news of my son."

Olympia bit back the urge to immediately call for Henry and reunite father and son. She studied the man shifting nervously in his seat next to Brant. He was handsome in that English country squire way was but tall and lean. She could see little Henry in the shape of his mouth, his fair hair that refuscd to stay where it was put, and his handsome blue eyes. She could also sense a deep need in him, one struggling with the fear and hope filling his heart. This man loved his son. What she needed to know was if he loved his wife so much he would refuse to see the danger the woman presented to his child.

"M'lord, I had not realized that you were in town," she said. "As you can plainly see, I was not at all prepared for your visit."

"So you do not know where my boy actually is, do you." He dragged his hands through his hair. "I cannot believe she did this. How could she do this to her own child? I had not realized how terribly ill she was."

"She?" Olympia prodded when he fell silent.

"I might as well tell you as I am certain the scandal will break soon if the whispers have not begun already. My wife. She took my boy away. Told me she sold him for ten quid and I would never see him again. I could not believe it, but the way she spoke of Henry . . ." He swallowed hard. "It was as if she had forgotten that he was her son, too. You would have thought she was speaking of some urchin I had taken in and was paying too much attention to. I fear I was too shocked to guard my words. I was harsh. Should not be harsh with a woman who has clearly lost her mind, should you. But I was."

"M'lord, I doubt that mattered and no one would blame you for lashing her with words after what she had done."

"She hanged herself," he whispered. "That very night as I worked to start the hunt for my son, she hanged herself in our bedchamber. Well, the window of the bedchamber. Tied the rope to the bed, then around her own neck, and then leapt out the window. Doctor Martin said she would not have suffered as she broke her neck."

"So she is gone?"

"Yes, buried her just outside the family plot as the church would not put her in consecrated ground and I was in no mood to argue for it. Then I came here to look for Henry but," his voice broke, "I cannot find him. He is just a little boy. Only five. How can he survive whatever she sold him into?"

Olympia looked at Brant, who nodded and quietly went to the door to call Pawl. Knowing it would not take long for the boy to come, she turned all her attention to the marquis. "She sold him to Dobbin House." The way the man paled told her that, at least once, he had clearly spent enough time in London to know of the place, and she wondered how so many could know yet not do anything about the place but shoved aside her anger over that as now was not the time to go on some crusade. "He was not harmed. There was a woman there who recognized that he could make her some money and kept him to herself. We suspect that she was waiting for news of a reward."

"So he was not hurt?"

"Nay, but he was very scared. I fear he also wondered why you had not come to get him. I told him it was just because you did not know where he was and needed time to hunt for him. He also knows that his own mother sold him, for she made no secret of it. She told him that he took all of your love from her and she would not abide it anymore."

"That is what she screamed at me," he whispered. "What could I have done? I love my boy. Of course, I love my boy, but I still loved my wife despite how troubled she had become. I confess, that love had dimmed as she was such a trial at times, so angry, so jealous, so temperamental, that it wore on me. This, what she did to my son, well, I think that ended what was left of my love for her. Mayhap she saw that and that is why she killed herself."

"One can never guess the reasons someone does such a thing. Do not carry the weight of it. It was the illness in her mind. If your son had not become the center of her delusions, something or someone else would have." She heard someone approaching and smiled at him. "We have the boy, m'lord. In hunting for some missing boys of our own, we stumbled upon your Henry. I but hesitated to tell you straight out for I was not completely sure why your wife had sold him."

"Of course. I would never have brought him back into a house with her in it. Not after what she had done."

"I am sure of that now, m'lord. I but needed that assurance for I could not send a child back into danger."

"I understand."

The door opened and the marquis leapt to his feet. Little Henry walked in and stopped to stare at his father. Olympia could see the child's unease, his gaze darting around the room as if to be certain his father was alone.

"You found me, Papa?" Henry asked as he slowly stepped toward the marquis. "Does Mother know you found me?"

"Your mother will never hurt you again, Henry." The marquis walked over to his son and crouched down in front of the boy, touching Henry's curls with a shaking hand. "Your mother had a sickness, son, and that made her do bad things. It took her from us in mind and then in body. It is just you and me now."

"I was afraid, Papa," Henry cried and threw himself into his father's arms. "I was waiting for you to find me but you did not come."

"I was hunting for you, son. I would have found you. We must be glad and thank God that Lady Wherlocke and Lord Fieldgate found you before you came to much harm."

He set Henry back on his feet, stood up but kept a hand on the boy, and looked at Olympia. "I can never thank you enough. Not for finding him, saving him, and not for being ready to keep him safe even from me if necessary."

Henry slowly released his tight grip on his father's

leg and looked at the food on the table. "Scones and clotted cream. May I have one?"

Pleased with the diversion, for the man's heartfelt gratitude, the tears in his eyes, made her a little uncomfortable, Olympia smiled at the boy. Henry had his father now and, in his child's mind, all would be right again. There would be wounds that needed healing but she could see the love between the two and knew that would be what would slowly ease the child's lingering fear and hurt.

"Only if your Papa says you may," she said.

It did not surprise her when, after one pleading look from the boy, the marquis nodded. As Henry clambered up on the chair next to her and helped himself to a scone and a lot of the clotted cream, the marquis retook his seat. She made sure the marquis had a fresh cup of coffee and waited for what he would say. It was easy to see by the way his expression grew serious and a little stern, that the man wanted more information. Olympia glanced at Brant as he sat down and he nodded, silently agreeing that there should be no secrets kept even though it would mean revealing his mother's part in it all.

"Who was the woman who planned to hold him for a reward?" he asked.

"My mother," said Brant and shrugged when the marquis stared at him in surprise. "She likes money and has no qualms about how she obtains it."

"She had to know that I would have paid but also that Henry is too young to have kept silent about her part in it. Once that was known she would be destroyed in society."

"Very true." He nodded when the marquis frowned

in thought for a moment and then paled. "I fear my mother is not well. Lady Wherlocke believes she is ill or just missing that part of one which tells you something is wrong and that you should not do it."

"And what do you plan to do about her?"

"Destroy her."

Although the marquis nodded in agreement, Olympia watched Brant. She could see the cold determination in him but had to wonder how this would affect him. His deadliest enemy was his own mother. Could he, when it came to it, do what needed to be done to end her threat to him and innocents like the children and young women she so blithely sold to the flesh peddlers? And if he could, how would he be once it was all over? She shook aside the thoughts, knowing there would be no answer until it was ended. All she could do was pray that he came out of it all with heart and mind not too badly scarred.

"She has been telling some rather horrific tales about you," the marquis said to Brant. "Although I go out into society very little, even I heard the whispers. I wondered but I could not actually bring myself to believe them as it seemed too great a change in a man who had never before been the subject of such tales. She was making sure that what she said was spread far and wide."

"I know. All doors are closed to me now. It is making it very difficult to get what is needed to end her malicious games."

"No doors are closed to me."

Olympia joined Brant in staring at the marquis who just smiled and then sipped his coffee, making a soft noise of appreciation for the brew Enid was so skilled with. "But, are you not in mourning?"

"I should be." He sighed. "But, when she told me what she had done, as I said, the last vestiges of what had made me shock society by marrying her, died a swift death. The fact that she ended her own life," he added in a soft voice, "will be enough to excuse me for not mourning her."

"That and the fact that you are a young marquis who is now without a wife," drawled Brant.

"True, although no matter whom I might meet, I believe I have had enough of marriage for a while. Also, it will take awhile for the news of her death to reach society as the people at Understone Hill are loyal and suicide is something so scandalous they will attempt to keep it a great secret. I am not worried that I will shock society too much if I wander through a few salons and ballrooms for a little while."

"Thank you," said Brant. "We need all the information we can get to bring her reign to an end."

"Do you try to make her fall from grace as quiet a one as possible?"

"For the sake of my younger siblings, yes. They should not be punished for what she has done. But, I also know that could be impossible. It will not stop me." He looked at where Olympia gently bathed clotted cream from Henry's face with a napkin she had dampened in the finger bowl. "I cannot allow it to matter for she cannot keep doing the evil things she has been doing. Too many are being hurt."

"Yes, they are."

When the marquis and Henry were gone, Olympia

moved to sit next to Brant and kissed his cheek. "It may be good to have his help."

"It will be. The scandal about his wife will break soon no matter how loyal his people are, but I do not believe society will care much that he is not following a proper mourning period. He married so far beneath him that they did not recognize his wife anyway. I suspect many will believe the woman deserves no mourning."

"Sad but true."

"You are afraid I will falter when it comes time to bring my mother down." He kissed her when she looked guilty. "I will not, Olympia. I will not say that it will not trouble me when it is done, but I cannot allow this to continue. I failed by not ending her reign after what she did to Faith and I will not fail again. All I can hope for is that I can do it without locking her in Bedlam or having her hanged."

And that, she thought, was a sad truth she could not argue away.

Chapter 11

Idly wondering if she needed more sweets for the small tribe of children she now housed, Olympia hesitated outside the shop, decided she had enough, and then began the short walk back to the Warren. She hoped no one had seen her slip out for there would be lectures about walking out alone to endure if someone had. She knew a lady should not go anywhere alone but she was not some virginal miss who needed protection just to keep the slurs of gossipmongers destroying her good name and it was still day, as well as only a short walk away from her home. Despite that stern talk, however, she began to feel both guilty and nervous about being out alone. Olympia prayed it was not some forewarning and quickened her step.

After three days of hard work, her house was not as full as it had been. One by one the children who could not or would not be returned home were being placed with her family but she still housed six boys, one girl who was close to being a woman, her four boys from the stews, and her two nephews living with her. The ones rescued from Dobbin House would need a lot of help no matter how good the situation they were placed into was. They had been born into the dark, dangerous slums of the city and had an acceptance, even an expectation, of the cruelty of life that the children of the more prosperous would never have, but they were still badly bruised in mind and spirit. She wanted to take everyone who had sent the children into that hell to be beaten until the skin hung in shreds from their bodies and she would like to see even worse done to the ones who had paid to make use of those poor children.

She took a deep breath and let it out slowly, fighting to clear the haze of anger from her mind. Just as she began to feel calmer she heard the sound of a cat. Olympia peered down the heavily shadowed alley between two aging buildings when a repetition of the noise told her it was not a cat but a kitten. Good sense and a creeping sense of foreboding, but good sense crumbled rapidly beneath the sounds made by a small animal in distress.

Cautiously, she entered the alley. The moment she was fully within its confines, she paused to allow her eyes to adjust to the near dark surrounding her. The first thing she saw clearly was a tiny yellow ball of fur hanging by its back legs from a hook high up on the side of the building to her right. It was frantically trying to free its back legs from the rope that bound them, the other end of the tether tied to the hook in the wall. Appalled by the cruelty of such a thing, she hurried toward the kitten.

Olympia was just trying to figure out how to reach the end of the rope the kitten hung from when two men rushed her from out of the deep shadows a few feet farther down the alley. She held her folded parasol out like a sword but it did not cause the men to hesitate in their advance on her for too long. Olympia began to use it as a club next, swinging it hard against any part of the men's bodies she could reach. All the while she kept them at a distance, she attempted to back her way out of the trap they had set for her.

A small misstep ended her escape. The heel of her boot hit a slick cobblestone causing her to stumble. It was enough to allow one of the men to grab her and the other to deliver a blow to the side of her head. Instead, just as the swing of his fist would have landed on her, she turned her head and caught a hard blow on the side of her face. Olympia had to fight hard not to give in to the searing pain of the blow. The force of it had pushed her hard against the man who had grabbed her and he stumbled, releasing her. She forced all her fear and outrage over the men attempting to hurt her and, as they tried to get hold of her again, she showed them that she could fight almost as well as any man. She also fought dirty.

"Bitch!" the taller of the two men yelled when she poked him in the eyes and he released her to cover his now streaming eyes with his hands. "She done blinded me!"

"Shut your gob, Will!" ordered the slightly shorter, more muscular man. "Ye will be drawing all eyes our way with all that noise ye are making."

His warning ended in a high-pitched squeal as Olympia rammed her knee into his groin. He stumbled back and she turned, intending to flee, only to be grabbed firmly from behind by the man whose eyes she had jabbed her fingers into. He could obviously still see well enough.

"Thought you said she was a lady," the man said, panting as he fought to keep a thrashing Olympia from escaping his grasp. "Ye said m'lady told ye that. Go kill the baroness, she said. Baroness?" His laughter was full of a bitter repudiation of the truth, that this woman trying her best to hurt him was no lady. "She near to took out my eyes, and done tried to push your cullions right up into your throat. She be no lady."

"Shaddup!" Will staggered over to her and raised his hand to hit her again. "M'lady wants her dead. Says she be trouble and she wants the trouble stopped." He pulled his fist back again. "Says her son must be alone." He smiled darkly at Olympia. "So ye, m'lady, must go."

Winded and a little dazed, Olympia stared at that filthy fist aimed for her face. The man holding her had too firm a grip on her for her to break it no matter how hard she tried. He even kept his head pressed against the side of hers so that she could not give him a sound blow in the face with the back of her head. She was helpless and she hated it.

Just as she drew a deep breath intending to scream for help, something she suspected would do her little good, there was the distinct sound of wood making hard contact with a person's flesh. She had heard enough fights to guess what had been struck was someone's head. The man preparing to strike her jerked, a look of utter shock on his face as he slowly fell to his knees where he swayed back and forth for a moment before falling on his face. Behind him stood Abel with a stout club in his hands and a savage look of satisfaction on his face.

Olympia tried to struggle free of the man still holding her only to hear two more blows strike flesh and, chillingly, the sounds of bones breaking. Her captor screamed and fell to the ground, releasing her to grab at his legs as he fell. She lost her balance and landed on her hands and knees. One quick glance at her captor who was writhing and moaning on the ground near her was enough to tell her that at least one of his legs was broken. Daniel stepped into view and hit the man on the head, stopping the man's noise and sending him into unconsciousness.

"Lady O," said David as he tossed aside the club he had clearly hit the man's other leg with, and crouched by her side. "Are you hurt bad?"

"Nay, not badly," she replied as she accepted his help to get back on her feet. "The kitten?"

"Kitten?" David looked around and, after a careful search of the alley, finally saw the little animal where it hung. "Ah, poor thing. A lure, eh?"

"Aye. Need to get it down."

Every part of her hurt for each time the men had grabbed her they had not done so gently, but she moved back to where the kitten hung, still conscious but no longer fighting, and trembling in a way that broke her heart. The side of her head throbbed badly enough to make her stomach churn, but she could not leave the animal where it was. What chilled her to the bone was the proof that someone had taken the time to learn enough about her to know she had such a weakness. Olympia vowed to herself that she would remember that and consider the implications of it later.

With the aid of the boys, she collected her shawl from the ground and wrapped the kitten up in it as David, with the help of Abel, untied the end of the rope secured on the hook. Daniel cautiously untied the kitten's legs. Olympia collected her bag, had the boys pick up her scattered packages, and forced herself to begin the walk back to the Warren.

"We should call a carriage," said Abel, hooking his arm through hers to help steady her.

"Nay, it is not far," said Olympia.

"Or get someone from Bow Street to come and pick up that scum what tried to hurt you," said David, quickly stepping up on her other side.

"We can do that later." When she saw the Warren come into view she heartily wished she had the strength to run to the safety it promised her.

She knew she was a mess and was staggering more than walking. That was undoubtedly drawing the attention of everyone they passed. The three boys helping her were sure to catch everyone's attention as well as they were not the sort of boys a woman of breeding would have anything to do with. There would be gossip from this misadventure but she was too sore to care. Then again, she thought as the boys helped her into the house, she was a Wherlocke and gossip about them never truly faded away.

"Ollie!"

She scowled at Enid who was rushing to her side even as a rushing noise began to fill her head. "Do not call me that." A moment later, as both Pawl and

Enid reached her side, Olympia knew she was about to collapse. "Kitten," she managed to say just before the blackness crowding into her mind took her under.

Olympia could hear people whispering. She did not want to open her eyes to see who it was, however. Her head hurt and she was certain that opening her eyes would only add to the pain she was in. Confusion settled in as she realized she was in a bed and, by the feel of it, had been stripped of her clothes and put into a nightdress. Then she slowly began to remember what had happened to her. Pushing back a wave of fear, she cautiously opened her eyes and was relieved to find herself in her own bed with only Enid and her nephews at her bedside.

"Kitten?" she asked as Artemis moved to help her drink some cider.

"It is fine," said Enid and she set the tiny kitten down on the bed. "I washed it."

Olympia stared at the small animal. It was a soft golden color and had dark gold eyes. Its fur was all fluffed out from its bath and it still trembled. She was wondering how someone could possibly have discovered that she had a large tender spot for animals when the kitten began to scramble toward her. A moment later it curled itself up in the curve where her neck met her shoulder. Although it still trembled a little, it began to purr.

Enid sighed. "I suppose we will be keeping this one, too. Now, tell us what happened, m'lady?"

"Did the boys not tell you?"

"They did but I wish to hear the story from you."

Lightly stroking the kitten and pleased when it slowly stopped trembling, Olympia told them what had happened to her. It was difficult to keep the fear at bay when she recalled her feeling of utter helplessness. Someone had attempted to hurt her or even kill her. As she remembered who the men had said was the one they obeyed the orders of, she suspected just who that might be. There was only one person such ruffians would call m'lady and she had to wonder if Brant's mother had decided she was a risk too big to keep alive.

"We sent word to Brant," said Stefan.

"Oh. I wish you had not. He is meeting with Andras today concerning what needs to be done to get his sister free of that wretched woman."

"He needs to know that you have been attacked. We all know who ordered it done, too. David heard them talking about a lady ordering it done. Something needs to be done about that woman."

"I know. I am just not sure exactly what can be done just yet."

"He is the earl. No matter what the woman has managed to get some fools to grant her, any true court, any true judge, would quickly end her rule in favor of the earl."

That was probably true, Olympia thought, but the moment they went to the courts, it would not be able to be done quietly. "It would be such a scandal," she murmured.

"Not as great a one if she ended up hanging for your murder."

"Ah, true. I best rest a little then, for I suspect he

will arrive soon and I shall have to tell my tale all over again."

Enid rid the bedchamber of her scowling nephews with an efficiency Olympia could not help but admire. She then forced Olympia to take a drink of a potion that would ease her pain. When she tried to remove the kitten from Olympia's neck, however, the animal hissed at her, and Olympia waved Enid away.

"Wretched beast," Enid muttered but there was no real anger in her voice. "Its legs were not hurt badly though the rope and its struggle left a wee burn. It was not worth your life, however, and that is what you would have lost if those boys had not been following you."

"Why were they following me?"

"Because I told them to. Now, rest."

"Such a tyrant," Olympia managed to say just before Enid's potion yanked her into sleep.

Brant looked at the young man seated across the desk from him. Andras Vaughn had the look of many of the men in the Wherlocke-Vaughn clan, that utterly annoying handsomeness with a touch of mystery that drew women to them like a flame drew moths. Andras was slender and tall yet Brant suspected there was a dangerous strength in that graceful body that would surprise many. He also had blue eyes that held a strong hint of green. Brant was tempted to ask the man what his particular gift was for he was certain it was one that suited his choice of profession.

"All of this information certainly paints a dire

picture of Lady Mallam but, if she has gained the power you believe she has, then it will do little more than hurt her reputation somewhat," Andras said.

"Only somewhat?"

"She is one of the reigning ladies of society. Women either fear her or revere her. You, on the other hand, have been marked as that most despicable of creatures—an ungrateful son who has sunk himself in sin thus breaking his poor mother's heart."

The Vaughns obviously had the same tendency toward ill-placed levity that their cousins the Wherlockes did, Brant decided. "What you are saying is that I must catch her with actual blood on her hands."

"Perhaps not but all of this, no matter how fascinating, will not be enough. It is weakened by the fact that most of your witnesses are not of the right social class. The only one who is, is young Henry Understone and he is but five years of age. Not a good witness against a woman of your mother's standing."

"And ending my mother's hold on my sister?"

"You would have to be a vicar for a few years to gain that because of your reputation. Or, your mother would have to have a quite spectacular fall from grace. I need a creditable witness. Well, perhaps need is not the correct word. It will make it easier to get what you want if we have a more creditable witness."

"Not very hopeful."

"No, but now that you have begun to gather such information, I may be able to use it to make the ones who gave her custody of your sister begin to change their minds. No matter how your mother has strengthened her place in society, you are still the earl and that will count for something."

"It has not managed to open a single door for me yet."

Andras opened his mouth to speak but frowned when there was a loud noise and shouting coming from outside the office door. He stood up and moved to open it. The moment he did so young Daniel ran inside and moved to put Brant between him and the harassed clerk who had followed him.

"That will be all, Carter," said Andras. "The boy was expected."

The moment Andras closed the door, Brant looked at Daniel. "Has something happened?"

"Lady O got hit in an alley. Me, Abel, and David saved her but she got a few hard hits," Daniel answered.

"How badly is she hurt?" Brant began to don his coat and hat.

"Not too bad, but she will have a lot of bruises and they knocked her about a bit."

"Go," said Andras when Brant looked at him. "I will continue trying to find something we can use against her to break her power."

Brant was hurrying out the door with Daniel at his heels a moment later. He knew the boy spoke true when he said Olympia had not been hurt badly but that did little to ease his need to see her as quickly as possible, his need to see for himself that she would be fine. By the time he reached the Warren he had regained most of the calm Daniel's message had stolen from him. Then he walked into Olympia's bedchamber and saw her.

She was asleep and Enid was just changing the cold pack upon Olympia's face, revealing the deep bruising on the side of her face. Brant stepped closer to the bed to look at her and softly demanded Daniel tell him what had happened. When the boy repeated what one of the men had said, anger quickly became a hot flood in Brant's veins.

"I will return shortly," he said and walked out.

It was not until he had gotten to the door of the Mallam town house that he was able to grasp even the smallest shred of control over his anger. He pounded on the door and pushed past the butler when the man opened it. Out of the corner of his eye, he saw a footman run toward the small blue parlor his mother favored and, shoving the butler aside once again, he strode toward it.

There were several new and expensive pieces of furniture in the small parlor he noted as he strode in. Sitting on a settee covered in a rich deep blue, his mother looked at him. For one brief moment he glimpsed surprise and then a hint of fear in her expression, but she quickly regained her control.

"You have been banished from this house," she said.

"'Tis my house, Mother. I but allowed you to bar me from it but that is not what I have come here to speak about. I will let my lawyers sort out such matters."

"Say what you will and then leave."

There was indeed a coldness in her voice, he thought. It went deep into the heart of her, although he had to wonder if she even had a heart. The cold had always been there, he realized. She had given none of her children any affection. Over the years that cold in her had grown worse, burrowed itself deeper into her heart, but it had undoubtedly been with her from the day she was born. Olympia was right. There was something missing in Letitia Mallam.

"You had Lady Wherlocke attacked today," he said bluntly and saw only the faintest of reactions to his bold accusation, the merest flicker of an eyelid.

"You are being quite absurd. Why should I order anything done to that woman?" She glanced at him. "Or is she just another one of your many doxies? I suppose she is of a slightly better quality than your usual choices although the Wherlockes are not highly regarded everywhere."

"Do not play this game with me, Mother. I begin to think you believe your own lies. I am not some dim-witted drunk you can fool. I may have spent far too much of the last few years steeped in drink but you should remember that I also managed the estate and my investments enough to send you a princely sum every quarter. Heed me now, I have sent away all your spies and retaken my home. Fieldgate, if you do not recall where I live, is no longer your little hunting ground. And, yes, I have also discovered a veritable horde of Father's bastards."

"He had no right to put his by-blows in my house."

Her voice was still so cold Brant was surprised he did not see her breath forming in the air. "Neither Fieldgate nor this house is yours and they never have been. It might be best if you try to recall that from time to time. I fear your allowance may be trimmed so that I may sort out all these half-siblings. It is something that is long overdue." He could see the smallest twitch at the corner of her left eye and knew the mention of his father's bastards was not a subject she could maintain that icy calm she could wear like armor. Nor was the threat of lessening her income something she would accept lightly.

"You have no right to do that. It was an agreement made between us and you must honor it. You are, after all, a gentleman born and bred. Perhaps you best read it."

"No, I do not have to read it as I helped write it up and read it most carefully. I will see that it is made null and void as quickly as I can. As far as I am concerned the attack upon Lady Wherlocke has ended all agreements between us. You did not hold up your end of the bargain.

"I was moving slowly to bring you down, but no more. I know what you have been up to, m'lady, and once you did not see it fit for you to obey the contract then neither shall I. I was willing to forget you even exist but you could not be satisfied with staying here, enjoying the place in society you have made for yourself, could you? You had to play your games again. Well, they will fail this time." He leaned so close to her that he could almost taste the fury he could read in her eyes. "If you ever try to hurt Lady Wherlocke again, I will do far more than warn you off. Do not believe, for one single moment, that the fact that we share blood will make any difference to how hard I will come down on you."

Afraid he was about to do something he would

forever regret, his hands actually itching with the need to slap her until the icy grip she had on herself shattered, he left. He had warned her. That had to be enough. He could not make himself feel confident of that, however, as he returned to the Warren and Olympia's bedchamber. His mother was arrogant and she had gotten away with her many crimes for so long it might well prove that only her own death would put an end to it. She probably thought herself too clever to be caught and too arrogantly sure of her own cleverness.

When he entered Olympia's bedchamber, he saw that she still slept and moved to pour himself a tankard of the cider she favored and kept in her chambers. He actually wanted a large drink of brandy but he resisted the urge. Instead he sipped at a nicely spiced cider and sat down in a chair close to the side of the bed.

Olympia's face was even more brilliantly bruised than when he had left. There was no swelling because of Enid's swift and judicious use of cold compresses, but he hated to see her this way. She had not deserved this, was only trying to help him. Brant felt the bite of another failure in keeping someone safe.

And then he saw the kitten. It was watching him, its golden eyes peering out from beneath Olympia's chin. Thinking it had to be uncomfortable, and probably unhealthy, for Olympia to have the creature so close, he reached out to move it and it hissed at him. Just as he thought to try and grab it by the scruff of the neck fast enough to avoid all those claws and teeth, Olympia opened her eyes and looked at him.

"They should not have dragged you away from your meeting with Andras," she said. "Did they tell you what happened?"

"It was only Daniel and, yes, he told me what happened." He frowned at the little cat. "Are you certain you should have that little beast so close to your face?"

"It was terrified. I fear it is why I was caught in that alley. I heard it cry out and, even though I knew it was unwise, I had to go and see if I could help." She quickly told him all that had happened and was not surprised to see the anger on his face. "I know I made many foolish mistakes."

"Aside from going out alone, no. You went to shops very close to here and in the day. It should have been safe or, well, as safe as this city can ever be. Daniel told me that it was a woman who had told the men to hurt you and that it was surely my mother as they kept saying, 'm'lady' told them to do it. That she wanted her son to be alone."

"Aye, they said that. I am sorry. What I would like to know is how she found out that I cannot ignore an animal in need. Someone has been finding out all they can about me. It appears we are not the only ones doing some spying."

"I cannot think how she found out about you at all."

"There are always ones watching in the city. It has been clear to us for a while that she is very skilled in gathering information."

"I was so angry," he murmured as he stroked her bruised face lightly, needing to touch her yet worried about adding to the pain she had to feel. "I went to see her. Stormed in and threatened her. Told her she is to leave you alone. Reminded her that she is only allowed to call that house hers on my sufferance, that now that I know about my father's bastards I will see to their care and that could well mean she gets a smaller allowance from me each quarter. A few other things as well, but that is the gist of it. Not a wise move at all."

"Considering all she has done and how she probably knows we are hunting her down, I do not think it such a bad thing," Olympia said and quickly smothered a yawn. "She was certain to find out about us and maybe even guess at our plans for her sooner or later."

"You were right."

"Then you must tell me what I was right about before I go to sleep. It should make for a few pleasant dreams. It is not often any man tells a woman she is right." She grinned when he just grunted.

"About the coldness in her. Both you and Artemis noticed it. I should have for she had no interest in us, her own children. It runs deep and I believe it has always been there. Not that I try to make apologies for her actions, just that I feel a bit of a fool for never seeing it at all. Simply believed she was not one who cared much for children but had done her duty to our father." He sat up straight and said firmly, "And now you see why you must never go anywhere alone. Not only has she turned her attention to you but she is more than willing to kill you simply for helping me."

"I will be most careful from now on. Did Andras have good news?"

"Not really but he is eagerly working on it." He stood up and kissed her on the cheek. "Sleep. You are yawning so fiercely there is a chance you could accidentally swallow your little companion."

He was pleased to see her close her eyes. Barely a heartbeat later she was sleeping soundly. Brant felt the sharp stab of guilt. He had failed to keep her safe. Each bruise on her fair skin was a slap in the face, a sharp reminder that he was failing her as he had failed so many others. For a brief while, after they had become lovers, he had thought he might be able to have all he had ever wanted in life, but the attack on Olympia had shown him that he was not a good protector. It was best if he remained alone. When that thought hurt more than he thought it ought to, he hurriedly left the room.

Chapter 12

"There is no need to follow me around as if you expect me to swoon at any moment," Olympia said as she entered the room where breakfast was being served, her nephews close at her heels. "I am fully recovered from my injuries after a full week of being kept captive in my bedchamber."

Brant stood up and held a chair out for Olympia, fighting a smile at the way she glared at Artemis and Stefan. He was surprised she had remained in her bedchamber for as long as she had, but it had been far from some sort of imprisonment. Olympia had used the time needed to recover from the battering she had suffered carefully finding safe places for the last of the children from Dobbin House and gathering every tiny whisper of information that the boys, Brant, and many another collected for her. She had spent more time at her writing desk than in her bed and had enlisted the aid of her vast family in the search for information on his mother.

"You are still quite colorful," he murmured as he

watched her fill her plate with food, fleetingly touching the fading yellowish bruise on her face.

"And shall be for a while longer, I suspect, but nothing hurts now," she replied as she poured herself some tea. "But, I begin to feel uncomfortably caged."

"Despite the veritable river of visitors coming to see you?"

She laughed. "True. There were a lot. Ask a Wherlocke to dig up anyone's secrets and they gleefully leap at the chance." Olympia looked at him and added quietly, "It should not be long now."

He nodded as he spread some freshly churned butter on a piece of toasted bread. "I should not have gone to confront my mother. I see that more clearly every day. It merely allowed her to begin to cover up her many crimes."

"Which is something she cannot do, Brant. There are too many crimes. Too many people she has bribed, blackmailed, or merely tempted into joining her in those crimes. We may have only a few witnesses to point the finger at her as part of such crimes, but the numbers are slowly growing and will continue to grow. Then there are all the ones she uses to gain information. In truth, I think most of those who bow down to her commands are coerced in some way. Dobson said he got very little information from any of the gentry caught at Dobbin House. They will not be of any use to her now, of course. They have all fled the city and gone into hiding." She scowled at the scone she was about to smother with clotted cream. "I would rather they had all been hanged."

"Dobson said something very similar. He was also pleased that you had settled all of the children rescued from that hell. True, he just grunted and nodded when I told him, but they were definitely grunts and nods of approval."

Olympia laughed, easily seeing the big, gruff Dobson doing just as Brant described. Although hardened to the plight of poor children to some extent, he had moved quickly once she had told him of the chains holding the children prisoner in Dobbin House. He further revealed his caring by helping her gather information on Lady Mallam. Hobson shared her wish to rid the world of that woman and undoubtedly shared her disappointment that it probably could not be done in a nice, permanent way.

"It but goes so very slowly yet I ease my mind by recalling that we are gaining allies."

"Exactly. And she is losing them." She began to slice an apple and set the slices on her plate. "I have to attend a tea at my friend Mrs. Poston's today," she announced and calmly ate her food as she waited for the many arguments against her plans.

They began immediately. Her nephews gave up quickly, well acquainted with her stubbornness. The five younger boys gave it an even greater try but soon quit as well, diverted by the need to fill their bellies until they ached. Brant did not voice his displeasure, or even argue with her, but the look in his eyes told her that he badly wanted to.

She thought about how their time as lovers had come to a rude halt with her beating. Even though she had certainly been healed enough to enjoy it, he had been hesitant. Since her company ceased coming around once it was time for dinner, he had had no real reason not to come round. She tried not to fear that he had already grown tired of her, but the fear kept slipping into her heart and mind at odd times and refused to be completely dispersed. A part of her urged her to make it very clear that she was healed and eager, while another feared he would reveal that her injuries were not the reason he no longer slipped into her bed at night.

"When and where?" he asked the moment the door shut behind the younger boys and he was left alone with Olympia and her nephews.

For a brief moment she feared he had caught wind of what she was thinking and had to fight a fierce blush. Then her good sense returned and she knew that was impossible. If he had any sort of gift, he would have told her. He knew a lot about the Wherlockes so he would know that he could be fully honest about such a thing. It took her a moment to recall what they had been talking about before she had become lost in her own thoughts.

"As I said, Mrs. Emily Poston," she replied. "She holds a little affair each year and I have only missed it once since I turned thirteen as she is both a friend and neighbor in the country." Olympia could tell by the way he looked at her, by the slight narrowing of his eyes, that he had guessed exactly what year she had missed.

"I know where that is. Not far from here. She and her husband live right at the edge of the best address in the city. I can make certain you reach there safely, and leave in safety as well," he said, silently cursing the fact that he could not attend, could not stand at her side throughout the event and watch for their enemy.

Olympia wanted to argue with his plan but bit her tongue instead. Most of the reasons she had for him not to go with her, even as an unseen guard, were ones born of the fact that his own mother had caused him to be so thoroughly rejected by society. That was finally beginning to ease, more and more people beginning to question the tales Lady Mallam told about her son. Olympia was certain they had the marquis of Understone Hill to thank for that.

It was not enough yet, though, and many a door was still shut to him. He never got an invite to any event. If anyone caught sight of Brant escorting her anywhere, whispers about what he and she might be doing together would begin to fly fast and furious throughout the ton. It was only her concern about his feelings that troubled her about that possibility, however, for she knew he would take on all the guilt for any damage done to her reputation. He need no more guilt wearing him down. It could also be just enough to destroy what few repairs had been made to his own thoroughly blackened reputation.

"Just as long as you do not allow yourself to be seen," she said, "for there have been a few who have begun to question all your mother has said about you and we do not wish to destroy that. We will be in sore need of it later, I think."

"I know that but I cannot just sit here and do nothing while you walk into that pit of vipers. And what of all your bruises? Do you think there will be no questions asked as to why your face is that color?"

"I shall just say that someone attempted to rob me as I returned home after doing some shopping. Not such a rare occurrence, sad to say. I will also dim the harshness of them with a touch of cosmetics."

Artemis shook his head. "That might work but I do not understand why you continue to go about just listening. There is little of import to be gained from gossiping."

"You are quite wrong there, Artemis," Olympia said and was pleased to see Brant nod in agreement. "While much of the gossip has little foundation in truth or is but petty, useless news, there can sometimes be the hint of a very interesting fact. It does tell you who society has turned against, however, and quite often gives you an idea about who is doing the slandering."

"We already know who is slandering Fieldgate."

"One also needs to know what lies are being told if one is to refute them." She smiled faintly. "And Emily has always been a friend. One must never treat the gift of friendship lightly. This is her one large gathering, all she can afford, which is why she chose a time when many in society are at their country houses. She never fails to invite me. Never. I *have* to go." She glanced at the clock over the mantelpiece. "And I had best go and begin the long, tedious process of preparing myself."

"There are times when a strong woman can be the very best asset any man can have," said Brant as he watched the door shut behind Olympia.

"And more times when it can be a royal pain in the arse," muttered Artemis and laughed along with

Stefan and Brant. "Why is this taking so long?" he asked as soon as the laughter quieted.

"If I was my mother's only child, it would be done and she would be gone. I would care nothing about scandal or a taint to the name for, despite that, my marriage prospects would not be dampened much. But I have a younger sister and two younger brothers. I also have two older sisters, married and in society. I am trying very hard to end this as quietly as possible."

"Which means you must slip through the legalities of it all with as few people as possible." Artemis nodded. "I can understand that. It is just that she had my aunt attacked and would have had her killed. That makes me anxious to have the threat removed."

Despite the fact that Artemis and Stefan were still boys by many people's reckoning, the looks on their faces as Artemis said those last words were not ones to be ignored. They wanted his mother gone. He doubted the boy was meaning a simple seclusion in the country when he spoke of having her removed. Once he had understood how easily Olympia could have been killed that day in the alley, he had begun to think the same.

"It may yet come to that. Again, once the truth was known, I would suffer no penalty for how I rid my family of a threat but the others in my family would. Through society, the gossip they so love, and the cruelty that can be all too prevalent, they would suffer."

Stefan shook his head. "Have never understood why anyone would fight so hard to remain a part of something that seems rife with backstabbers and liars and worse."

"For marriages, information, alliances that might fatten one's purse. Many things are there that are useful if someone wishes to take the time and effort to wade through the muck to find it. My first investment, the one that helped Ashton get out of debt, was something we began upon meeting a man at a society event."

"Ah, there is that, I suppose."

"And," Brant grinned, "many of us do not have so many relatives we can fill a large ballroom by just inviting direct family and first cousins." As the boys laughed, Brant wiped his mouth with a napkin and then stood up. "I neglected to find out exactly when Olympia intends to leave for the Postons'."

He escaped the breakfast room before either young man could question his excuse. They were not stupid, however. Brant was fairly sure that everyone in the Warren was aware that he and Olympia had become lovers. He had missed her in his arms this last week. His body ached for her. Their affair was still new but he was certain he had never hungered for a woman as he did for Olympia. Since she would be preparing for an afternoon at a tea, he knew she would not be giving him what he ached for now but that did not slow his step at all. He just wanted to hold her, kiss her, and if she was healed enough to go to some society event, she was healed enough for that as well.

Brant nearly choked on his tongue when he stepped into her bedchamber. Olympia was standing there in nothing but a large drying cloth and carefully

adding some scented oil to a large bath, the scent
quickly wafting through the room along with the wisps
of steam rising from the water. Her rich, black hair was
pinned up in an untidy manner, long, wavy tendrils
dangling down to brush over her shoulders. It might
be impossible to stop at just one kiss. When she suddenly turned to look at him in surprise, his need for
her became painful for the swell of her full breasts
rose above the wrap and there was still the glow of
color from the steam.

"I but wondered when you wished to leave," he
said as he walked closer and lightly ran his knuckles
over her cheek. "And you are correct, you look
healed enough to do as you please."

The hunger she could read in his eyes made her
bold. "I fear what I would be pleased to do would
mean all this lovely bathwater would cool before I
got to it."

Even though her words struck him like a blow to
the stomach, he grinned. "Such a bold lass. If I did
not fear we would have some unwanted company in
the midst of it, I would show you how much fun it
can be to share a bath." He brushed a kiss over her
lips. "And you might wish to grab that little cat
before it falls in."

Olympia blinked and it took a moment before she
caught the meaning of what he had said. She gasped
and grabbed her cat, which was balanced precari-
ously on the edge of the tub. As seemed its habit, it
immediately curled up against her throat and began
purring thunderously.

"I do not believe I have ever seen a cat be so

affectionate but then I have mostly only known barn cats which are nearly feral."

"Oh, cats can be affectionate. It is just that many of them decide when they wish to be and care little for your schedule. But," she said, rubbing her chin against the cat's head, "if you get them as small as this one is, they can turn into very affectionate animals as you become, well, their mother in a way." She glanced at the big tabby cat sleeping on a blanket in the corner. "This little one may nurse off the garden cat but it still comes to me more than to the tabby."

"Mayhap it has enough sense to understand that you saved its life." He reached out to scratch the cat's head and, even though the animal allowed it, it watched him carefully and growled softly. "Hmmm. Jealousy." He glanced at the tabby, which was watching him closely as well. "Mother may not be this one's first choice but it still watches out for its charge."

"Come along, Lure. Settle down with Dinner." Olympia put the kitten on the blanket with the mother cat and watched as it was subjected to a bath.

"Getting my scent of it," Brant said as he stepped up behind and kissed her bared shoulder. "Time you wish to leave?"

"Three. Emily likes me to get there a little early so that we can talk and, I think, she likes someone to look over what she has done and approve before company begins to arrive."

He nodded and headed for the door, certain that if he did not leave soon he would be pushing her down onto the bed, but he paused, frowned, and looked back at the cats. "Lure? Dinner?"

"Well, the kitten was a lure, was it not? A lure to pull me into that alley. As for the tabby, she lives in the garden now and shows up at the kitchen door just as dinner is being put out to be served, faithfully, every night and right on time. She lost her kittens shortly after they were born. So, Enid felt she would be able to care for this one."

He laughed. "As good a name as any. I will be here with a carriage at three."

Olympia sighed when he was gone. He still wanted her. She wished she was not slated to go somewhere and the house was not filled with wide-awake boys who did not always remember to knock before entering a room. She could think of nothing she would like better at the moment than to spend the rest of the day rolling around in bed with Brant.

"You have become a wanton," she muttered, shed the cloth wrapped around her, and climbed into her bath. Duty called. Playtime would have to wait until later.

Brant watched as Olympia came down the stairs. He wondered if she knew that a little gold cat followed her. Then he looked her over from head to toe and wished he did not have to send her into the jaws of society without him at her side. Dressed in a blue gown, white lace at the neck and ends of the sleeves, she was beautiful. The gown also showed to advantage all those curves he was hungry for. He re-

alized he was feeling very possessive of her and tried
to kill the feeling. She deserved better than a man
who could not seem to protect anyone close to him.

"Do you know that you have a shadow?" he asked
when she reached the bottom of the stairs, and he
nodded toward the hem of her skirts.

Olympia looked down and sighed. "Lure. Bad
kitty." She picked the kitten up, caught sight of Pawl
lounging in the back of the front hall reading a book
and called, "Pawl, can you put this little demon back
into my bedchamber?" She heard a yowl coming
down the stairs. "Best be quick about it or Dinner
will be trying to claw her way through my door.
Mother cat gets very upset when she cannot find this
little bit."

As soon as the kitten was gone, Brant helped her
into her coat and escorted her out to the carriage. It
had curtained windows if they were needed so that
he could remain hidden as he left her at the Poston
house, something that galled him. He should have
paid more heed to what his mother had been up to
but had to admit that it had never once occurred to
him that his mother would find any reason to make
him such an outcast amongst society.

The ride was pleasant enough but only reminded
Brant of how much he wanted her. Her scent, the
brush of fat, black curls against her shoulders, and
even the way she occasionally bit her bottom lip as
she thought on the visit facing her made him eager
to push her skirts up and take her right there in the
carriage. Tonight, he promised himself.

"When shall I collect you?" he asked as the carriage pulled up in front of the Postons'.

As she leaned forward in preparation of getting out of the carriage, Olympia was about to answer when there was a soft tap at the window. She was even more startled when Brant pushed his body forward, hiding her behind him as he looked out the window. Over his shoulder she saw the marquis and wondered why Brant did not relax at the sight of a man he knew fairly well now.

"M'lady?" said the marquis, or Stone as he preferred to be called. "I thought I recognized you."

"Brant," she whispered and nudged him, hard, in the ribs. "I think it wonderful that he is here and can serve as an escort if needed, someone to shelter behind if I find reason for that as well."

Brant sighed and pulled away from the window, knowing that he was risking being seen. He knew she was right, just as he knew he had no reason to be jealous of the marquis. The man was eager to make someone pay for what had happened to his child. Even better he fully understood why it all had to be done so carefully. Yet, he was young, handsome, and of a higher rank. Undoubtedly far richer as well, he thought a little sourly.

"I am willing to bring her home, Brant," the marquis said as he helped Olympia out of the carriage.

The word no was on the tip of his tongue but he bit it back. That would be convenient and would lessen the risk that someone would recognize him with Olympia. It would also give her an added shield from gossip if all saw that the marquis friended her.

"That would be convenient. Thank you, Stone."

As the carriage pulled away Brant decided he would use his time to prepare a romantic night for

Olympia. Their time as lovers had not only been short, but a bit rough, their hunger for each other too new and hot to allow much seduction and romance. He smiled, his good mood revived by the idea and he began to make plans.

"It is very kind of you to offer to escort me home, Stone," Olympia said as the butler collected their coats.

"I fear Fieldgate was not so pleased by the offer." He laughed and shook his head at her look of confusion. "He conceded but I could see that he did not want to hand you over into my care."

The thought that Brant might actually be jealous of Stone was a heady one. Olympia wanted to consider it some more, but her friend hurried up to her and a moment later, just long enough to settle Stone in the library with a drink, Emily had her looking at all the arrangements she had made and talking of everything that had happened in her life in the months since they had seen each other.

Emily had a full, happy life and Olympia admitted to a fleeting twinge of jealousy. Her friend's husband was a good man, faithful, kind, and madly in love with his wife. They already had two beautiful, healthy children, a boy and a girl. It was all Olympia had once thought would be her future. Despite the dismal fortune her family had with husbands and wives, she had never let go of that dream, not until the night Maynard had destroyed her innocence.

"So, is the marquis courting you?" asked Emily and then she blushed at the startled look on Olympia's face. "I realize he is but newly widowed but from the whispers I have been hearing it was an ill-fated match, unequal if you will, and the wife was, well, ill."

Since Stone had given her permission to speak of it all if asked directly, Olympia told her a very discreet version of what had happened. Henry had just been tossed out in the city, not sold, and Polly had committed suicide but not in the rather gruesome way she had. She made sure she also left a large hint of extreme marital discord woven into the tale.

"So sad. He is a very good man. He has never acted as if he is too far above us to bother with us as many of his rank would and I know he loves his boy. I believed he loved his wife but if she had been ill for a long time . . ."

"She was. And, it wears on one, Em. Wears on one every day and night for as long as the couple remains together. He is a good man, and there was still some love there, but there was no chance of fixing what ailed that marriage for she was sick in her mind and there is rarely a cure for that. What she did to Henry killed the last vestiges of that love."

"I can see how it would. Well, go join the marquis as my footmen just gave me the signal that my guests are arriving." She winked at Olympia. "I think the marquis will appreciate a little protection."

Olympia went to sit with Stone and almost laughed at the sigh of relief he gave. He might not be in mourning but he was not ready to be looking for another wife. She hoped he did not give up all thought of one for she had the feeling that Stone was one of those men who liked to be married. Subtly patting his hand and grinning when he chuckled, she turned her attention on the guests arriving.

It did not take long for Olympia to sense that a few of the guests were cool to her. They did not openly snub her because she was a friend of the hostess and the marquis. For a moment she wondered if they feared she had already taken the excellent marriage prize off the market but soon realized it was more. Lady Mallam had turned her slanderous talents her way.

"I will not stand for this," Stone said in a cold voice that starkly reminded her that this man was one step away from being a duke. "Do they think I cannot see what they are doing?"

"Take no mind of it, Stone. She is still trying to separate me from her son, to steal away what appears to be his only ally. This will not work for long if I keep from being seen with Brant very often." She sighed as a worried Emily hurried to her side.

"What is wrong?" Emily whispered and slipped her arm around Olympia's waist. "Who has been saying things about you that have these silly cows acting as if they might catch some dreaded disease if they get within feet of you?"

"It is nothing, my friend." She kissed Emily's cheek. "Someone wishes to send me running home and I refuse to do so. I will tell you the why of it all when I can."

"I know who spreads the tales. It is that nasty Lady Mallam. She wishes you to be barred from all the best homes and that means it is something that would be to her advantage. Everything she does is to better herself or fatten her purse. I have never understood why anyone listens to her. My darling tells me that she has destroyed several good men and then slipped right into the investments or business they had before she began her hateful campaign against them."

Seeing a wonderful source of some of the best gossip, Olympia pressed her friend for more. As the afternoon wore on, Emily divided her time between seeing to her guests and filling Olympia's ears with all kinds of fascinating information. By the time Stone settled her in his carriage and they started on their way to the Warren she was eager to get it all written down. There was some pattern there she was not seeing yet and she was certain it would lead her to a way to cut Lady Mallam off at the knees.

"A fruitful day, I gather," said Stone.

"I think so but I need to study it for a bit before I can be sure. How is Henry?"

"He sleeps with me every night. I will allow it for now as he wakes terrified if I am not close at hand but I shall have to break him of it eventually. He does not miss his mother much at all. I realized that he loves his nursemaid, Moira. My wife must have ceased to care for her child a lot earlier than I had thought."

"It will pass, Stone. He is little more than a babe and he was terrified. He was also deeply hurt. I am glad he has his Moira even though it is sad that he turned to someone else for the caring he needed. Being with her again will soften some of those hurts he suffered."

"I hope you are right. Henry would like to come

and visit you. He says he misses Enid's scones and playing with the boys."

"He is welcome whenever he wishes to come. Ah, here we are."

"Take care, Olympia," he said as he helped her out of the carriage. "A woman like Lady Letitia Mallam is a dangerous enemy to have. It appears she may see you as a threat. This attempt to blacken your name is but a minor salvo in her war against you."

Olympia nodded and headed up the steps to her home. It had hurt a little to be snubbed on the basis of one cold woman's words, but she found it easy to push the hurt aside. Her friends had stood firm at her side. The only real problem she had concerning what Lady Mallam was doing was that she now had to report that behavior to Brant. She hoped he was past being hurt or shamed by what his mother did.

Chapter 13

The aroma of expensive scented candles struck Olympia first as she entered her bedchamber. She shut the door behind her and looked around but did not see anyone. Taking off her gloves and tossing them onto the desk, she moved toward the candles lined up on the hearth. They were lovely and the scent was just enough and not too flowery. She was just about to go and find out who had put them there when Brant entered the room followed by Pawl carrying a tray that was so loaded with food and drink she was surprised he could carry it. It was then that she noticed someone had set a small table and two chairs to the side of the fireplace.

She said nothing as the two of them set out the food and a grinning Pawl slipped away. She had not eaten many of the dainty treats at Emily's and the scent of roasted chicken had her stomach rumbling with hunger. Brant held out the chair for her and she smiled at him as she took her seat.

"It is a little early for such a meal," she said and

then frowned and looked around. "Where are Dinner and Lure?"

"In with Enid and Pawl. I tipped him well for the favor, too," said Brant as he sat down across from her. "I thought such a meal would prove more temptation than they could resist."

"I confess that I am quite hungry. Emily always has wonderful delights at her teas but I rarely get a chance to eat many of them. Many are a little too sweet for my tastes anyway."

"And how fares Stone?" he asked as he cut some meat and set it on her plate.

"He uses me as a shield. A very few have already heard that he is a widower and do not seem overly offended at his lack of mourning. But then, he is young, wealthy, and in line for a dukedom. My standing by him does not deter everyone but it helps. He did ask if Henry could come to visit as the boy wants one of Enid's scones and wants to see the boys staying here."

"Does he suffer from his ordeal?"

He listened as she repeated what Stone had said about his child and that small jealous part of him relaxed at the tone of her voice as she spoke of the man. Stone was a friend to her, no more. Brant knew it was selfish of him as he could not keep her but he did not want to see her with another man, either.

"I discovered something else," she began tentatively, reluctant to spoil the enjoyable time they were spending together.

"I am not going to like this, am I?"

"How can you know?"

"Something in the way you are looking at me. What has my mother done now?"

"I fear she has decided that since she cannot attack me physically she will do so by ruining me in the eyes of society. By linking me to you."

"Why would anyone heed her? No one has seen us together." Brant realized he was gripping his knife so tightly the handle was impressed upon his palm and he forced himself to control his anger.

"That does not seem to bother anyone. Emily made quite a show of favoring me and I hope it does not cost her too much. And, of course, I did have a marquis at my side. It was still little more than a whisper and the hint of a snub from a very few people."

"Why does anyone listen to her? Some are already seeing that what she said about me could be all lies and yet they now heed what she says about you?"

"Gossip, especially the dark sort that can ruin people completely, is the life's blood of the aristocracy. Stone made his disapproval very clear although he rarely had to say a word against anyone who was trying to whisper anything in his ear. It made a great difference. The sense of being almost snubbed began to disappear quickly. I think she might fail at her trick this time."

"Perhaps if I banish her to her country house."

"She would soon begin her games there and then you would have to be constantly watching her. I do not think you wish to do that. I did get some information though, from Emily herself." She told him all she had discovered about some men who had lost their business, investments, or even, in two cases, their inheritance. "These may be the people with

some credibility that we could use to bring her to
justice."

"Do you know, if she had put all this guile into
honest investments and business she could have
become very wealthy without hurting anyone or
breaking the law."

"I have discovered over the years that many see
those things, investments and business, as a worse
mark against you than any criminal venture one
might have gotten caught up in."

"I am sorry you were hurt by this latest trick of
hers."

"Oh, it was not so bad. I did feel a pang at first but
the way Stone and Emily showed their approval of
me in ways that began to become a little embarrassing," she grinned when he laughed, "but touching
as well. It also worked. Most of the ones spreading
the tales quickly closed their mouths and refused to
listen to any more or repeat them. It will be fine. It
was just a surprise. But, I really must make notes of
all I heard concerning those businesses and all."

"Later. Eat, woman." He winked at her. "You will
be in need of your strength."

She blushed and turned her attention to her
meal. Her heart was pounding for she suddenly realized what Brant was doing. He was seducing her.
She was more than ready to be seduced. Glancing at
the candles, she realized he was also trying to be a
little romantic.

By the time they finished the meal and sat on the
rug before the fire sipping wine, Olympia realized
she was probably not one inclined toward long, slow
seductions. Her whole body was aching to be rid of

her suddenly too constricting clothing and to rid Brant of his. She wanted to be skin to skin with him.

"Relax, Olympia," he said as he leaned closer and kissed the side of her neck. "Are you uncertain now that we have been apart for a while?" he felt compelled to ask but he prayed she would say no.

"I was just thinking that I may not be a woman who enjoys what I believe is a slow seduction. Or"— she turned her face toward his and brushed her lips across his—"it has just been too long since I felt your skin beneath my hands."

He shuddered. "Wretched woman. I wanted to go slow. To show you how one can build that delicious heat slowly, savor it, revel in it."

"Oh. That does sound lovely but perhaps it is all too new for me."

He began to unlace her gown. "This is new to me as well." He noticed how her eyes narrowed in suspicion. "Not an empty compliment, I swear. I rutted, Olympia. That is all. I am embarrassed to admit that a lot of times I was so drunk I remember little of what happened. You? I ache. I want. I remember every touch, every kiss, and want more."

She thought about that as she undid his waistcoat. It made sense even though she hated to think of him with those other women. They were no more than a different kind of drink for him. He lost himself in the pleasures of the flesh but had no interest in who gave him that pleasure. One thing she was certain about was that he enjoyed her company. It seemed an odd thing to be so happy about when he offered no more than the delights of lovemaking, but it did make her happy. She opened his shirt and kissed his chest, enjoying the faint tremor that went through him.

"Olympia," he whispered and tried to remove her gown with some skill even though his hands were not as steady as they should be. "I begin to think you may be right."

"Oh, how nice." She took off his waistcoat and tossed it aside. "I truly do love to be right. Even more do I enjoy the fact that you actually say I am. The men in my family can be very reluctant to say such things." She took off his shirt and tossed it after his waistcoat.

The touch of her mouth against his skin had his blood running so hot, Brant could not think clearly for a moment. He tossed her gown to the side and stared down at her lacy shift and a lacy style of drawers, something considered outrageously scandalous by most of proper society. There was a naughty side to his Olympia and he decided he liked it very much indeed just before he began to remove the last of her clothes. He was a little surprised at how skillfully and quickly she removed his as well, his boots the only thing that caused them to have to pause in undressing each other.

"I shall have to remove them the moment I am alone with you," he muttered as he tossed them aside and then sat still as she removed the last of his clothes.

"It would not take long for my family to guess why you are always in your stocking feet around me."

"I know. Even the boys are a little too clever by half."

"Kiss me," she whispered as she put her arms

around his neck and pressed her body against his, savoring the feel of his warm flesh against hers.

He did as he pushed her down onto the soft carpet. The soft warmth of her flesh was enough to strain his control. He wanted to be buried deep inside her now but grit his teeth and struggled to get his runaway desire under control. Olympia had a true skill for making him lose all finesse in the art of lovemaking. He grew wild with need and suspected it was partly because she did. Olympia was a very passionate woman.

Olympia hummed with delight as he kissed and stroked her breasts. She had the fleeting thought that it was a good thing she had never had any idea of how much pleasure could be found in a man's arms or she would have become notorious in her greed. Then she accepted that it was just Brant who made her feel this way. She knew she ought to think about that for a while but then he took the hard tip of her breast deep into his mouth and she forgot everything but how her desire was racing through her body, settling in a hard ache of need between her thighs.

He began to kiss his way down her body and she shifted slightly beneath his kisses and caresses. Each touch of his mouth against her skin was like the flicker of a flame, heating her, adding a sharper edge to her passion. When he stroked her between her thighs with his long fingers she opened to his touch. It was as if he was petting her in just the way she needed to keep her desire running hot.

It was not until he touched his mouth to the place where his fingers had been playing that her desire was checked a little. The intimacy was so deep she was shocked yet intrigued. Then he thrust his tongue inside of her and she lost all ability to think at all. A small part of her passion-clouded mind was disturbed by such an intimacy but that hesitancy faded rapidly as he kissed and stroked her so intimately. When her belly grew tight with an ache that was both pleasure and pain she tried to pull him up into her arms so that he could join their bodies, but he resisted. Then she broke, crying out his name as her release tore through her. She grabbed him and held on tightly as he thrust himself inside of her and rode the wave of pleasure with her, calling out her name as he shuddered in completion while he held tight against her body.

Brant could not move but managed somehow to shift his sated body to the side so that he was not resting all of his weight on top of her. Olympia was pure fire in his arms. He did not think he had ever bedded a woman who so enjoyed lovemaking or was so ready to return kiss for kiss and touch for touch. Women whom one paid often had some training but that training actually tainted their touch for one could feel the practiced art of it even as it stirred one's passion. Olympia had no more than a natural skill and a hunger that equaled his.

"We should move to the bed," Olympia said when she was finally able to find her voice. "The carpet is nice but one realizes how hard the floor is after awhile."

"I am comfortable," he said and grinned when she slapped his backside.

He stood up, picked her up in his arms, and ignored her protests as he carried her to the bed. Her

beautifully done hair was not so tidy now and he
loved the look of it. Tossing her onto the bed, he
quickly joined her and pulled the coverlet over
them. The moment he was settled on his back,
Olympia curled up in his arms.

"I had not realized that when one made love one
could kiss a person everywhere," she murmured
against his chest.

"When one makes love there are many things one
can do but only if both wish to do it."

"Such as having two women at once," she drawled
and almost laughed at his blush of embarrassment
for it was enough to soothe the anger that memory
brought with it.

"Many men think that is the best thing that can
ever happen to them. I rather wish I recalled the
incident."

"You recall none of it?"

"Not a single kiss but then there may not have
been any kisses. I will not say that there are not some
unfaithful wives walking around out there who
have known me well, or a few widows, but mostly it
is the ones a man pays for who have all the skills.
And then that is what it is like. A session with someone who has been taught some skills." He grimaced.
"Not something I should be discussing with you."

"Do not forget what this place was, Brant. The
Wherlocke Warren. Filled to the rafters with the
by-blows of my family. While I will admit to some
ignorance on the methods and positions and all, I
have never been ignorant of the act or talk of desire
or pleasure or all the rest."

"The men in your family should, perhaps, take a

little more care in how they speak before the women in the family."

"Why? Are not all women expected to become wives? To bed down with their husband every night?"

"And you think knowing about such things while still innocent is a good idea?"

"I think too much ignorance is a bad idea. Be honest with me, Brant. Were you disappointed that I was not a virgin?"

"As good as," he murmured and thought about it for a moment. "No. I was not. Bedding a virgin, something I have never done but have heard a lot of talk about, does not sound like it is so very enjoyable. I even had one friend whose wife swooned at the sight of him naked on their wedding night. Turns out she thought he had some strange mutation." He grinned when she started giggling. "Yes, we all laughed, too, but thinking on it, it isn't all that funny when you are the man standing there with your new bride, a woman he loved dearly, so he said, in a limp pile at your feet. So perhaps some knowledge would be good but I suspect few will ever get it. It would worry parents that their virginal little darling might attempt to find out for herself if all they told her was true."

"Foolish." She trailed her fingers up and down his belly. "So kissing one anywhere is acceptable? Like riding you is acceptable?"

"Yes. If both enjoy it, it is acceptable."

He gasped when she suddenly dove beneath the coverlet. Brant then tensed when he felt the warmth of her lips and tongue on his stomach. Although he was hoping she intended to do what he hoped she would do, he promised himself he would not press her to do so. Then she ran her tongue up the length of his already hard shaft and he closed his eyes, losing himself in the pleasure of it.

"Olympia!"

She swatted at the hand shaking her shoulder. "G'way."

"Wake up. Something has happened at Myrtledowns."

Olympia woke up and sat up. She was groggy but growing less so by the moment as fear pushed aside her sleepiness and invaded her heart. Quickly rubbing the sleep from her eyes she looked up at a half-dressed Brant standing by the bed.

"What do you mean something has happened at Myrtledowns?"

"Someone tried to take your son," he answered and quickly grabbed her by the arm when she went pale as he was certain she was about to swoon.

"Who brought the message?"

"One of your stable hands. Hugh Pugh, I believe he said."

She leapt out of bed and began to dress. "That is his name. I need to speak with him and then pack and get down to Myrtledowns."

"I will take you. I can have the carriage here in a very short time."

Olympia watched him throw on his shirt and hurry out the door. So much for their love affair being a secret, she thought, and then shrugged.

Trouble from her family over her taking a man to her bed was the least of her worries.

She yanked on her slippers and hurried out the door. Hugh stood at the base of the stairs looking tired and sweat-soaked. Olympia nearly leapt down the rest of the stairs and grabbed him by the arm.

"Ilar?"

"He is just fine, m'lady. Just fine. Magistrate has one of the men who tried to take the boy locked up. May be something he can tell you."

"How did they get to him?"

"Came in as men delivering the coal. Old Moll was not paying attention for she was making the bread for the parish poor—her turn you know and all— and so they slipped right inside the house. Knocked out poor Moll and then went through the house. The boy was napping in the library. Said the book he was trying to read had put him right to sleep." Hugh briefly grinned. "Then he woke up to find two men trying to hogtie him. He managed to get loose and then the fun began."

"Oh, dear, he used his gift," she muttered and ran a hand over her hair. "That news could spread fast."

"Who will be believing a couple of fools who could not even kidnap a skinny lad, eh? Folk will just think the men are trying to hide the fact that they are such poor fighters they could not even hold fast to a child."

"I have the carriage, Olympia," Brant said as he reached her side and held up a small bag. "Also packed a few things."

"Of course. I must do the same."

She raced back to her bedchamber, looked at the

remains of Brant's lovely dinner for two, and sighed. It was nearly dawn and she had looked forward to waking up in his arms for one more bout of lovemaking before he had to slip back to his house. Then again, now that everyone undoubtedly knew he had been in her bed, that slipping away before everyone woke up could stop, she decided as she began to throw some clothes into a bag.

Once she brought the bag downstairs, she looked at Hugh, Pawl standing beside him. "You rest, Hugh. Come back to Myrtledowns after you have had a rest and a good meal. Brant and I will be fine."

"I will do that then, m'lady. And you are not to worry, the boy is fine."

Easier said than done, she thought as she climbed into the carriage followed by Brant. There were several things to worry about. Who would try to steal her son? In all the years they had lived at Myrtledowns, the baron's ancestral home, no one had troubled them, not even Maynard's family who had resented the loss of title and land a lot in the beginning. Nor did they have the kind of fortune that would prompt an attempt at kidnapping. They had never even dealt in politics. That left only one thing.

Lady Mallam had tried to steal her son. The woman was either going to do to Ilar as she had done with so many others, or use the boy to make Olympia do as she bid her to. If it was not so frightening it would be funny. The woman had no idea what she had been about to steal or that hell would rain down on her because she had attempted such a thing.

Taking a deep breath she told Brant all Hugh had

said and he frowned. Then a tight look came over his face and she knew he had just reached the same conclusion she had. She moved to sit beside him and, after a moment of tense silence, he put an arm around her shoulders and held her close. He may have thought he had understood the full truth of what his mother was, but, even if he did, it had to sting to hear of yet another sin she had committed.

Or tried to, Olympia mused, and actually smiled. Letitia had just poked the wrong wasp nest. Now her family would come in droves and what she had not already found, they would uncover for her.

"I am so very sorry," Brant said and kissed the top of her head.

"You have nothing to apologize for. Believe me, Brant, our family is littered with bad mothers, and fathers, and a few others, and when a Wherlocke is bad, it can get ugly. Our mothers walk away from husband and children. Our fathers walk away, too, but not as often. One cannot choose one's parents. We do not all get someone like Stone."

"No, we do not. Henry is a very lucky child. Stone not only loves his son and has no trouble revealing that but he is a good man, a stable man who does not shy from work, drinks little, and, I suspect, was utterly faithful to his mad wife."

"They are a treasure. Most of the men in my family, when they wed, they hold to vows taken. I think that is one reason the wives walking away because they cannot abide what we are, thinking we are all Satan's children or some idiotic thing, is such a hard blow. It is also why so many of the men in my family are rather slow to marry."

"Who can blame them?"

"Well, we have instituted a few new family rules. The one who wants to marry someone who is not gifted is to tell the person they want to wed before the wedding. On hand will be one of the ones who have Argus's gift. In most cases, the proposal, sometimes even the intent to wed, can be taken from the person's mind. Not completely, of course, but it is not something I can understand all that well, either because it is beyond my ken or because the ones who have the gift just cannot explain it clearly. As we all agreed, better the heart break before the wedding and the children."

"It truly can be more of a burden than a gift then."

"Aye, although acceptance gets easier with each generation, with the distance from the past of witch hunts and fears of Satan in anything or anyone unusual. Your mother, however, well, I could easily be made to believe she is the child of Satan."

"I begin to think she is ill in her mind."

"But not in the usual way. There has never been anything to make people think her even a little odd. I still believe she was born with something missing."

"Like a conscience."

"You are certain her men did not hurt the boy?"

"Hugh would not lie about that. My other concern is how Ilar managed to escape being taken. He used his gift. I gather my library is now a mess. They even managed to capture one so we might finally have some answers, some witness we can use against her."

"That would be a good thing but I believe I will not get my hopes up."

Olympia rested her head against his shoulder and tried to still the fear writhing inside her. She needed to make plans to keep Ilar safe until Letitia Mallam was no longer a danger. She could not do so when she was so tied up with fear for her child.

Brant's mother had borne six children yet she had not one maternal bone in her body. The woman treated children, even her own, as nothing more than merchandise. Coming from a family that, despite a long history of one parent deserting the other and fearing the children, loved children dearly, she did not understand such a woman, could not understand her. It was going to be difficult to defend against such a woman. Olympia found comfort in the thought that Lady Mallam was not a woman to do her work herself.

"She fears you," said Brant as he rested his head back against the squabs and closed his eyes. "That is what this is all about."

"Do you think she believes what is whispered about the Wherlockes and their cousins the Vaughns?" Olympia asked, fearing that her son's gifts were why the woman wanted him.

"I would not have thought so. She does not have any imagination so why would she believe in something that even those who do possess imagination question and fear?"

"True. That is relief. If she ever discovered that what is whispered about us is true," Olympia said, shuddering faintly as a wave of cold fear went through her, "I do not think any of our children would be safe. Your mother knows how to get people in and out of places, or she hires ones who do."

"Well, except for one of the ones who went into your library."

Olympia grinned. "Very true."

"I think we should rest. It is not a long journey to your home but it will give us a nice rest so that we can face the trouble at Myrtledowns with a clear head."

"Agreed," she said and bit back the urge to tell him that he was now using the word *we*.

She closed her eyes but doubted sleep would come. After hearing that someone had tried to take her son, Olympia suspected there would be a lot of nights ahead where she would find going to sleep difficult. There had never been a threat to him before and she had no knowledge of how well she could arrange things so that he need never fear a threat again.

Ilar was also going to be quite full of himself, she mused, and found she could smile about it. Since the use of his gift had saved him, she would not be able to scold him for using it before strangers. She also suspected that her aunt was spoiling the boy right now. Even Tessa might be there doing the same by the time Olympia arrived.

She wanted to hold her boy right now. Wanted to hear his heartbeat and watch him breathe. The thought of anyone taking her child, of hurting him in any way, terrified her to her very soul. He was her treasure. She had always doubted that she would ever have another child. And now, with the man she loved snoring softly beside her, she was even more certain that her future was a barren one.

For a moment Olympia just stared at the coat her cheek was resting against. The thoughts continued to swirl through her mind until she actually realized what she had just admitted, silently, to herself. She loved Brant.

"Oh hell."

Chapter 14

Brant stared at the house the carriage rolled to a stop in front of. It was built of a soft gray stone, elegant, and massive. He was a little surprised there was no moat as there were turrets on each corner of the square building. What could have been a rather stark home had been softened with trees and flowers. It welcomed despite the austerity that one first saw.

Olympia leapt out of the carriage and he quickly collected her bag. Telling the driver to wait for a moment and he would find out where the man could bed down and get some food if he preferred, he followed Olympia into the house.

The inside of the house revealed that one of the barons had once had a lot of money or had blithely sunk his whole family deep into debt. The floors were black-veined marble, polished to a shine except for where Olympia's shoes had left a mark. The walls were all wood, a dark wood, but he was no expert on how to guess what wood it was. It just looked warm and rich to him, expensive. All the doors he could see were heavy oak with carvings. Whoever had had this house built had buried a fortune into it.

A tall, lean man hurried toward them from the back of the hall. "M'lady! We had not expected you to come so quickly. Hugh must have flown to London."

"I suspect he did, Jones Two. He certainly looked exhausted. I told him to rest before attempting to return. The fact that he did tells me that not only was he tired but he believed the horse needed a rest as well. Hugh babies his horses," she told Brant with a glance over her shoulder and then she turned back to her butler. "This is the Earl of Fieldgate, Lord Brant Mallam."

"My lord, I will see that a room is readied for you."

"Thank you, Jones Two." Brant handed the man their bags when he reached for them. "The driver of our carriage will need a place to sleep and some food."

"That will be seen to as well. M'lady, the young master is in the library with your aunt and cousin, attempting to clean up in there."

"Thank you, Jones Two."

Olympia was already striding along the hall as she spoke and Brant hurried to catch up with her. She stopped before two elaborately carved doors depicting nymphs romping in the water, took a deep breath, and opened the doors. Brant followed her into the room and looked around at utter chaos. Most of the shelves in the library had been cleared of books. Several chairs were set in a far corner and he could see at a glance that they would need some repair. Piles of books were stacked up near the shelves but many still littered the floor. He looked up at Olympia and watched her turn slowly, surveying every inch of the room.

"I am pleased to see that you did not break the lamps this time, Ilar," she said and smiled at the tall, thin boy rising to his feet from where he had been on the floor stacking books.

"Mother!" He ran into her arms. "I am so glad you have come home. We had a great deal of excitement here."

"I can see that." She held her son close for a moment, reassuring herself that he was alive and all too painfully aware of the fact that just one more surge of growth and he would be taller than her. "I have brought some company with me." She turned Ilar toward Brant and introduced them to each other. "And this is my aunt, Antigone Wherlocke." She nodded to the older woman who now stood next to her. "And my cousin, Mrs. Tessa Vaughn."

Brant bowed to the woman who watched him a little too closely with her deep brown eyes. "I am pleased to meet you all."

"Are you certain you are Fieldgate?" Tessa asked, wiping her dusty hands on the voluminous apron she wore over her green gown.

"Tessa! Of course he is," snapped Olympia. "Do you think I would not know?"

"Nay. 'Tis just that he does not look or feel like the drunken debauchee one hears about."

"Oh. Well, no he is not a drunk. As for the debauchee," she said and grunted when Brant elbowed her in the back. "No more than many another man of the gentry."

"Thank you," muttered Brant. "You are too kind."

Olympia exchanged a grin with Tessa before looking at her aunt. "Do you have any idea why someone would try to take Ilar?"

"None. I believe the trouble came down from London. The men had the city manner of speech. I heard quite a bit when the one who was caught was threatening us all."

"Then let us have something to eat and drink and Ilar can tell me his part of the tale. Then I should like to hear yours, Aunt Tig."

"I could tell you a tale or two as well," offered Tessa.

"You were here when it happened?" Olympia asked, knowing it was rude to keep Brant tromping along at her heels like some pet dog but she was unable to release her son yet.

"Nay, but I could still tell you a tale or two if you would like." She winked at Olympia and they both laughed.

Brant felt a little ignored at the moment but he understood. He doubted a team of oxen could drag Olympia's arm away from her son. He was a good-looking boy with his glossy, wavy, black hair and eyes just like his mother's. His features were beginning to lose their boyish softness and he would be as handsome as so many of his other relatives. What was easy to see in the way the boy held Olympia and smiled at her, was that Ilar loved his mother very much.

They entered a room that had a great deal more of a feminine touch than the library. It had drapes in a soft blue, matching one of the colors in the carpet, and the walls were painted a soft rose color, not one he had ever seen before. Olympia waved him to a seat next to her, seating Ilar on her other side, her aunt at the head of the table, and the irre-pressible Tessa in the seat opposite her. A few mo-ments later the butler led in three servants who unloaded a great deal of food plus coffee and tea onto the table. A quick look out the window told Brant it was indeed time to break his fast.

"So, Ilar, tell me what you recall," said Olympia as she piled some eggs on her plate.

"I was sleeping in the library," the boy said. "I had not intended to have a nap but the book I chose to read was very, painfully boring. Anyway, I woke to the sound of a footfall and a sharp sense of some-thing just wrong. As I got up off the settee and set my book down on the table I got the distinct feeling that someone was watching me. I opened my eyes and this huge, very hirsute fellow was reaching for me. I leapt off the settee and started to run but one caught me. The other tried to get a gag over my mouth for I was making a lot of noise. I was kicking and screaming and then I thought to myself, well, why am I getting all asweat?"

The way he was looking at her, a glint of mischief and unease in his eyes, eyes just like hers, almost made Olympia smile but she knew she had to be firm, serious. "So what did my sweaty, screaming son do then?"

"Cleaned off the bookshelves," he said a little warily. "I was aiming as best I could for their heads. Got a good blow in on one of them but the other became all terrified and started praying and ran away. By then the others came in."

"You did well, Ilar. Very well indeed. You fought, called for help, and then used what you had to to make certain you did not get dragged out of reach of the help you needed." She smiled at him. "You also sent for me and began to clean up your mess."

"With a lot of kind help," he said and smiled at both Tessa and Antigone with a sweet charm that had her aching to pick him up and hug him as she always used to when he was small. She frowned and tensed as she heard a noise coming from outside the room. "Now what has happened?" Just as she stood up to go and look, Jones Two walked in, his hand behind his back. "Jones Two? Is something wrong?"

"We were tending to your luggage, m'lady, and m'lord. I believe you may have had vermin get inside."

"Vermin?"

Jones Two drew his hand from behind his back and held it out. Dangling from his hand and trying to look fierce was a small golden cat. "Vermin."

"Lure!" She hurried over and took the cat from her butler. "How did she get in my bag? I was certain she was not even in my bedchamber last night." Olympia recalled why the cat had not been in her bedchamber and fiercely held back the blush she felt stirring.

"If m'lady does find out how that creature got in your bag, then it may explain the other one." He held his hand up and snapped his fingers and a lanky, grinning footman walked in carrying Dinner. "This was in his lordship's bag." He looked at Brant. "I have one of the lads already brushing the fur from your clothes, my lord."

"M'lady?" asked the footman and held out Dinner.

"Just put her down, Morris," Olympia said, struggling not to laugh. "I will arrange something for them in my bedchamber after I have finished eating." She sighed when the kitten wriggled free of her hold, climbed up on her shoulder, and then up to sit on her head. "There goes my dignity." She joined in with her family and Brant who started laughing. "Someone take this foolish creature off my head, please." Once her son took the kitten down, she returned to her seat as the servants left, shutting the door behind them.

"More cats," muttered Antigone but Olympia saw her aunt surreptitiously drop a small piece of ham down to Dinner.

"They must have gotten out of Enid and Pawl's room while we were running around packing things," Olympia said and then frowned at Brant. "That does not explain how Dinner got into your bag, however."

"I set it down in the hall as I waited for you and it was open," he answered. "I did not notice that until we were in the carriage. I am surprised I did not see a cat that large, however."

"A cat is a master of the art of hiding, m'lord," said Antigone. "And, Olympia, m'dear, why are the cats called Lure and Dinner?"

Olympia decided to explain Dinner's name first and then, taking a deep breath, told them how Lure got her name. She put an arm around her son when he quickly moved to sit by her side. It was still a horror new enough to make her shiver in remembrance.

"So as we rode here, it occurred to me that what has just happened to Ilar could be a part of what is happening to me. It really would not take long for anyone to discover I have a son and where he might be. I just wonder how they knew I would never be able to leave that poor cat stranded there."

"That would not be so difficult, either, m'dear. Anyone just needs to speak to someone here or in the village. Even the Warren has its fair share of animals you have collected. Not only animals but many are the sort of animals most people would simply kill or toss away."

"That was what I feared. The moment Lady Mallam decided I was Brant's ally she went hunting for anything she could find on me. She discovered a weakness before she set her men on me and, I strongly suspect, she then discovered you, Ilar." She lightly smoothed her hand over his hair. "If she had found you first, I think we would have seen this attack much earlier. I am just not all that sure of what she hoped to accomplish by getting her hands on you."

"Use him to tame you," said Brant. "Who can be certain what she would decide was the best way to use your child against you? She saw the possibility of a good, heavy club to beat you into service for her and reached out to grab it."

"The first thing we need to do is get some more men here to guard the house," said Olympia. "Having never had any trouble, it is too easy to get in here, as we now know. So, some guards. Then, back to London to stop this woman."

Ignoring the people sharing the table with them, Brant reached out and patted her hand where she rested it on the table, her fist so tightly clenched that her knuckles shown white. He could see a lingering fear in her eyes. This was a true mother, he thought. This was a woman who cared for the child she had borne, would fight for that child, and comfort that child if he needed it. This was a woman such as his mother had never been.

Brant shook off a moment of self-pity and asked, "Are there strong men in the village that you can trust? This is not forever, merely until we can stop her. There may be some who would welcome the extra coin to act as a guard for your son, Olympia."

"There most certainly would," said Antigone. "Jones Two and I can see to that today. In fact, why do we not all take a walk into the village together. The magistrate has a nice home at the far end of the village and the man who was captured here is locked in his wine cellar."

"A splendid idea, Auntie. I will finish this fine food, put those foolish cats away in my bedchamber, and then we shall all go to the village," Olympia said, sighing when Lure pulled her small golden body up her skirts to sit on her lap. "I think I am going to have trouble with this one." She smiled when Ilar began to lightly stroke the cat and it began to purr its very loud, too-big-for-its-body purr. "Aye, I am definitely going to have trouble with this one."

* * *

Olympia wanted to hold Brant's hand as they followed Peter Jenkins down into his wine cellar but knew she could not. This was the local squire, a man who might live on the fringes of society but still moved within it. He would not be able to resist telling his wife about the baroness and the earl, about how they held hands. His wife would tell her sister, who would tell her dearest friends, who would tell their dearest friends, and so on until the whole of society would begin wondering just what was going on between "that strange Wherlocke girl" and that wretched, dissolute child of Lady Letitia Mallam. She stiffened her spine and hoped her face held the calm, sweet expression she was struggling to hold.

"Here he be, m'lady," Peter said. "Real sorry I did not get there to catch the other one but your lad did himself proud."

The man in the cell stood up and stared at Olympia. He was of medium height, thinning brown hair, and pale hazel eyes. She saw fear in his eyes and knew he saw her son when he looked at her.

"Why did you try to take my son?" she asked.

"The lady told Jake that she wanted the boy so she could rule the mother." He looked around. "You find Jake?"

"No," answered Peter. "He left you here to hang for him."

"Better to hang than go back and tell that cursed bitch that we failed." He looked back at Olympia. "You got yourself a brave lad but I be thinking he be a might strange, too. Best you keep that boy out of that bitch's hands."

"What is the woman's name?" asked Brant.

"You think you can stop her?" said the man. "Think you can make her go away? Nay, lad. She be a coldhearted devil of a woman and she means to rule. Best you and the lass stay tucked up here because of the lady who has your eyes. She hates men, that she does, but she sure hates you, lad."

"Now you be quiet," said Peter. "They were asking for a name."

"We have it, Peter. We have it," Olympia said and gave up on discretion by taking Brant's hand in hers. She knew this had to hurt. At the very least it had to pick at the wound in his heart that had never had the time to heal properly.

"Fine then. I will be judging this fellow on the morrow and I suspect he will be hanging from the tree in the square soon."

"No, he must stay alive, Peter. I may have need of him when I capture that woman. She came into my home and touched my child, and I mean to see her pay dearly for that. This fellow, since he knows who she is, could prove to be a great help in the doing of that."

"M'lady," the man in the cell called when Olympia turned to leave.

"Are you about to tell me that you cannot help me?"

"Oh, I can help you but the magistrate there should also have himself a few new guards."

"Are you threatening him?"

"Not at all. Seems a good fellow. Nay, her ladyship is not fond of leaving folk around who can talk. I can talk. The magistrate there can talk. M'lady prefers silence. Jake has not gone back to tell her he failed. He is running for his life."

Olympia was silent all the way back to the house and then joined her son in putting away the books he had used in his fight to save his life. She was sitting on the floor in the middle of several stacks of books and wondering which ones should be put back on the shelves first when Brant arrived and sat down next to her. He looked thoughtful but no more. She had to wonder if he had become used to hearing bad news concerning his mother.

"You threw all these off the shelves?" he asked.

"I did." Ilar looked at Olympia and she nodded, silently giving him permission to speak of what he could do. "It was all I could think of. I had no weapon."

Looking around at all the nearly empty shelves and the books on the floor, Brant shook his head and smiled. "Oh, I think you did."

With Brant's and Ilar's help, they had returned nearly all the books to the shelves when the dinner bell was rung. Olympia hurried to her bedchamber to clean the dust and dirt off. As she washed her hands and face, she told herself not to find anything hopeful in how well Brant and Ilar got along. It could simply be because Brant had a skill at talking to a young boy on the cusp of manhood and Ilar was hungry for some male company.

By the time she reached the dining room everyone else was there waiting for her. She took a seat next to Brant and across from her aunt, Tessa, and Ilar. It was a pleasant meal and Olympia enjoyed hearing all of the latest news about various family members but she could not stop thinking about the man the magistrate held.

"Do you think that man meant that your mother will kill them because they failed? That he wants extra guards for the magistrate mostly because he is afraid of someone coming into the magistrate's and killing him for it?" Olympia truly wanted him to say no.

"Yes, I fear so. Oh, she will not dirty her hands with such a job, but she will know someone who would."

"We should warn Peter more firmly so that he understands that there is a real threat to him."

"The man Peter is holding will tell him."

"I hope so because Peter is a good man."

"If my mother sends someone to silence that man, she will have it done in such a way that Peter will know nothing about it until he goes down in that cellar to see a body there instead of the man he had brought in." Brant helped himself to some roast beef, realizing that he liked the way the Wherlockes had no servants standing silently at their backs as they ate. The servants came in, set the food down on the table, and left the sorting and serving of it to the people at the table. It let everyone be at ease while at the table.

"You think she is that good?" Olympia simply could not see Lady Letitia Mallam killing anything.

"I think she knows who to hire who will be that good. If not for Ilar's gift, those men would have gotten away with him."

"That is very true," said Ilar and then stuffed his mouth with some tender roast beef.

Olympia shivered. If she had known how far Lady Mallam's reach was and how lethal the woman could be, Olympia was not sure she would have been so eager to help young Agatha. A moment later she decided she was fooling herself. No matter what the risks she knew she would not have been able to stand by and watch a young girl be forced to marry a man as filthy and lacking in morals as Lord Sir Horace Minden.

"This mess just keeps getting messier and more complicated," she muttered and sat back in her chair when Jones Two and two young maids came in to clear away the meal and leave the varied desserts for them to choose from.

"My mother has always been efficient and thorough in every endeavor. She will be an efficient and thorough criminal. I know only one thing for a fact, have no doubt about it, and that is for as long as she has people she can use, she will never dirty her own hands. What she will do when we rob her of all those carefully chosen accomplices, I do not know."

"She will become very angry," said Antigone as she spooned some stewed apples into a bowl and poured some thick cream over them.

Brant looked at the older woman with her thick black hair lightly sprinkled with gray and her handsome features, the most striking of which was a pair of bright green eyes. "I suspect so as we will be robbing her of her source of income."

"Nay, you will be robbing her of her power."

It was hard but Brant bit back the string of curses that rose to his tongue. The woman was right. His mother would never accept a loss of her power. She had spent her entire adult life gathering that power, something she had always craved.

"Pick a dessert, Brant," Olympia urged, pulling him free of the anger that was twisting his insides.

He served himself some cake, covered it with some of the stewed apples, and then stared at it for a moment. There was one good thing he could see in all the trouble that now swirled around them. They were very close to breaking his mother. Brant was just not certain how he should prepare himself and the others for that eventuality. This time it seemed he was not only going to fail to keep those close to him safe, but was bringing that trouble right to their door.

Olympia smiled as she relaxed on Ilar's bed and listened to him read to her from *The Taming of the Shrew* by Shakespeare. He had always liked the plays even as a small child. Glancing at him where he sprawled at her side, she could see more of the man in him now than the child he had been.

"You are leaving tomorrow," Ilar said as he set aside the book, turned on his side, and studied his mother.

"I must, love," she said. "I gave Brant's sister a promise. Her mother is planning to marry her off to an evil man who is old enough to be her grandfather. She came looking for help and I said I would do it. I cannot leave her at the mercy of that woman and we are too far away from the city here for me to rush to her side if she is in peril."

"Then take her away from the woman."

"We are working on doing just that. Brant has hired Cousin Andras to bring the girl under his guardianship."

"Oh. That is very good for Andras is very smart." He yawned.

Olympia got off the bed and kissed him on the cheek. "Rest, love. You used your gift a lot lately and that steals a lot of strength from ones like us."

"I will. I am glad you came home for a little while."

"So am I, Ilar. So am I."

She slipped out of the room and headed for her own bedchamber. The need to get up and start the journey to Myrtledowns at such an early hour and then rushing around trying to sort out what had happened and what needed to be done had exhausted her. She stepped into her bedchamber and smiled faintly at the sleeping cats. Then she saw that she had company for Brant was sprawled on top of her bed. Since he was fully dressed she suspected he was not there to try and seduce her into making love, something she could not do when they were in the home she shared with her son.

"How did you get into my room with no one seeing or hearing you?" she asked as she walked to the bed and settled herself beside him.

"I can be very stealthy if I wish." He tugged her into his arms and kissed her.

"Brant, I cannot," she began.

"I know but I wished for a good-night kiss."

She laughed and gave him one. It quickly turned into a deep, passionate kiss and she was breathing very unsteadily when she finally pulled away. "This is very unwise."

"Probably but I will not misbehave. Is your son as calm as he appeared?"

"I believe so. He was more startled than frightened or hurt. He also discovered that his gift gave him the strength needed, the weapon he needed to use, to free himself and that is a heady thing I believe. He could have made a more tempered strike at his attackers, but this was good."

"I can see why you are cautious about bringing him to the city." He kissed her again, then got off the bed before he gave in to the strong urge to help himself to far more than kisses. "I am more sorry than I can say about how my mother threatened your son."

She sat up and took his hand in hers, placing a kiss upon his palm. "No more apologizing for what is none of your doing. This wrong belongs to your mother. Never you."

He was not sure he believed that but he smiled, brushed a kiss over her mouth, and left her room as stealthily as he had entered it. It was hard to leave her side. Brant surprised himself with the realization that he liked curling up with her in bed for the night. He had never spent a full night with a woman except for the few times he had been so drunk he had taken his pleasure and fallen into a stupor almost immediately.

"Are you dishonoring my mother?"

Looking into the eyes of the angry boy who had the voice of a man and promised to be tall, Brant inwardly cursed but kept his voice calm. "Never. I but came to say good night to her, and apologize for what my mother tried to do to you, and to her." He bowed to the boy. "I apologize to you as well."

"There is no need," said Ilar. "I was not harmed." He grinned. "And I discovered that I am far from helpless as well. That is a good thing."

"Yes, it is."

"Is my mother in danger because she is helping your sister?"

"Yes, she is but she will not stop until this is done no matter how much I tell her she should. She says she has given my sister a promise and will see that it is fulfilled."

"Ah, of course. My mother would never break a promise. I understand now. Good night, m'lord."

Brant murmured a good night and watched the boy return to his bedchamber. He had known almost from the start of their adventure that Lady Wherlocke was an honorable woman. The confidence her son had in her keeping of a promise revealed that her honor was a deep part of who she was. He found that a little too alluring.

Just as he was starting to remind himself for what he thought had to be the hundredth time that he was no good for her, something brushed up against his leg. Brant looked down at the tabby that had been brought in to feed the kitten. A quick glance around revealed no small shadow and he looked back at the cat.

"You should return to the room and to your new child," he quietly told the cat and the cat responded with a slow blink but never moved. "I have no box of sand in my bedchamber." Still the cat did not move. "Well, come along then."

The cat followed him into his bedchamber, looked at the bed, and jumped up on it. After several moments of circling, it settled down right in the middle of the bed. Brant shook his head, prepared himself for bed, and then, after losing a staring match with the cat, he slipped beneath the covers, contorting his body a little to fit in around the cat. Lady Olympia Wherlocke, the beautiful baroness of Myrtledowns, had a lot to answer for, he thought before closing his eyes. He just hoped he did not wake in the morning too stiff to move.

Chapter 15

Pawl met them at the door as they pulled to a stop before the Warren. He looked at the two cats in the small cage Olympia carried and scowled. "So that is where they went."

"Sorry about that, Pawl," said Olympia as she let him take the cage from her. "Just put them back in my bedchamber."

"How is Ilar?"

"Just fine but it appears the enemy has upped the stakes." She frowned as she heard female voices coming from the drawing room. "I have company?"

"Your cousin Quinton Vaughn has arrived. It seems he saw to a small bit of business for you in Scotland."

Olympia turned to smile at Brant who stood behind her. "He found the stolen girls." She hurried off to the drawing room hearing the click of Brant's boots as he followed her.

Inside the drawing room were seven girls. He doubted any one of them was older than fifteen. Thomas sat next to a thin, frightened young girl with curly brown hair and huge brown eyes, holding her hand and patting it. Brant supposed that was his other aunt.

And then the man in the room stood up and smiled at Olympia. She gave a glad cry and hurried over to hug him. If not for that very distinct look of a Wherlocke, Brant knew he would be suffering far more than the small pinch of jealousy that he was. This had to be Quinton and, if Brant was any judge, Olympia's cousin was the sort of man women flocked to. He was not only well over six feet in height, he had broad shoulders, long black hair that he did not bother to tie into a neat queue but let flow over those big shoulders, and was impeccably dressed. When the man looked over Olympia's shoulders and studied Brant like he was some new kind of bug, Brant had to fight to quell the urge to go over and punch the man right in his elegant nose.

The introductions took awhile as each girl was identified. Thomas took them off to find some place where they could all clean up and rest while Pawl arrived with some food and drink. When Olympia sat down on the small settee, Brant was quick to sit by her side. He just smiled at the cold look Quentin Vaughn gave him as her cousin settled his big body on the settee facing Olympia. As she told Quentin a severely edited version of everything that had happened so far, Brant poured himself a cup of coffee, briefly wondering if he could get Enid to teach his cook how to make the brew. Then he recalled that he was in dire need of a whole new roster of servants at Fieldgate and would undoubtedly have to replace many of the ones at the town house as well.

"There were only six girls?" asked Olympia as she poured tea for the men.

"No," replied Quentin. "There were twenty but several were from the port town the ship was docked in, a few more had me leave them at their homes along the way as we traveled here. Aside from Thomas's aunt, the rest live in the city. They all made it very clear who had stolen them away from their homes."

"My mother," Brant said and sighed.

"If your mother is somewhat slender, not too tall, and still a handsome woman despite her age, then, yes, I suspect it was your mother. Young Anna, Thomas's aunt, said the woman acted toward them all as if they were no more than cattle. She arrived in a carriage with a huge footman, looked all the girls over and then demanded payment from the ship's captain."

"That certainly sounds like her. Did you see my mother then?"

"No, that description was given me by some of the girls as they were all in the hold and the woman actually came down to inspect them. One lass said that from the way the woman looked them all over she had expected her to ask them to show her their teeth next. I do believe I got them all out of there before any physical harm was done to them. They were soon to be shipped out when I arrived with my men and then they did not have to worry any longer. The captain does not either," he added with a cold smile.

"Thank you so much, Quentin," said Olympia. "We must have done her some damage now since we emptied that Dobbin House. I just wish we could rescue everyone."

"The rescue of the girls did not hurt her finances, Olympia, as it is clear she had already gotten her payment for them," said Brant. "The loss of the captain might be more damaging. If nothing else, it will mean she must arrange something else. I just wish I could say for certain that that will be a difficult thing for her to do."

Quentin finished off a small cake and then shook his head. "It is a filthy trade but it has gone on forever and will continue to go on. We saved some and those we saved will be much more aware of the dangers out there. I did discover, Fieldgate, that many of the girls were taken from lands belonging to you, the Earl of Fieldgate."

"She means to help herself to all of my people then, to treat my lands as if they are some market." He sighed. "I had thought it was just the bastards my father bred but Thomas's little aunt is no blood of mine. She is just a pretty young girl."

"Pretty young girls have been victims before and will be again. That is something you will never stop. So how do you intend to stop your mother?"

The fact that none of the Wherlockes appeared horrified that a genteel woman, a mother and pillar of society, would do such things as sell children told Brant that the family had suffered. They had also seen a lot of suffering. Olympia had also been told all of that had happened when Ashton had met his Penelope and saved her from trouble.

At times Brant still reeled in shock over all his mother had done when he thought about it. He did not even wish to search for other crimes she may have committed in the past for he had too much to accept now. More horrors would surely break him. He carefully explained yet again how he was trying to soften the blow to the family for the sake of his siblings and the name of Fieldgate. With each new thing he discovered about his mother, those reasons began to look selfish and uncaring.

Quentin nodded. "You have three who have not even stepped out into the world much yet. To suffer the kind of scandal this could bring down on their heads could break them. One needs some tempering before standing straight and proud while the storm rages over your head. And your sister deserves her chance to make a good marriage."

"Mother feels she has taken care of that by negotiating a marriage agreement with Lord Sir Horace Minden." Brant nodded when Quentin stared at him, his eyes slowly widening. It appeared Wherlockes and their cousins the Vaughns could indeed be shocked.

"That is something you had best hurry to stop. He is filth and it is a wonder he has not been gutted before this. From all I know and have heard there is no perversion the man will not try or does not like to indulge in. I have also heard that he likes virgins because he thinks bedding them will rid him of the pox that is eating away at him."

"Lord Fieldgate?" Pawl called from the door. "Andras Vaughn has just sent you a message. He would like to meet with you as soon as possible. Do you wish to reply? The boy he sent is waiting." He nodded when both Brant and Olympia paled.

Shaking free of the horror of his mother selling her child to a man riddled with the pox and sensing his hopes rising, Brant went to talk to the boy Andras had sent, made sure he understood the reply, and gave him a shilling. He hurried back into the drawing room and smiled at Olympia. Perhaps matters would now begin to go their way.

"I must change and go speak with Andras," he told her.

"Of course." Olympia stood up and, not caring what Quentin thought, gave Brant a brief hug and a kiss on the cheek. "I will pray that this is the news you have been looking for."

The moment Brant left and Olympia retook her seat, she could feel Quentin's gaze on her. She idly wished she did not have the sort of family that felt it had the right to stick their long noses into all private business within the family. She could not complain too much, however, for she was guilty of that little sin herself.

"Just how good a friend is Fieldgate?" demanded Quentin.

"Do you forget that I am a baroness," she said, ignoring his snort of laughter over her announcement, "and a widow of six and twenty? I do not believe it is necessary for you to know such things. What goes on between me and Brant is none of your concern." The look on Quentin's handsome face told her he was just patiently waiting for her to finish and not really listening. She wanted to hit him.

"And he has a mother who sells babies to the flesh markets."

She sighed. There was that to consider. Her family

would not be the shelter it was to all of their kin if they did not worry when one of their own became connected to such a man.

"Brant is not involved in all of that."

"Oh, I know that. Could see that right away. He does not have that taint."

"He would be pleased to know that as I know he worries. How could one not when it is the person who bore you? But, he will end her crimes in one way or another."

Quentin nodded. "I could see that as well. Honest man. Good man. Also a man so stuffed with guilt that it could take form, step outside of him, and walk along his side as a brother."

"That much?"

"He is fair to choking on it. He believes he is a failure," Quentin said, his eyes taking on a faraway glow. I suspect it is for far more than that girl of his Penelope and her man found, what, two years ago?"

"Yes, it has been that long at least. But, he did not fail her. Her father was a vicar, and when he told Brant Faith had run off with a soldier, what else could he do but accept it? He had no reason to believe such a well-respected man of the cloth would lie to him."

"No, he did not, but that does not stop a man from thinking he could have done more." Quentin smiled at her. "We are what our nature makes us, love. We believe it is our duty to protect the smaller and weaker." He laughed when she glared at him. "You can get as angry as you wish. It will not change that, either. I doubt you will find any man who would not believe what a vicar said but there will still be that little voice in a man's head suggesting he could have done something else, asked one more question or done one more small thing that might have shown him the truth in time for him to save her."

"Men can be such foolish creatures."

"We can but can you honestly tell me that, if any harm had come to your son, you would not have had the weight of guilt upon your own heart? You could not have changed what happened. You could not have even guessed that that woman would try to take the boy."

"I should have," she said and then grimaced when she realized she had just proven Quentin right in his assumptions. He did not have to look so smug about it, however, she thought and then asked, "I know it is wrong to use our gifts in such a way yet cannot seem to stop myself from asking what else you saw. I so want to ease his heart and mind, foolish as that might be."

"It is the guilt I see that weighs on him the most. It is as if he carries the ghost of all he believes he has wronged or failed. The man needs to learn to forgive himself."

"But he has done no wrong."

"No, he has not, but unless he forgives himself for not being right there, sword in hand to protect everyone close to him, that guilt will remain."

"Bugger."

Quentin laughed. "Now, tell me how my daughter is. I mean to go see Juno while I am in the country and should like to be warned if there is anything troubling her. And then you can tell me how your son managed to keep himself from being taken away by that demon that calls itself Fieldgate's mother."

Brant stared at Andras and then at the papers set before him before looking back at Andras again. "It is settled?"

"You must just sign the papers." Andras smiled and Brant thought the man was a little too close to being beautiful when he did. "I had not expected it to go so smoothly, either. I went to our cousin Leopold. He works in the government, although not in such things as this. I but felt he could name someone I might be able to talk to, maybe even get some help from so that we did not have to drag this all through the courts. The man was far more than helpful."

"I notice that you do not mention his name."

"And I will not as I promised him to keep his part in this as quiet as was possible. He is *barely gentry* as he likes to say it and cannot afford to be seen to be using his knowledge or skills to aid in anything that interferes with the affairs of ones as high up as a countess."

Brant nodded, still touching the papers that gave him care of Agatha as if he feared they would disappear. "It could end his career."

"Exactly. He did not think helping in this matter would hurt him but he could not risk it. He means to marry soon, you see. And, it appears that one of those children you rescued and returned to their family was the son of his closest friend."

"How fortuitous for me then."

"Exactly, although I believe he would have helped me anyway. He said that even though you had, er, misbehaved of late there should never have been any question of who was head of the house, even as concerned the youngest daughter, your sister. You are, after all, the earl."

"So how did he reverse all the decisions made?"

"First he sniffed out the one who had made the final decisions, and why he would have done something so contrary to what any other man in that position would have done. Then he went and had a chat with the man. Of course that man dared not change his decision openly for the secrets your mother has on him could destroy his new marriage to a woman he dearly loves." Andras frowned. "My new friend," he grinned, "told the man to cease being a coward and tell his wife for even if your mother is declawed, others could find out the same secrets and try to use him for their own gains as well. Then it was off to a man one step higher up than that one, a man my new friend is very close to, and all was rescinded. That man has no secrets your mother could use against him. He is a rare creature in the halls of power, a blunt, honest, thoroughly clean man."

"It sounds as if there may be a few others. Sad that one has to hunt them down in such a convoluted manner though."

"So what do you plan to do?"

"Go and kick my mother out of my house." He grinned. "I shall thoroughly enjoy that."

"You do not think it would be best if she remained where you could find her? You have not yet gained

what you need to hold her own crimes and the
threat of punishment over her head and thus con-
fine her."

"Not quite." Brant frowned even as he took the
quill Andras offered and signed the papers. "I will
give her a reprieve of a few weeks to pack her things,
sort her affairs, and then move to one of her dower
properties. My mother would never just flee. She requires her comforts, her society, her shops. She
would never just run and hide, either, for she is
blindly arrogant. I think she has held power over too
many for too long and thinks herself beyond punishment." He grimaced. "She may even not fully see
that what she has done is wrong."

"Or care if it is," Andras added softly. "If I may be
direct . . ,"

"You may say whatever you wish."

"We are not our parents. While it is true that some
illnesses of the mind and body can be carried
through from parent to child, each child born of
that parent does not have to carry the bad seed, if
you will. You have no taint in you, m'lord. Your
mother, however, does but I do not believe it is one
that can be passed from mother to child."

"When did you meet my mother?"

"Never. I but made it my business to be where she
was from time to time after you came to me. Always
know your enemy. I can see the taint in a person, the
stain of guilt or madness or just disease. I can also
nearly smell a lie. Your mother was a very difficult
person for me to be close to but what twists her into
what she is is not one of the things that can be
passed on to a child. I think you are very fortunate

that she was never maternal for such a taint could, through many different means, eventually stain a child even if it does not come through the blood."

"I have slowly come to realize that. None of my siblings have her coldness, as Artemis calls it. Not one. My older sisters are hard and bitter but that is the fault of their husbands. My younger brothers are good boys and Agatha is a sweet, loving girl. None of that came from my mother." He smiled a little sadly. "It is sad, is it not, that one can actually find oneself grateful that one's parents never actually had anything to do with them."

"M'lord, if you remain close to my family for a while, you will find that many a person has that feeling and, yes, it is sad."

He stood up, and when Andras did the same, shook the young man's hand. "Thank you. Send the bill and," he hurried to say when Andras began to protest, "I will hear no argument on it. You have, in a way, saved my sister. This will also give me power over my mother again and who knows how many that will save. I have a nicely full purse as well so can well afford to pay my bills. You earned your fee. You have also earned my hearty recommendation if anyone ever asks me about a solicitor."

"Thank you, m'lord. Oh, and how fares young Ilar?"

Brant stared at the younger man in surprise. "How do you know about what happened to Ilar? Olympia and I have been back in the city for only a short time."

Andras just grinned. "We have our ways."

"Ilar is fine. More than fine. As he told me, he

discovered that, with his gift, he has the ability to protect himself from ones bigger and stronger than he is. I suspect that was a discovery that came as a great comfort."

Brant stepped out of the carriage and stared up at the façade of the family town house. It was clean, well maintained, and gave off the air of wealth. He could not complain about how well his mother had tended this piece of property. She was going to hate the fact that he actually had the full legal power to kick her out on the street now and he savored that for a moment.

He went up the well-swept steps and rapped on the door. When the butler opened the door and then hastily tried to shut it in his face again, he just grinned and kicked it open so hard the man went stumbling backward and fell on his backside. Brant stepped in and looked down at the man.

"I suggest you find yourself a new position as soon as possible," he said. "I would not be comfortable having a servant who once tried to keep me out of my own home. Oh, and do not think to weigh your pockets down with my goods as you flee this place for I have an exact accounting of all that is here." It was a lie but he was not very concerned about that. "So, I believe, does my mother."

When the man paled and then scrambled to his feet to run to the back of the house, Brant shook his head. It was sad when a man's threat carried less weight than the threat of his mother. He grabbed the arm of a young footman who was cowering in an alcove a few steps away from the door. There had to be a reason the servants were all so terrified of the countess but he would dig for the why of that later.

"Where is my mother?" he asked.

"In the conservatory, m'lord. Just down there and to the right." He blushed. "Oh, suspect you know that."

"I might have except that I suspect this conservatory is a very new addition to the house."

"It is about two years old, maybe a few months less than that. Do you want to be announced?"

Brant smiled and when the footman paled and stepped back a little, he suspected it was a very predatory smile. "No, thank you, lad. I will show myself in. Since she will not be in a very good humor soon, you might wish to find some place to be out of her reach. Name?"

"James. James Tompkin. I was just hired last week. Seems the last footman disappeared all sudden like."

"Ah, I understand. Hide for a while, lad." He paused and decided he could trust the boy, and boy he was for Brant doubted he was much over eighteen. "If anything happens that you think is wrong once I leave here, I can be reached at the Wherlocke Warren which is number 10 Bennington Road."

The boy nodded and ran off. Brant continued down the hall until he came to the door the boy had indicated. He stepped into the room and nearly swore. He was not one who knew much about the cost of things such as conservatories or furniture, but he recognized when something was expensive. He did not want to think of how much his mother had spent to add this room to the house. There was even a small fountain somewhere in the midst of all the plants for he could hear the water as he stood there studying the green marble floor.

Shaking his head, he began to wander through the place until he found his mother. It was not that she sat there wearing what was no better than a nightdress and robe made of silk so fine he could actually see the shape of her form through it. Not something a son wishes to see, he thought, and averted his eyes. It was the shirtless man sitting at her feet being fed grapes that shocked him. He had never considered his mother a sensual woman but then he realized it was not an act of lust he was seeing so much as an exertion of a woman's power over a man. The Countess of Fieldgate had discovered a way to keep a man enthralled. It did not surprise him to see that the man she currently had at her feet was the huge footman she had been seen with many times.

"Hello, Mother," he drawled as he stepped into her view. "Enjoying your morning, I see."

The fact that she did not even look embarrassed disgusted him. She simply waved the footman away. It was only the man who revealed any hint of emotion and that was with a glare of such frustrated anger that Brant thought he might be drawn into a fight. Instead the man grabbed up his shirt and boots and walked out, never hesitating to obey the countess.

"What are you doing here?" She smoothed her hands over the skirts of her scandalous outfit with all the calm and poise of one wearing a proper gown. "I believe I made it clear that I do not want you in this house."

"And I believe I made it clear that you are here on my sufferance."

"Ah, yes, well, I am working to change that."

"Too late. I have it all in writing. I also now have full parental authority over the boys and Agatha."

For a moment there was such fury on her face that he had to beat down the urge to take a step back. And, then, just as quickly, the cold, aloof expression he was accustomed to returned. It was, perhaps, small of him, but he was going to thoroughly enjoy taking this house away from her. She had made it her own, done just what she pleased with it even though she had always known that she had no claim to ownership. He had allowed it simply because it had been too much trouble to do otherwise. The little house he had bought to house his occasional mistress had suited him more.

"You are an unwed man and one whose profligate ways are well known. No one would give you full power over a girl of sixteen."

"The girl is my sister and I am head of this household. Now, I am willing to give you a few weeks to get your affairs in order before you must retire to one of your dower properties, but that marriage contract you are negotiating with Minden is ended. There will be no negotiations with that man and he is, in fact, forbidden to come to this house."

"I will see your proof of power first." She held out one hand, the rings on her fingers heavy with jewels and gold.

Brant showed her the papers. The way her hands

tightened on them, her knuckles whitening, made him pleased he had asked for two copies for himself. There was a good chance this copy would soon be in shreds. Nevertheless, the moment her grip eased on the papers, he took them away from her.

"I do not recognize that name," she said.

He was not sure how but he knew she was lying. "You do not need to know him. The only thing that matters is that he is higher up the ladder than the man you used to usurp my place in this family. He is also incorruptible."

"No one is."

"Except perhaps a man who had his woman's child stolen and placed in Dobbin House by you." He noticed she did not even attempt to deny her part in the evil of that house. "I would like to see Agatha now."

"That will have to wait. She is out for her morning ride with her friends."

He wanted to question that but decided he had pressed her enough for now. "Then tell her when she returns that I will come calling on her at three."

"As you wish."

That bland acceptance sent a chill down his spine, but Brant again decided it would be wise not to push. His mother was not completely sane and he did not want to cause Agatha any more trouble. He had no doubt his mother would make Agatha suffer in her anger at her loss of the house and her power over the girl. Brant could see the coldness Olympia and Artemis had talked about in the gray eyes fixed upon him now. If his mother had had a weapon he knew he would have been fighting for his life.

"I will leave you to plan your retirement to the country now," he said and, after giving her a bow that was so shallow and quick it was equal to a slap in the face, he started out of the room. He could not resist pausing just within her sight one last time and smiling at her. "I approve of this room and am certain I shall enjoy it to its fullest when I move in after you are gone."

He heard the first crash of something breaking before he shut the door behind him and smiled. There was no one near her that she could hurt so her anger could be enjoyed for now. The footman who had been at his mother's feet slipped past him, obviously hurrying back to her side. Brant was eager to return to the Warren so that he could share his good news with Olympia and, pushing all thought of his mother's fury from his mind, he hurried back to his waiting carriage.

Chapter 16

"Bastard!" Letitia picked up the small pot of flowers she had set on the table and hurled them across the room. "He thinks he has won? He thinks he can do this to me?" She found another pot, a little bigger than the first and hurled that as well but the sound of the destruction did nothing to cool the fury burning within her. "We shall see who holds the power."

"M'lady?"

She turned to see the big man she had taken as a lover standing a few feet away watching her as if he expected her to do more than throw pottery around. "Has he gone?"

"Aye, m'lady."

Letitia took a deep breath and carefully pushed the hot fury down until it simmered just below her skin. She had learned at a young age that anger should be kept cold. Hot rage made one make mistakes. She needed to plan now. Brant had found a way to take away her power and that could not be tolerated.

She looked around at the room she had built. Such places required a lot of money to build, were a new fashion just beginning to take hold and so expensive that few could really afford them even amongst the most prosperous of the aristocracy. To her it was a sign that she had succeeded, that she had the fortune and the power to do as she pleased. That she did not need a man to become a person one feared. She could not allow Brant to place her back in that position where her only power came from the man who was her husband, father, or, in this case, son.

It was going to take time to reverse this setback, however. Her son had already cost her too much and she had lost a number of her most useful people. With the fall of Dobbin House, the raid on the ship, and even the rescue of the marquis's son, she had suffered too many losses to recover too quickly. Worse, the ones she dealt with were now wary of doing business with her, afraid that somehow her son had discovered all of her dealings and would soon be coming for them.

Brant and that Wherlocke bitch he was rutting with needed to die, she thought viciously and, again, fought to cool the heat of her anger. Until she could find a way to accomplish that she needed something to set him back for a change, to let him taste the bitter flavor of defeat. She also had to do it in such a way that no one could prove she had any part in it.

She looked at John, her current lover and, she

admitted, slave. One thing she had learned from her lecherous bastard of a husband was how to play upon a man's true weakness—his lusts. John could refuse her nothing. Even if he grew enough backbone to try, she could see him hanged a dozen times over for the blood on his hands. He was a reluctant killer, however, and would need persuasion when the time came to send him after her son and his woman.

Letitia actually wondered for a moment if she should just burn the house down. It would deprive her son of the pleasure of it. She looked around again and knew she could not do it. This was her monument to her success and she fully intended to keep it, even if she was forced to give it up for a little while.

That left the other prize Brant had stolen from her. Agatha, her soft, weakling of a daughter. Or, perhaps not as weak as she had thought, for the girl had somehow managed to get her brother to London to help her. However, Minden desperately wanted the girl. He had convinced himself that such a young, innocent girl, one of excellent breeding, would be the cure of the pox that was eating away at his body and mind. It was a foolish belief, for nothing could save the man now, but Letitia had seen a chance to gather a hefty purse from the man. Now she both would get the money and spit in the eye of her arrogant son.

"John," she said, and smiled at him in a way she knew would stir his lusts, "I have something I need you to do."

"You know I will do anything for you," he said as he stepped closer and pulled her into his arms.

Letitia swallowed the wave of distaste that always swamped her the first time any man held her close. She hated sex. Hated the mess of it, the sweat, the smell, and the need to have a man so close to her to achieve what she needed. It had taken her a long while to sharpen her seductive skills and learn how to hide the fact that she hated everything to do with lovemaking and even hated men themselves. But the first time she had realized that she had something that men desired, she had begun to use it to her advantage and it had worked very well for her.

She slid her arms up around his neck. "I need you to go and find Minden. You must tell him that unless he acts quickly he will lose Agatha. All he needs to do is bring me the sum we last agreed on and he can take her away today."

"I know right where he is, m'lady." He kissed her neck. "You want me to leave right now?"

She could feel the hard ridge of his manhood pressed against her and nearly cursed. There were a lot of things she would require of him in the near future, the sort of things he always needed to be persuaded to do. It would be best if she began the persuading now.

"No, I believe we have time."

Brant found Olympia in her bedchamber at her writing desk. By the look of it, there had been a lot of letters recently delivered. Her family was proving to be frighteningly skilled at unearthing every secret his mother had as well as the ones she had used to force people to do as she wanted. Very soon they would have more than enough to get the woman hanged or transported. He was thinking the latter would be good for, even if she managed to escape her chains, it would take her a very long time to get back to England.

He walked over and kissed her on the side of her neck, breathing in the scent of her and feeling his body tighten with need. "Busy as always. Do you know, you, with the help of your family, could be a very good investigator?"

Olympia laughed. "So I could although my family might soon get weary of my requests for information on various things."

"Maybe not. You told me they all love to pry into people's secrets."

"True." She turned in her seat to look at him. "You are looking very pleased with yourself. Have you found out something that will finally end your mother's games?"

He took the papers out of his pocket and handed them to her. He was eager to give her the gift he had taken time to find before coming to the Warren but that could wait until a more appropriate time. Right now, it was a pleasure to watch her face as she read. The smile she gave him when she was done made him even more eager to get her into his arms.

"You have done it," she said and leapt up to throw her arms around him and kiss him.

"Andras has done it," he corrected. "When I first went to him I thought him too young, perhaps even too gentle of nature, to deal with this but I trusted in your judgment and am very glad I did. He knows what paths to take to get information and, in this case, where to go when the authority you need to circumvent is corrupt."

"So she did have a secret she held over the man's head."

"She did and he refused to change his decision because of the fear that she would tell his secret to the one person he did not want to know it, a young wife he loves very much. Your cousin accepted his refusal, told him he needed to get the secret told or he would always be used as a pawn by someone, and then sought out a man with the power to change the decision the other man had made. Mother will soon have to leave the town house and she has no authority over Agatha from this day on."

Olympia kissed him, unable to resist him when he looked so pleased and relaxed. It took her only a moment to realize that both of them were far too hungry for each other to be satisfied with only kisses. She had wanted him very badly when they had been at Myrtledowns, wanted the pleasure he could give her to wash away the fear she had felt for her son. Yet they had had to sleep apart and could not even attempt to steal a little privacy for themselves in order to feed their need for each other.

Brant knew he had to have her now. It was not going to be any sweet and tender bout of lovemaking, either. He was too hungry for her. The look in her eyes told him she shared that greed.

"Door needs to be latched," he said, reluctant to let go of her and move to do so.

"Hurry then." The moment he stepped back she began to unlace her gown.

He secured the door and, even as he removed his coat and waistcoat, he walked back to her. "Not sure I want to wait until you undress no matter how much I like to see you naked."

"Fast then."

"Very fast. So fast I should probably be ashamed of myself."

He kissed her and picked her up in his arms. The moment she twined her arms and legs around him, he walked until she was pressed up against the wall. The little pantalets she wore were easy to remove and when he slid his hand between her legs he found the hot, damp welcome he needed so badly. He growled his approval against the hollow at the base of her throat as she undid his pants with her long, nimble fingers. The moment he was free, he shifted her against his body until hers was wide open to him, and then thrust inside.

Olympia held on tightly as Brant thrust into her again and again. It was a rough lovemaking, fierce and with little finesse, but her body had no complaint. The hunger within her was so fierce that she quickly began to feel that tightness inside her that told her bliss was just around the corner. She kissed him and a moment later cried out into his mouth as pleasure washed over her in hot waves. He joined her in that sweet place a heartbeat later.

Brant carefully eased himself from her body and, still holding her in his arms, staggered over to the bed and fell onto it. He liked the feel of her soft laughter against his throat as she adjusted her position so that she was sprawled more comfortably on top of him. Olympia was the perfect lover, he mused. She matched his passion to perfection and was so free with her own that he still marveled over the fact that he was her first real lover.

"Well, that was a fine celebration of a victory," she said as she stroked his chest, idly wondering if she should undo his shirt so that she could feel his skin beneath her hands.

"A worthy effort, but, perhaps, if we rest a little, we can try to surpass it."

The laughter bubbling up in Olympia's throat suddenly vanished and a coldness swept over her. She stared at the headboard but did not really see it. What she saw was a terrified Agatha fighting an ugly old man. Behind them stood a smiling Lady Mallam with a nearly naked footman at her feet. And then, just as quickly as it came, the vision was gone. She sat up on Brant, fighting the dizziness that always accompanied the rare visions she had.

"You now control all that happens with Agatha, correct?" she asked.

Something in her voice caused him to tense and he gripped her hips a little more tightly. "Yes. Whatever my mother was negotiating with Minden is now null and void for no agreement can be made without my complete approval."

"And where is Agatha now?"

"She was out riding with friends but might have returned home by now. Why?"

Olympia leapt off him and grabbed her pantalets off the floor to slip them on. "You have to go back."

He stood up and began to redon his waistcoat. "Why? How do you know I have to go back?"

"Occasionally, actually, rarely, I have a vision. Not like my cousin Chloe's, of course, but quick, sharp pictures or even just a sharp demand that I do something or go somewhere. I just saw Agatha fighting with a nasty old man. Your mother was standing there watching, a smile on her face. And, for some odd reason, there was a big, somewhat handsome footman, kneeling at her feet."

He threw his coat on and started toward the door. His fear for his sister renewed. "It would be just like my mother to try to punish me by destroying Agatha."

Hurrying after him, Olympia said, "You took her power away and her symbol of her power, that damned house. She is probably trying to dim your victory over her."

Once in the hall, Olympia called for Pawl, Artemis, and Stefan. "Do not argue," she said when Brant frowned. "You do not know what you might find when you return to that house. It would be wise to have someone at your back."

"Agreed," he said.

"And it would not hurt to have one of these as well," said Pawl as he walked up and handed Brant a pistol.

"Good man," he murmured as he pocketed the gun but Pawl had already run out to call for a carriage. "Let us just pray we are not too late." He looked at Olympia. "How soon do you see something before it actually happens?"

"I have so few visions it is difficult to say. Not long, if I recall correctly. So, go, and this time bring Agatha back here."

"I will."

He would not leave the girl within a mile of his mother ever again. As he leapt into the carriage Pawl had already called for, and the others joined him, he cursed himself as an idiot. He should have known his mother would seek some revenge for what he had done. What better way to strike at him than to hurt the sister he had been trying so hard to save. His mother knew the house did not mean all that much to him.

"You got this carriage quickly, Pawl," he said, hoping talking would keep his mind from preying on all that could be happening to his baby sister. "They are usually a bit slower to answer a call."

"Did not call," said Pawl and grinned. "Saw it sitting outside m'lady's cousin's house and told the man Sir Orion had told us to take it."

Artemis and Stefan laughed and Brant found he was able to smile. "I hope this Orion does not scold Olympia too much for this theft."

"Nay," said Artemis, "especially not when he learns why we stole it."

And that quickly his mind returned to thinking on all that could be happening to Agatha. He was so tense by the time they reached the street where Mallam House was that his bones ached. Just as the carriage rolled to a halt behind another carriage parked before the house, Minden threw a screaming Agatha into the carriage and leapt in behind her.

Brant leapt from his carriage but it was too late for the driver on the other one whipped up the horses and Minden's carriage lurched into motion.

Brant leapt up next to the driver of his carriage. "Follow them!"

"'Tis dangerous to go that fast through these roads," the man protested.

"I will pay for any damage. Now, move!"

"M'lord," he began again.

"Move now or I will kick you off this box and drive the cursed thing myself. That is my sister that swine has just run off with."

The driver did not argue anymore. Brant soon realized that, despite his hesitation, the man knew how to handle his team on the narrow roads and do so at high speed. From the look of the carriage they chased, Minden's driver was not as skilled. Brant could only pray that his sister was not harmed during what was supposed to be her rescue.

Minden's driver did his best but disaster struck quickly. In turning a corner, the man judged wrong and Brant held his breath as the carriage teetered on two wheels and then fell over. He could hear Agatha screaming and watched as the horses dragged the tipped carriage a little ways farther before stopping. The fact that the driver had fallen off the box and the reins were no longer held in anyone's hands may have helped that quick halt, Brant thought as, the moment his carriage stopped, he jumped to the ground.

His driver, Pawl, and Olympia's nephews were right behind him as he ran to the fallen carriage.

"See how the driver is," he told Pawl and then looked at his driver. "Can you do anything with the horses?"

"Aye, m'lord," the man said and hurried over to calm the frightened animals.

Brant approached the fallen carriage slowly, Artemis and Stefan flanking him. The silence inside made him uneasy. Carriage accidents caused too many deaths for him not to be afraid for his sister. He was only a foot away when the door, now situated at the top of the turned-over carriage, opened and Minden scrambled out.

Brant lunged forward but, for an aging roué, Minden proved very nimble and went down the other side of the carriage. He ran around it and saw Minden hobbling away. It was easy to catch him but, as he drew close, Brant was reluctant to touch the man. Minden could no longer hide that he had the pox. He looked wretched and unclean. Either he had been in such a hurry he had not bothered to try and hide the sores on his face or they were so bad now that he could not hide them any longer.

"Give up, Minden," he said.

"I had a right to the girl. Your mother took good money for her and signed the betrothal papers," the man said, looking all around him as if some magical doorway would open to help him escape.

"My mother had no right to negotiate with you and well you know it. What? Did you think despoiling my young sister would cure you?" He could tell by the look that passed over the man's ruined face that Minden had thought just that. "Idiot. All that would

have happened would have been that you would
have infected an innocent with your disease. I think
the madness that comes with the rot has already
seeped into your mind."

"It was worth a try." Minden shrugged and then
pulled out his pistol.

Brant reached for his even though he knew he
would not have time to pull it from his pocket and
aim before Minden shot him. As he thought which
was the best direction to move in, a shot rang out.
Minden stood for a moment and then slowly col-
lapsed on the ground. Brant saw Pawl standing
behind the man with a pistol in his hand. He hurried over and took it from Pawl.

"Best if we say I shot him," he said and handed
Pawl his unfired pistol.

"It will certainly save me having to talk to a lot of
folk. Your sister is fine. A few bruises and a few rips
in her gown, but nothing else. Artemis and Stefan
are keeping her behind the carriage so she cannot
see this."

"Minden's driver?"

"Dead. Head split open when he hit the road.
Making certain your sister cannot see that, either."

Brant saw Agatha standing between Olympia's
nephews, each boy speaking softly as they tried to
ease her fear. She saw him and raced to his arms. For
a moment, Brant just held her, thankful she had not
been harmed. Once his own fear was calmed, he
held her away from him and looked her over, seeing
only what Pawl had said was there.

"Did he touch you?" he asked her.

"Not as I think you mean. He was so ill, Brant. Wretchedly ill. Each time he spoke you could nearly smell the rot inside him. Mother gave me to him anyway. He handed her a bank draft and she handed me to him." She shook her head. "I do not know that woman," she whispered.

"Nor do I and that is probably a very good thing. Wait with the boys, Aggie," he said quietly when he noticed a man with silver hair and an air of authority walking toward them.

As Brant had expected, the man was a magistrate. Even more convenient for Brant the man had also seen everything from his window as he had struggled to dress. It meant he had seen who had shot Minden but he said nothing as Brant confessed to the shooting, just wrote it all down and then told him he was free to leave. As Brant walked to his carriage, he watched the magistrate touch Pawl's arm, stopping Olympia's cousin for a few words before smiling and letting Pawl go.

"I do not wish to go home where our mother still is, Brant," Agatha said the moment he climbed into the carriage.

"I will take you to the Warren and soon I will take you out to Fieldgate if you like," he said as he sat down next to her and put his arm around her.

"I think I would like that," she murmured and rested her head against his shoulder.

Brant looked at Pawl. "What did the magistrate have to say to you?"

Pawl smiled. "Asked me if I was ever a soldier. I

said no and he said that was a shame as the military could use a man with such a good eye for shooting."

Shaking his head, Brant laughed. "I knew he had seen it all but when he never questioned my claim of having shot Minden, I assumed he was just going to let it stand."

"Why would it matter?" asked Agatha. "Minden was about to shoot you, was he not?"

"Pawl is a servant," Brant answered. "It should not matter but it does. Easier to try and just slip around it with a small lie."

The moment they reached the Warren, Brant handed the care of his sister over to Olympia. "I will need to go back to Mallam House. I have to make certain my mother does not slip free."

"What will happen to Mama?" asked Agatha from where she pressed close to Olympia, willing to accept the comfort she offered with an arm around the girl's shoulders.

"There is a lot that could be done. I was thinking the best would be to send her to the most remote of her dower lands with a few guards who can be trusted. I will make it clear to her that she must stay there and cease what she has been doing. If she breaks away or begins to play her vicious games again, I will see her punished as the criminal she is even if it sends her to the hangman."

"And would you? Really?"

"If she does not stay where she is put and tries to return to what she has been doing here for years, yes. Without hesitation. I am offering her a comfortable prison. She would be wise to accept that."

She would, Olympia thought as she watched Brant leave, but Lady Letitia was not a woman who would accept her fall from power with dignity and grace. A chill of foreboding washed over her but she fought to ignore it. Olympia told herself it was just a fear of what Lady Mallam was, a cold, evil woman, and meant nothing. She turned her attention to Agatha.

"Let us go to my bedchamber and you can have a bath," she said as she walked the girl to the stairs.

"Oh, yes, please, that man was diseased," Agatha said and shuddered. "He had sores on his face and he smelled as if he was already dead but someone had forgotten to tell him to lie down."

Olympia bit back a grin. There was spirit in the girl. A little time without Lady Mallam looming over her and controlling her life, and the girl would quickly blossom into the woman she was meant to be.

It took awhile to get Agatha clean enough for her own approval. Olympia understood. Even though the girl had not been raped, or even fondled, she had been in the presence of a man who planned to do both. Worse that man had been obviously diseased and anyone would want to be sure none of that infection had touched them. Olympia was not about to explain to the girl that touching was not the way one got a disease like Minden had, at least not simple touch such as a hand grabbing a clothed arm, which was apparently all he had done to Agatha.

"So, Brant is now the true head of the house?"

Agatha asked as Olympia helped her get dressed in an old gown of Olympia's.

"Yes, he has the papers all signed to prove it as well."

"I hope he chains her up somewhere."

"To your mother, being confined to the remote countryside, unable to rule over the society she lives and breathes for, will feel to her as if she has been chained."

"Good."

"It will certainly make life more peaceful."

"I think she was a very evil woman. I do not know all she did but I can guess. There were a lot of children that just disappeared while she had the rule over me."

"Did you tell Brant?" Olympia could not believe he would have ignored such a thing.

"Yes, but I am now sure that all my letters to him were read and any that said anything Mother did not want known or did not like, were destroyed. I would get so hurt and be angry at Brant and he did not deserve it. It was all my mother's doing."

There was such fury in the girl's voice that Olympia wanted to hug her but knew that comforting words and touches would not cure it. Agatha had to mend her own heart. Time without her mother around would help tremendously. A firm but loving companion or governess would also help and she had a few people she would recommend to Brant when he returned.

Just mentioning his name made her shiver but this time it was not from pleasure. Olympia paused in brushing Agatha's hair and studied what she was feeling. The chill was not leaving, was only growing worse. The brush fell from Olympia's hand as she realized what that meant. Lady Mallam was not done getting her revenge.

Chapter 17

"I want you, Pawl, to see to what servants are left and make certain none of them can come up behind me. And I think you can probably tell which one of those may or may not be worth keeping," said Brant.

"Aye." Pawl nodded. "That I can do. Do we go in now?"

Brant sighed as he stared at the front of the house, one he feared had been irrevocably tainted by his mother over the last few years. He would never know all that had gone on in that house or all that had been bought with money made by the selling of innocents. There had to be some way he could make it new again for it held a lot of the history of his family and he knew he would hate to give it up.

"Yes, best we get this done with," he finally said.

Pawl, Artemis, and Stefan followed him into the house. Once inside the three of them went off to find whatever servants they could. Brant had to decide where his mother might be.

"Her ladyship is in the drawing room."

He looked up to see the same young footman who had helped him before. "Have you been told to leave?" he asked, a little surprised for he was certain this was a good man and one he would not mind having in his service.

"No, I was told to come down and go to the kitchens as I told the young man upstairs that there would be a few in there he would be wise to send packing."

"Go on then. The house will soon be mine alone again and you shall have a job if you wish it."

"That I do, m'lord. Have to help my family. Have eight siblings, I do." He sauntered off to the kitchens, obviously more than ready to help in the weeding out of the bad from the good.

Brant made his way to the drawing room. He stepped inside and saw his mother immediately. She stood by the window dressed in a lavender gown that must have cost more than many made in a year, even amongst the gentry. It was elegant, made of the best material and dripping with the most expensive of laces but all he saw was the misery of the children she had sold to pay for it. Just when had she begun to hate children, he wondered, for he had no other explanation for how she could treat the young and innocent as she had.

"Mother, it is time," he said.

"Time for what, you ungrateful child?"

There was no anger in her voice yet Brant was sure that she was viciously furious and that false calm made him uneasy. "For you to pack to go to your country house."

"You told me I had time to put my affairs in order."

"That was before you sold Agatha to Minden. You knew you had no right to do that, knew it went against all the legal papers I had said were right, yet you handed her over anyway."

"She is of an age to be wed and start bearing children."

"She is sixteen. Just. Minden was also diseased, riddled with the pox, and you knew that as well. You were selling her to a man who would begin to kill her with the first bedding."

"Is that not a woman's lot in life?" She turned to face Brant and could see her husband in him, something that made the fury she was fighting to control churn inside of her, demanding release. "I was not much older when my father sold me to yours. Even as your father bedded me and made me bear his children he was bedding everything else in skirts he could get his hands on. When he grew too old and too poor to play amongst the courtesans he came home and did it again. Bedded me, bedded the maids, bedded the village girls, and made us all bear his children. Then he put those children bred on other women right in front of me, making them our servants so that I had to see them every day."

"A wretched situation but you cannot blame it for the things you have done."

She shrugged. "I needed money."

"Money made off the backs of innocent children. You knew what Dobbin House was. You had been inside. You knew what fate those children would suffer yet you sold them and bought expensive gowns."

"You did not give me very much to live on, did you? I had a position to maintain."

He shook his head as if he could shake her words out of his memory. It would be comforting in a way to think that she had completely lost her mind but, although he would freely admit that there was something amiss with her, he did not think she was insane. She was a cold, mercenary woman who did not care what she had to do and who she had to hurt to keep what she considered was her proper place in the world. That, and all the expensive things she felt were truly important in life.

"And now you try to blame me," he said. "You did what you did for yourself. I begin to think everything you have ever done has been for yourself."

"I did not go through the hell of childbirth for myself."

"In a way, I think you may have. It was not only Father who wished to be certain he had an heir. You needed one, needed a son you could mold as you pleased so that you would forever be the true power. Agatha, Emery, and Justin were just security. Two more sons in case I did not turn out as you wished, and another daughter. After all, look how much profit you gained from selling off the others."

"Your father sold Mary and Alice."

"No, I begin to think you had a firm rein on Father and knew how to lead him to what you wished him to do. The unfaithfulness? I do not believe that troubled you at all for it left you free to do as you liked, to take control of everything. Father was so busy rutting, drinking, and gambling, he was more than happy to hand you all the work. I should have seen it before but it was easy to just think that Father was a fool.

"And so was I for I never truly looked at how you had your dainty little hand in everything. I realized but recently that you have been stealing from all of us for years. I mean to gather all the papers from all the properties and pay a visit to your solicitor, for instinct tells me that there may have been something left for all of my half-siblings. It would be like you to see that they got nothing, even the pittance Father probably left for them."

"I did all the work. I built everything that made Fieldgate profitable. I was more the earl of those lands than he ever was and yet he felt he could give the profits of my hard work to his bastards? Fool. I have ruled his solicitor since shortly after you were born."

There was the ghost of a bubbling fury in her voice and Brant wondered just how far he could push her. For the first time he was getting some information that he needed. Now he knew that his feckless father had indeed left something for all the children he had bred. There could even be an accounting of where each of those children, or men, were.

"Do Agatha and the boys have anything left? So easy for you to steal from them since by the time they were born you truly were in full control of all the accounts."

"I needed nothing to sell Agatha to Minden, did

I? He was willing to pay for a well-bred virgin in the vain hope that she would be his cure."

"No, you did not need anything." He sighed. "So that answers my question. You have bled their inheritances dry."

"I did not bleed them dry. I made sure they never had one to begin with."

"I will sort that out. Now, I suggest you go and pack for you are going to Hillsbury House."

He was not surprised to see her shudder. It was a lovely, roomy cottage in a beautiful area in the Lake Country. It would have nothing remotely resembling a society, however. There would be a natural beauty but his mother was not one to care for such things. She would be completely isolated from everything that had ever interested her. And he would make very sure that the guards she had were not the sort she could seduce as she had her footman.

Thinking of that big man, Brant looked around. "Where is your lover?"

"He is gone. He has no wish to leave the city." She pulled her hand up from where it had been tucked into her skirts and pointed the pistol she had hidden there right at his heart. "Nor do I. I do not intend to waste what remains of my life in a tiny hovel in the middle of nowhere."

"You would kill your own son to escape that fate?"

"Actually, Brant, at the moment I would kill you just for the pleasure of it."

Olympia raced out of her bedchamber calling for Pawl. Halfway down the stairs she remembered that

Pawl had gone off with Brant. It only calmed her a little for she did not think she would have had such a strong foreboding if Pawl was close at Brant's side.

"What are you bellowing for my husband for?" said Enid as she came hurrying out of the kitchen, Thomas and the other four boys right behind her.

"I need to get to Brant," Olympia said.

"Is something wrong?" asked Agatha as she reached Olympia's side.

"I just know that I have to get to Brant."

Enid stared at her for a moment and then nodded. She marched to the front door and looked across the street to Sir Orion's home. "You are in luck. Your cousin's carriage is still out there." She looked at the boys. "You lot go with her."

"What is wrong?" asked Agatha. "Is Brant in trouble?"

"Well, that is what Olympia is about to find out. Now come to the kitchen with me and we can get that hair to dry faster if you sit by the stove."

Olympia grabbed her cloak and raced across the street. She saw the driver eye her and the boys nervously. The poor man had already had one adventure with her family. She suspected he had no great wish to have another.

"I need you to take us to Mallam House," she said as she opened the carriage door and all five boys leapt in.

"I have just got back and rested from doing that once. I am not of a mind to do it again."

"If you do not and Lord Fieldgate is hurt, I will hunt you down and shoot you like a dog."

"Get in," he said in a resigned voice.

"And you must get there as quickly as you can."

"Of course. None of you lot seem to want to go slow."

Olympia jumped into the carriage and sat down between Thomas and David. As the carriage began to move, she glanced out the window and saw her cousin Orion step out to gape at the sight of his carriage racing off down the street. It might have been a good idea to ask him to come along but she shrugged. It was too late now.

"Exactly why are we rushing to that place to find his lordship?" asked Abel.

"I have a feeling he will be having need of us very soon," she replied.

"You got one of them gifts the others have?"

"Yes, although I do not often have visions. I just *know* that we have to get to Brant as soon as we can."

"Then we will although I be thinking this driver will be running from the sight of us for many a month after this."

Olympia actually laughed. "Yes, quite possibly."

She knew the man had gotten them to Mallam House with astonishing speed but it still felt as if hours had passed. With every turn of the wheels she had feared that she would be too late. She was not sure what help he needed but the chill in her blood was too sharp to ignore.

"Thank you!" she said as she leapt from the carriage. "Stop at the Warren and tell my maid that you need to be paid." She ignored his muttered curses and ran into the house.

Just inside the door Olympia nearly ran into a tall, thin footman. "The countess?"

"Who are you?"

"The baroness of Myrtledowns and I need to see the earl right away. I know he is with the countess."

"Drawing room," he said and pointed out the way to go.

Olympia allowed her instincts to direct her. She did not race up the stairs as her heart demanded but went slowly and silently. It surprised her a little at how quiet each of the boys was. Signaling them to halt when they were near the door, she crept closer. As she heard what was being said her heart hurt for Brant.

"I do not intend to waste what remains of my life in a tiny hovel in the middle of nowhere," said Lady Mallam.

"You would kill your own son to escape that fate?"

"Actually, Brant, at the moment I would kill you just for the pleasure of it."

Those words sent a tremor of fear through her body, and Olympia chanced moving a little closer. Lady Mallam stood facing Brant, a pistol in her hand. The woman had a faint smile on her face but nothing else about her expression revealed any emotion whatsoever. What concerned Olympia, however, was how to stop what was about to happen without getting herself or Brant killed.

A tap on her back made her slowly move away from the door and look at Abel. "She is going to shoot him."

Abel grabbed her by the arm and made her move even farther away from the door. "He will keep her talking in the hope someone comes. I feel sure in my bones that we have some time. How are you at climbing?"

"Excellent. Why?"

"There be an easy climb up the wall right and into the window right behind where that b- er-witch is standing. Can you get up there in those skirts?"

"I can but would it not be better for one of you boys to . . ." She stuttered to a halt when she saw the fear in their faces that they all fought to hide. The climb up to that window was obviously a height none of them could stomach. "I can do it. But, what do you plan to do? I do not want any of you to put yourselves at risk."

"We will be fine. David, go find Pawl as I know he has a pistol." He looked at Olympia. "The window, m'lady?"

She nodded and hurried away as fast as she could without alerting Lady Mallam to her presence. Abel would make a very fine soldier she thought as she ran out the door and around to the side of the house. She fleetingly noticed that the carriage they had stolen from Orion was still there and the driver was watching everything. Curiosity or a need to be certain he was paid, she supposed. Stopping beneath the window, she tied up her skirts and silently prayed no one was looking out their windows in the neighboring houses.

Looking up, she realized it was an easy climb. There was so much decorative brickwork on the side of the house that it was almost as if someone had put steps up there. Just as she began the climb she glanced around to be certain there was no one that could be a threat to her in the area. Something caught her eye near the garden wall and once she was a little farther up, she looked again and nearly gasped. A large man was sprawled on the ground just inside the garden walls and even from up where she was she could see that he was very dead. Lady Mallam was cleaning house, she decided.

Praying every step of the way, she climbed up to the window. It was not until she got there that she realized she had trusted Abel too much. She had not even asked him if it was open. To her relief it was and she suspected he had seen that as well in the brief peek he had taken into the room. Olympia told herself that she had to remember to mention those skills to Brant and perhaps one or two of her family. Abel had great potential.

Peering over the sill, she inwardly sighed with a relief so strong she had to tighten her grip on the sill. Brant was still alive. He was talking, making time for some chance of rescue just as Abel had predicted. She just wished she had asked what he expected her to do now that she was hanging on the wall of the house behind Lady Mallam.

Brant stared at his mother and read the intent to kill him in her eyes. He waited for that to hurt and found nothing. Over the past days as he had discovered more and more about the woman who had borne him, the very last of his bond to her, thin though it had been, had been cut.

"I did not come here alone, you know," he said. "You cannot kill me and walk away. This time you will hang for your crimes, as I begin to think you should have hanged many times before."

"I never killed anyone."

"No, I suspect you never dirtied your own hands although not for lack of the stomach to do so. You just wished to make sure that if a body was found and all signs pointed to you, you could turn around and point the finger at someone else."

She shrugged slightly. "Sacrifices must be made."

"Do you truly believe all you say or do you just not care?" He thought about what she had replied when he had asked about her lover. "You have killed. You have murdered your lover. Afraid he knew too much to let him live?"

"As I said, sacrifices must be made. Now, for my own well-being, you are forcing me to kill one of my own children. You should have just stayed in the country drinking and wenching and slowly becoming just like your father. Either that or you could have done as a good son should and married the woman I had chosen for you."

"Which is why you saw to it that Faith died."

"She was clearly weak. I lost a lot of money when you refused to get yourself betrothed to Henriette."

"My apologies." He knew he was not as successful at keeping all his emotion, all of his disgust and fury, out of his voice when she looked at him as if he was some odd curiosity. "You must know you cannot win this. You kill me and you will hang."

"It is a gamble but one I am willing to take. I have grown quite good at judging the odds." She frowned as there was a soft noise out in the hall. "What was that?"

"I told you I had not come here alone."

"Well, it does not matter as I can shoot you dead before anyone can get in here to stop me. I am actually a very good shot."

Brant wanted to ask her if his father had really died of heart failure as they all thought when he noticed an all too familiar face appear over the edge of the windowsill behind his mother. His heart stopped in his chest for a moment and he had to fight hard to keep his fear for Olympia off his face. Not only had she risked herself climbing up the side of the house but she now risked being shot by his mother. If they got out of this alive, he was going to throttle her.

And then he knew. It was an incredibly awkward time to have his heart reveal a truth to him, one his mind had tried to ignore. He loved the woman now slinging one stocking-clad leg over the windowsill. Loved her more than his own life.

"Pleased to hear it. I would hate to have you wound me and leave me to suffer pain and possible infection."

"You have developed a very sharp tongue. It is not becoming in a gentleman."

He blinked and was not surprised to see Olympia pause in her stealthy entrance to stare at his mother in open-mouthed shock. Lady Mallam had sounded very much like some scolding mother for a moment. She was about to shoot him dead and she was concerned about how gentlemanly he was behaving? Brant wondered if he had been wrong in his assessment of her mental state.

Then the faintest sound of cloth tearing broke

the silence. Brant cried out as his mother turned toward the sound. He lunged toward her but she fired her pistol before he could reach her. Olympia cried out and disappeared beneath the sill. Brant, not even considering the fact that he was giving his mother a chance to reload or rearm, raced toward the window. The sound of another shot halted him but he felt nothing. He looked behind him to see Pawl standing in the doorway. He then looked for his mother and saw her on the floor, one pistol by her feet and another held in her hand. She had been ready to shoot him again.

Brant went back to the window. He took a deep breath to steady himself. He dreaded seeing Olympia's broken body on the ground.

"Is she dead?"

He jerked back a step with surprise. "Olympia?"

"Aye, and could you hurry and give me a hand up, please? I am not sure how much longer I can hold on and I am certain someone must have looked out their window by now."

He leaned out the window and saw her hanging by her fingertips from the narrow edge just outside. Brant was so relieved to see her alive, he was shaking. He bent over, grabbed her by the wrists and pulled her in through the window. The minute her feet touched the ground he hugged her until a soft squeak from her told him he was hugging her too tightly.

"Your mother?" Olympia asked.

"Dead," he replied and thought Olympia was looking a little pale.

"Not yet," said Pawl from where he crouched by

Lady Mallam, "but there is no saving her. Sorry, m'lord."

"There is nothing you need to apologize for," Brant said as he reluctantly released Olympia and went to kneel beside his mother.

Letitia Mallam, Countess of Fieldgate, was dying. He could see it in her eyes and in the way she was breathing. It would be hard on the younger Mallams but he suspected not all that hard. One thing it did do was give him the opportunity to hide all the crimes she had committed. He only had to come up with a very good reason why she had been shot in her house.

"I think her footman is the dead man I saw in the garden," said Olympia as she hurriedly put down her skirts, knowing that she could not hide her own condition for too much longer.

"A lovers quarrel?" asked Pawl.

"Excellent," agreed Brant, "and I know just the man to help us make that happen." He looked toward the boys all gathered in the doorway. "Can one of you get Dobson for me?" he asked.

"I will," said Abel and frowned at Olympia, "but . . ."

Olympia shook her head, silencing him, knowing that he had sensed that something was wrong with her. "But you may have to give him some money. The carriage we came in has not been paid for and the one you came in will also require some money to take the boy to get Dobson." She sat down beneath the window and leaned against the wall to preserve her strength.

Brant hastily held out some money for Abel, which the boy took and then ran off to fetch Dobson. He turned his attention back to his mother who was watching him with that same, unsettling little smile. It was as if she still knew something he did not and he had the feeling that he did not wish her to tell him, either. He managed to hold back the urge to ask for several minutes as he watched her slowly die with such quiet calm that he was uneasy about it. Yet, when he looked again, he had no doubt that the wound was fatal, that it was actually very surprising that she had hung on to life for as long as she had.

"You were going to shoot me in the back," he said.

"Yes." Her voice was soft but steady despite the pain he knew she had to be in. "I know where to aim so that the bullet would still have gone through your heart."

"An admirable skill for a countess. I do not suppose you are going to ask for forgiveness before you die."

"No, I think not. I have known for a very long time that I was headed to hell. You see, I lied when I said I have not killed anyone. I killed your father."

"He died of heart failure. The doctor—"

"Was my lover and had an extensive knowledge of poisons, especially those that left no hint that poison was used."

"That doctor died of heart failure a year later."

"Yes, I learn my lessons well, always have, and it was such an easy poison to obtain."

"Foxglove," Olympia said and nodded when Brant glanced her way.

"No surprise that a witch would know."

"Olympia is not a witch."

"Of course she is but all I find distressing about

her Wherlocke blood, the blood of witches and sorcerers and said to give them all such powerful gifts, is that she makes no real use of that power. Very disappointing. I would have welcomed such power. There is one last thing I do need to tell you."

"And what is that?"

"Emery is not your father's son."

Brant frowned and thought of the nine-year-old Emery. The boy was tall for his age and held the promise of being a big man. He had brown hair so light it held blond streaks when he had been out in the sun. And his eyes were a hazel color with a great deal of brown in them. Then he realized where he had seen such coloring before.

"Your footman. The affair is quite old then."

"He was a very obedient lover and a great resource for me. Of course, when he decided that he did not love me enough to leave London, his usefulness ended."

A moment later she died. Brant sighed and reached out to close her eyes. "Bitter and vicious right up until the end."

"Calm, too, for a body that feels sure she is going to hell and that the trip will start with the next breath."

A moment later Dobson strode in. "You Wherlockes do tend to attract the bodies," he said as he walked up and looked down at Lady Mallam. "Your mother?"

Brant nodded. "Yes, she was about to shoot me in the back when Pawl shot her. Was hoping you might know a way to help us keep that sort of thing from being known."

"Well, there are all her crimes to think on but, this does save a hangman's fee, so I will think of something."

"Her lover's body is in the garden. She shot him because he did not really wish to go into exile with her."

"And there is your answer. Scandalous. A lovers quarrel between a countess and her footman. She shoots him but he lives long enough to shoot her and they both die. It will be scandal enough to whet the appetites of all the gossips so well they will look no further. Might have to wait awhile before we bring up the footman's body though. Good idea, m'lord."

"It was Olympia's idea. She saw the body as she was climbing up the wall to try and help me."

Dobson looked over at Olympia and then frowned. "Is that when you got shot, m'lady?"

"Shot?" Brant said and heard Pawl echo his cry as he spun around to look at Olympia.

He hurried to her side and then he saw it. Her gown was a dark green so he had not noticed the blood at the shoulder. Now, however, there was a lot more of it.

"Why did you not say something?" he demanded as he tore the sleeve of her gown to look at the wound.

"Your mother was dying and in the mood to tell you secrets." She winced as he gently tugged her away from the wall so that he could make certain the bullet had passed all the way through, which it had. "I thought she might actually tell you something of importance but it seems she remained petty right up until the end."

"I need to get you home and seen to by the doctor."

"Can you walk?" asked Dobson.

"I can carry her," said Brant.

"Would look better if she walked out." He rubbed his beard-darkened jaw. "A little more difficult to come up with a good tale that would include her being shot as well."

Seeing the sense of that, Brant still insisted on carrying her right to the front door. He then held her arm to steady her as she walked to the carriage. He told the driver to take them to the Warren as he settled her comfortably in the carriage and then climbed in to sit beside her.

"I cannot believe you climbed up to the window," he said as the carriage began to move.

When she did not answer, he looked at her and his heart stopped for a moment. She was unconscious and her face was as pale as the snow. He leaned out the window and told the driver to hurry. Returning to her side, he held her close to ease the roughness of the journey even though he knew she was feeling no pain.

"Do not die on me, Baroness," he whispered into her hair. "Do not dare. I will drag Penelope off her birthing bed to come and hunt your spirit down so I can scold you until your ears burn. Please, Olympia. Do. Not. Die."

Chapter 18

Brant paced outside Olympia's bedchamber. He had barely gotten her settled on the bed when Enid and Merry evicted him from the room. People soon began to arrive, some staying downstairs but several coming up and being allowed into the room. Stefan was in there as well as Doctor Pryne. He had also recognized Septimus Vaughn as that young man was hastily allowed into the room. Yet he was still banished.

"Come down and have a drink."

He turned to look at the man who had spoken. There was no question he was a Wherlocke as well. He even had eyes similar to Olympia's save that they were a darker blue. Suddenly, Brant knew who all the people were that he had heard arriving. He recalled from the time he had helped Ashton that the Wherlockes and Vaughns appeared to know when one of their own was hurt.

"They will not let me in there," he said.

"Not yet. I am Orion, Olympia's cousin."

"Yes, I assumed you were related. There is a look you Wherlockes have."

"A look? I hope it is a good thing." Orion took him by the arm and tugged him along down the stairs. "Come have a drink. They will let you know when you can go in there. With Septimus, Stefan, and Doctor Pryne all in there, plus Enid and that little maid, it would be too crowded anyway."

"She bled a lot," he said, worry softening his voice as if he feared to even say the words.

"She will be fine."

"Do you know that for certain?"

"Ah, no, just feel it to be true. I do not really have the sight. However, Chloe and Alethea, more cousins, have already sent word saying it will be fine. They do have the sight. They knew she would be hurt but the family is so scattered at the moment we could not get here in time to help with the trouble she was dealing with."

"Ashton and Penelope sent her brothers. I thought that was because Olympia had called for some help." He looked around at all the people gathered as Orion led him into the drawing room. "Although there were many who found out things we needed to know."

Orion handed him a drink of brandy. "We are very good at that. It is why there are so many of us here. We were not so far away anymore. Unfortunately, not close enough to stop this or able to know it was coming. Or that he would come," Orion muttered and looked toward the door.

Brant felt all the hairs on his arms lift and idly scratched at one. He looked in the direction everyone else was just in time to see a tall, black-haired man step into the doorway. The look the man fixed on him made Brant have to fight the urge to step back.

"So you are the one who got my sister shot," the man said as he strode over to stand in front of Brant.

Argus Wherlocke, who had recently married the daughter of a duke, Brant thought as he stared into the man's dark blue eyes. The urge to confess all rose up in him and then Orion stepped in front of him and held a hand in front of his eyes. That urge to spill his innards to this man slowly faded and Brant frowned.

"There is no need to do that, Argus," Orion said. "There have been no secrets here and you know it."

"My sister is hurt, cousin. I have a right to know everything that happened."

Suddenly recalling what Ashton had told him about his uncle-in-law, Brant sighed. "You could have just asked," he said and took a sip of his brandy. "My mother shot her. Olympia saw that my mother was planning to shoot me, climbed up the wall of the house and was coming in through the window when her skirt tore. The noise was enough to draw my mother's attention and she shot her. Unfortunately, your sister decided she could wait to have her wound seen to because my mother, who was shot by Pawl, was speaking and let free a few more nasty secrets before she died. None of which were worth your sister bleeding quietly in the corner. Something I mean to tell her if they ever allow me in to see her."

Argus studied him for a moment, glanced to the door as if he thought to run up the stairs and see to matters himself, and then looked back at Brant. "It sounds like what she would do." He looked at Orion. "Who is with her?"

"Septimus, Stefan, Enid, a young maid, and Doctor Pryne."

"Good enough. Any of that brandy left?"

Brant tried to relax as he stood waiting for Orion to get Argus some brandy. It was not easy to relax around a man like Argus, even if he was not already a mass of conflicting emotions concerning Olympia. When he finally got the courage to look at Argus, the man smiled, and Brant knew it was not a friendly expression. A man did not feel chills run up and down his spine when a man gave him a friendly smile.

"Just why was my sister involved in your troubles, m'lord?" Argus asked as Orion handed him his drink. "I do not recall that the two of you were particularly well acquainted."

"We were not." Brant was not surprised to see Argus's eyes narrow but he would not retract the implications of that *were*. "My sister came here to find Ashton but found Olympia instead." He carefully told the whole tale, ignoring how the room had gone silent as everyone listened even though he suspected a lot of them already knew much of what he was saying. Olympia had been sending messages out to her relatives concerning the matter from the beginning.

Once he was done, he took another careful sip of his brandy and waited for Argus to weigh every word he had just said. Brant knew the man would recognize the truth, but suspected Argus was looking through the whole for any hint that his sister had been unwillingly dragged into danger. When Argus quietly swore, Brant nearly smiled. The man knew his sister well enough to know that no one could force her to do anything she did not want to, just as no one could convince her to sit back and stay safe if she did not want to, either.

"That fool sister of mine should have just handed the mess over to you," muttered Argus.

"She made a promise."

That soft, female voice startled Brant as much as it did Argus and Brant turned to look at his sister. Agatha was a little pale and, to his disgust and anger, he could see the hint of bruising on her throat, but she was standing calmly with her hands folded in front of her skirts. She was also meeting that dark, intimidating gaze of Argus's with no sign of fear.

"To you," said Argus.

"Yes, to me. And to my maid when her brother was taken and to many another one, I believe. I know she would have helped me no matter what, but as it became clear that children were in peril, she was even more determined to do something. Anything." Agatha shrugged, but there was a hint of tears in her eyes. "My mother was an evil that needed to be ended."

Brant put his arm around his sister's shoulders. "She has been, Agatha. I am sorry. I should have come right to you and told you everything but . . ."

Agatha smiled. "I was not bleeding. I do understand, Brant. Pawl told me all that had happened for he felt the need to apologize for being the one who shot her. I think I have convinced him that I feel no animosity toward him for that and would never, ever try to make him pay for something that, I think, was long overdue."

"True, I can sense that but something still troubles you, child," said Orion.

It surprised Brant a little to see a flash of anger in his sister's eyes when Orion called her a child, but then the trouble the man referred to darkened her eyes again. "Only what anyone would feel when she is made to face the fact that her mother was so evil. Worse, I am not sure she was actually insane, just thoroughly bad, without conscience. It is hard to be sensible and convince oneself that such bad blood is not running in your veins as well."

"Do not worry about that," said Argus. "Not all such illnesses carry on through the family. Trust us to know that." He smiled when there was a ripple of laughter through the room. "Some people are just born with their conscience missing, m'lady. Some have it destroyed when they are a child or not even taught to use it. There are many reasons for a person to become what your mother was but I can say, without a doubt, that taint is not in you." There was a murmur of agreement from the others.

"Thank you, that is a great comfort to me." She looked at Brant. "How is Olympia?"

"I have not been allowed in to see her yet but no one here seems particularly worried so I shall find comfort in that," Brant said and glanced at Argus, "as well as in what he said."

"Huh." Argus smiled that smile that made Brant uneasy. "Do not believe I said the same about you." He grunted and whipped around to glare at the tall woman behind him. "Aunty Gone, what are you doing here?"

"Do not call me that foolish name," she said without heat and then looked at Brant. "I came because of Ilar. He needs to know how his mother fares and he is not yet allowed into the city. To bring him into this turmoil as well would be even worse."

Brant bowed to Olympia's aunt Antigone. "All seem to believe she will be fine. She lost a lot of blood though."

"Sepitmus and Stefan are up there," said Argus.

She nodded. "Good. Fetch me some of that brandy, Argus."

Much to Brant's surprise, Argus obeyed without hesitation. He turned to Antigone only to find her staring at Olympia's four waifs from the streets of London. Before he could tell her who they were, she marched over to them and stared hard at young Giles Green.

"Orion!" she snapped.

Unable to resist, Brant followed Orion over to Antigone's side. He knew Agatha was right with him and briefly considered telling her to wait. Then he considered all she had gone through in her young life and said nothing. She might still need protection in many ways, but not from the scandalous or ugly parts of life.

"Yes, Aunt?" Orion looked at the boy she was pointing to. "Ah, one of the ones who makes a habit of stealing my carriages."

"I am not surprised," said Antigone. "He is of your blood." Ignoring how pale Orion had gone, she looked at Giles and tilted her head. "Definitely of your blood. How old are you, lad?"

"Eight," answered Giles. "Just turned it, we think. Not too sure when I was born for I was still no more than a babe in arms when my mam left me in the alley. I did have a note on a ribbon round my neck. Said my name was Giles Green." He eyed Orion warily. "What do you mean I am of his blood?"

"Just what I said. He is your father."

"How do you know?"

"I just do, lad. I can always scent a Wherlocke or Vaughn touch in the blood and, if I think on it real hard, I can tell which one of the rogues left that touch. With you, it was this rogue. Sir Orion Wherlocke who was obviously misbehaving as always about eight years and ten months ago." She looked at Orion who had begun to regain his composure. "Do you even recall a lass with the name of Green?"

"I am certain I will figure out who his mother is before long," said Orion.

Antigone nodded and then started toward the door. "I need to see how Olympia fares."

Before she reached the door, however, Enid stepped into the room and announced, "My lady is fine. The wound has been tended to and the doctor says she will heal nicely if she takes it easy, rests as she should, and eats well. She is awake right now if any of you wish to say a word or two, but keep the visit short."

Before Brant could move Argus strode out of the room with Antigone at his side. He sighed and looked for a seat in the crowded room. It would be awhile before he could go and see Olympia. Her family would take precedence over him, as they should when he was not officially attached to her in any way. He smiled at his sister when she squeezed in beside him on the settee that also held Orion and Giles, who were talking in low voices as they became acquainted with each other.

Brant looked at the other boys and felt a pang. They looked pleased for Giles but that happiness had a touch of sadness behind it. Abel looked the saddest and Brant realized it was because the older boy had been almost a father to Giles, raising him from that babe in arms left in an alley. He hoped Orion was the type of man to understand the bond the four boys had.

"I think Sir Wherlocke will see that he must aid all of the boys, Brant, and not just take the one away from them," said Agatha in a voice soft enough to carry only to his ears.

"I hope so," Brant replied with equal softness and then glanced toward the door.

"You will see her soon."

Soon turned out to be four hours later. Not wishing to drink too much brandy, Brant had begun to drink tea and was heartily sick of it by the time the relatives had ceased to visit, Olympia had had another rest, and he was finally allowed in to see her. He stepped up to the side of the bed and much of his fear for her eased when she smiled at him.

"You do not have a family; you have an army," he said, then felt guilty for making her laugh when she winced and lightly touched her heavily bandaged shoulder. "I am sorry."

"For what?"

"Well, just now, for making you laugh. But, I am sorry you got pulled into this tragedy."

"Agatha is safe now as are a lot of children. A bullet wound in the shoulder is a very small price to pay for that."

"True but I would wish you had remained safe. I wish I could have kept you safe."

And now she had added to all that guilt he clutched to him like some cherished talisman, she thought. "One is never truly safe, Brant, and no one can keep a person safe for every minute of every day. She was going to shoot you. The boys and I could not stand there and do nothing."

"Why did none of the boys climb the wall?" he asked, trying to ignore what she said.

"It appears they have a small problem with heights. At least heights such as the one they would have been at if they had tried to climb the wall. I was the only one who could do it, although the plan did go a little awry."

He sat down on the edge of the bed, took her hand in his, and kissed her palm. "More than a little. Poor Pawl is probably very glad this is over. He will be more than happy to see the last of the Mallams."

Olympia felt her heart stutter with pain, but fought not to ask what he meant by that. If he was intending to end their association now that Agatha was safe and the problem with his mother was ended, she was determined to take the loss with all the dignity she could muster. Pride would give her the strength not to let him see how much that would hurt her.

"Pawl was trained as a guard. He is, in many ways, a soldier as much as a footman." She smiled faintly. "And occasionally a coachman and has held many another position in my household since he joined it. You have seen to it that he is not the one known to have pulled the trigger."

"I have. With Dobson's help this will all end as a horrible tragedy filled with the delicious scandal of a love affair gone wrong between a countess and her footman."

"Good. It will be difficult for Agatha when she finally has her come-out but not as difficult as it would be for your family if the full truth were known."

"We are not the only ones who know it though."

"The others will not talk for they will then have too many looking at them, at how they knew such things. If the full truth were told, every single person who had anything to do with your mother could be tainted and suffer for it all. I wish some would but this is for the best. The ones who were involved with her in any of the things she did will be very certain that the tale you have come up with gets their full support."

"How fare you? In much pain?"

"Septimus took most of it away and the doctor has left a potion if I need it. I will be fine." She could not fully subdue a yawn.

"Rest, Olympia." He leaned forward and brushed a kiss over her mouth. "That is the best cure. I will go now and get Agatha settled but I shall be back to see you on the morrow. Oh, one thing you might be interested in," he said as he stood up. "According to your aunt Antigone, Orion is Giles's father."

"How wonderful. She did not say but she was more interested in how I was faring so that she could tell Ilar. Orion will be good to the boy. I suspect he will take over the care of all of them as they are a family in many ways and should not be separated. Orion is wise enough to see that."

"Good. I wondered about that. Rest, love. I will see you again soon."

Olympia watched the door shut behind him and sighed. There was no doubting his deep concern for her but she had hoped for more. She almost smiled for in her few moments of clear thought as her wound had been tended to, she had imagined him having seen where his heart lay the moment he realized she was wounded. She had envisioned a tender moment with words of undying love as he came to her bedside to see that she would indeed survive. Olympia would never have imagined she would be prone to such girlish flights of fancy.

But it had been no more than a silly dream, she mused, and closed her eyes. Even if Brant had declared his undying love, she would have hesitated to fully accept it. He did not see it but a ghost lived in his heart. Faith was there even though she knew the woman did not want to be. He still carried the guilt of what had happened to her. Now he added the guilt of not having seen what his mother truly was, of not protecting Agatha enough, and, now, not protecting her enough. It was not something she could rid him of. He had to do it himself.

The question was, should she accept any declaration of love from him, stay at his side, and hope he found the strength to shed the guilt he did not have any reason to cling to? It was a poison in many ways but he was the only one who could rid his heart of it. Too tired to decide, and knowing it was all speculation since he had not declared any sort of love for her, Olympia decided to just deal with getting well and strong again.

Brant took Agatha back to the town house. He knew they could not stay there for long. The memories of all that had happened there were still too strong. Yet, he had to stay in town until he knew Olympia was well.

As he and Agatha settled in the small salon to share some tea and food, he looked at her but saw no sign that she was suffering in any way. "How fare you, Aggie?"

"I will be fine, Brant. It was frightening when Minden tried to steal me away. It also hurt to know my mother gave her full approval for it to happen. Yet, that pain was fleeting. I learned long ago that she has never really cared for any of us." Agatha sighed. "That was hard for I was still very much a child and eager to please my mother. It eventually became evident that there was nothing I could do, nothing any of us could do, to please her unless we could advance her place in society or fill her purse. An ugly truth but one I accepted."

"I should have been here, should never have left you in her grasp."

"Brant, you seem very fond of shouldering guilt for things you could not have changed. She would do what she would do no matter where you were, she would just have done it differently. And, I lived with her more than you did, yet even I did not truly grasp how evil she was. That is a shock it will take time to overcome."

"I think you pardon me too quickly. I was sunk in my own little world, paying no heed to anything but what I wanted. Too often I was sunk in drink as well and more useless to everyone who needed me than I care to think on."

Agatha smiled at him and patted his hand. "You were grieving. I think you were also trying very hard not to believe that our mother knew exactly what would happen to Faith when she sold the poor girl to that house. I think she did but it took this latest trouble for me to accept that."

"You know about Faith?"

"Oh, yes. Mother liked to keep her secrets but she was too arrogant, and too dismissive of me, to do it well. I know far, far more than she would have ever allowed if she had been paying attention."

Brant forgot all his guilt for a moment. "Just what do you know, Aggie? Enough for me to see to some punishment for those who worked with her or knew what she was doing? Those who may have helped her hide her crimes?"

Agatha smiled even more. "Oh, yes. I know a great deal. Where would you like me to start?"

Brant soon discovered that his little sister was not

making an idle boast. He did not wish to think on how young she must have been when she had begun to spy on their mother. The things she had learned about were not ones any young girl should have ever even heard about. Yet, he could not completely still his excitement as she spoke, telling him names, informing him of where he could find the papers to back up any accusations he made, and even how much money his mother had gathered and where it was.

"My God, Agatha, why did you not tell us this before?"

"You would never have been able to get to it. That much she was careful about. She also did not trust you and, for all her lack of care, she did respect your brain and your strength enough to be wary about you, to be on her guard." Agatha shrugged. "I was nothing she ever saw as a threat."

"More fool her," he muttered and ran a hand through his hair. "It will take some time for me to sort this all out. Are you uncomfortable in this house now?"

"No, it is just a house. True, it carries her mark but she did have good taste. It will be awhile before the chill of her presence leaves, but if we must stay here for a while, do not fret that it will disturb greatly."

"Good, for I have a need to bring some of these men to justice."

"And to see Olympia, I suspect." She laughed when Brant blushed a little. "She is a very good woman. Strong and clever, but with a very big heart."

"I am not good enough for her."

"Nonsense. You are more than good enough for her especially if you love her as I think you do."

"I failed her as I have failed too many others." He started in surprise when she gave him a light slap on the cheek.

"You need to rid yourself of that guilt." She stood up and brushed down her skirts. "It is useless, un-earned, and it will be a poison to whatever you might wish to build with Olympia. Do you love her?"

"Yes."

"And you believe she loves you?"

"I feel that she does." He was not about to explain why he felt that way since it involved matters much too personal to share with a girl of sixteen.

"Then you must go to her with a clean heart and mind."

"What the devil does that mean?" he asked himself after Agatha walked away.

He sighed and realized he was utterly exhausted. Tomorrow would be soon enough to deal with this treasure of information his sister had handed him. He might even have to bring Dobson back into the mess his mother had made.

As he made his way to his bedchamber, he decided he would fix his mind on making some of his mother's allies pay for their crimes. He would visit Olympia as often as he could as well. Once she was well enough, he would declare himself to her. As for all the rest, the talk of the guilt he carried and clearing his heart? There was time enough in the future to deal with that once he figured out how to do so.

Chapter 19

"Careful with that trunk, Pawl. I have some breakable things in there."

Brant slid in past Pawl and stood in the front hall of the Warren looking around. Trunks and boxes filled it and his heart sank. Olympia was leaving. She had not said a word about that in the fortnight since she had been shot but he should have known she could not stay in London indefinitely. She had a son who was undoubtedly eager to see her, if only to see with his own eyes that she was well again.

"Olympia?" he called, and smiled when she turned from making sure a trunk was securely closed to look at him. "You did not tell me you were leaving."

"I hinted at it many times, Brant," she said as she took him by the hand and led him into the parlor. "Ilar has been very patient but I have been gone from home for far longer than either of us had anticipated."

"I know." He waited until she took a seat on the settee and sat down beside her. She was looking very healthy again and his body tightened when he thought of all the ways he wished to take advantage of her good health. "I had just thought we would have a day or two to enjoy your recovery before you left."

Olympia knew that the heat his words stirred in her body was coloring her cheeks so she turned her attention to pouring them both a small glass of wine. She would like nothing more than to slip upstairs with him. It had surprised her how much she ached for his touch even though she knew she loved him. Having had nothing to do with men, never feeling any great passion or even mild desire, she had never thought it would be something that could plague her night and day. It did though, and it plagued her dreams as well.

For a moment she faltered in her decision to leave but then straightened her backbone and shored up her determination. This was the best way to handle this matter. He was the man she wanted and she doubted she would ever want another but he needed to heal himself. She wanted him whole and loving her and he was not here yet. Even Artemis, before he had left for home, had told her that the sorrow in Brant, the heavy, dark guilt, had actually grown, not lessened. She was not the one who could clean him of that darkness no matter how much she loved him.

Brant put his arm around her and tugged her close after she had finished filling the glasses. "I need to speak to you of something."

"You have finished seeing to the punishment of all those who shared your mother's guilt?" Despite her best intentions, she leaned into his hold, savoring the heat and strength of him.

"Nearly done. No, I meant I wished to speak about us."

This was not the way he had planned to do this, he thought a little crossly. Brant had planned a romantic dinner, lovemaking, and soft words of love followed by his proposal. Sitting in the parlor while the sounds of people packing echoed through the door was not romantic. There was no time to waste, however. He could not take the time to go to Myrtledowns and court her for several weeks yet but he did not want her to leave without knowing how he felt.

"Us?" Olympia said and met his gaze. "What of us, Brant? You have never really indicated that there would be an us after Agatha was safe."

"No? I became your lover." He grimaced when she just cocked one brow at him. "Fine. That may not have been the greatest of clues, all things considered. Curse it, Olympia, I love you."

She was both thrilled and amused. "Curse it, Brant, I love you, too."

"You do?"

"Aye, I do."

"Then you will marry me."

"Nay."

He sat back, more shocked than hurt for he was sure she had just confessed to loving him. "You do not wish to have a husband, is that it?" He knew she was a very strong, independent woman but he had never considered the possibility that she would not want to marry.

"I want a husband if that husband is you." She

reached up to stroke his cheek with her hand. "I said I love you and I do not toss those words about lightly as some do. I love you to the depths of my soul."

She allowed him to silence her with a kiss, sinking into his embrace and soaking up all the pleasure she could from his kiss. Once he ended it, however, she moved out of his arms and stood up. A little uneasy about what she had to say next, she picked up her glass of wine and downed it all. Carefully placing the glass back on the table, she looked at him, not surprised to find him scowling at her in anger and confusion.

"I love you. Never doubt that. I will not marry you though. Not yet. You see, I will not tie my life and my heart to a man who carries around a ghost."

"A ghost?"

"Faith's ghost or rather the grief and guilt over her death that you have never let go of. And, oh, how you have added to that load in the past few weeks. You carry so much that it is as if you have a whole other person inside you, one bent beneath the weight of it all."

"Olympia . . ." He stopped talking when she touched her fingers to his mouth.

"Listen to me. I will love you forever but I want the whole man. I will not share him with the ghost of another woman or that living, breathing guilt that lives deep in your heart. Clean your heart, Brant. Shed that hair shirt you wear like some armor. Say good-bye to Faith and beg her forgiveness if that gives you ease, although I have never thought you had much to be forgiven for. Come to me when you are ready, when there is not such a weight on your heart, and I will marry you without hesitation."

He watched her walk out of the room, unable to think of a thing to say to stop her. He was still sitting there when he heard the carriages pull away. Brant drank his wine, stood up, and left the house. For a moment he just stood on the side of the road staring blindly in the direction she had gone.

"I hope you are not thinking to take my carriage again," said Orion as he stepped up to Brant's side.

"It would do no good to chase her down," Brant said. "She will not marry me."

"Truly? I am surprised."

"She said I have to come to her with a clean heart." Brant could feel himself start to get angry.

"Ah, of course."

He glared at Orion. "Of course? Of course? What docs that mean? A clean heart? Did I not just offer it to her? Is that not enough to show it is hers? She speaks of ghosts and guilt and all and then leaves."

"Did she refuse your marriage proposal completely or only for now?"

"Only for now. I am to clean my heart. Sister told me the same and damned if I know what they are talking about."

"The past, m'lord. You are clinging to the past. As for guilt? Oh, yes, you carry a load that should have broken you by now. I have heard all about what you have endured and what your mother was. Time you fully accept that, with an enemy like that, sometimes one can only accept that nothing could have been changed. And sometimes, ugly as it is, Fate herself has a part. Your mother is at fault for all you suffered. No one else. That is what you have to accept.

Cast aside the I-could-have, I-might-have, I-should-have thoughts and accept that it happened."

"There are a lot of I-could-haves."

"And there always are and always will be. But they are just guilt's voice. It happened. Simple as that. It happened and you have done all you could to fix it. If it requires you to bleed yourself dry reliving every single thing you feel guilty about, do it. You will be the better for it for you will see that you weigh yourself down with unearned guilt. Then you can go and get your Olympia."

Brant watched the man cross the street and climb into his carriage. Inside were Olympia's street boys and he returned their waves. Brant wondered if Orion was nursing a few I-could-haves concerning how Giles had been treated. Then he realized the man probably was, but had the sense to shed them as useless.

"Clean my heart," he muttered as he told his driver to take him home and climbed into his carriage. He had a faint idea of what needed to be done now but was not sure how successful he would be. If it was the only way to make Olympia legally his, however, he would work until he got it right. And then he would go and get her and she had better have meant it when she said she would marry him without hesitation for he would allow her none.

"Are you certain that was the right thing to do?" asked Enid as the carriage left the city and headed toward Myrtledowns.

Olympia sighed and rested her head back against

the squabs. "Yes. It is. I thought it over and over and over. I know he loves me and that, by the way, is the most marvelous of feelings." She smiled when Enid nodded. "But he is allowing guilt over so much to eat at him, day after day, and that will be a slow poison to whatever we might be able to share. He has to shed it."

"I suppose you are right. In a way, it would be like having the ghost of some other woman in your bed. He is still tied to his Faith because of guilt."

"Exactly. She will always be in his heart. I know that. I can accept that. But, because he will not accept that he did no wrong there, that he could not know that a vicar, her father and a highly respected man, would lie to him, he holds himself responsible for her death. That keeps her chained in his heart and makes it hard for me, for Ilar, for any children he and I could be blessed with, to find our place.

"And because the guilt appears to come from his inability to protect everyone close to him all the time and from everything," she nodded in agreement with Enid's scornful noise, "he could act in ways that slowly strangled the love I feel for him."

"Ah, of course." Enid nodded. "For you to tie yourself to a man who will hunch over you, watching your every move, and perhaps restricting you in any way, would be pure poison to what you feel for him. He would slowly squeeze the love, and life, right out of you."

"Better a little pain now than a lot later, and pain that could extend to whatever children we share. I can but pray that he knows what needs to be done, does it, and comes after me."

"How long will you give him to come after you?"

"Are you insinuating that I will do something if he does not?"

"No, I know you will do something. So—how long does he have?"

"Two months and then I will hunt him down."

Brant looked around his home at Fieldgate and suddenly had a bad feeling. He had thought about it before but forgotten the hard work he had done in the past three weeks consuming all his energy and thought. It had not been easy to bring to justice the ones who had shared and profited from his mother's crimes but he had done it. Now he carefully studied his house and knew that every place in it would carry some memory of his debauched ways. He had not done anything to anyone in the master suite or the mistress's bedchamber but there was hardly any other place Olympia could touch that would not give her some vision of the past he really did not want her to see. It was bad enough that she knew what he had been up to for the last few years.

He marched off to his library and quickly penned a note to Argus. The man knew what Brant had been doing for the last few years as well so would not be surprised by the request. Brant just prayed that, amongst all those gifted Wherlockes and Vaughns, there was someone who knew how to dim or vanquish all those little memories staining the beds, walls, and elsewhere. When he brought Olympia here, and he would, he wanted the house to be so clean she could touch everything. Any memories that would linger in the air or on the furniture would be ones that he and she made.

Once he sent off the message, he went to work on hiring new staff. He and Agatha could be served just fine with the ones that had been left after he had cleared out all his mother's spies and allies but he would be adding more to the household soon. His determination to ready his house for the bride he meant to have consumed his attention well into the evening. It was not until he was alone, sitting in his neglected garden sipping some cool cider, that he finally turned his mind to the other thing he had to accomplish, cleaning his heart.

It hurt, almost more than he cared to endure, but he did as Orion suggested. He relived it all from the moment he had found poor Faith's body to Olympia being shot. Every painful, gut-wrenching moment. He let all the what-ifs parade through his mind and did his best to look at them with only logic, no emotion. It was not until he felt a small hand on his shoulder and was handed a delicate, lace-trimmed handkerchief that he realized he was weeping.

"Sorry," he muttered as he wiped the tears from his cheeks.

Agatha sat down next to him. "Does Olympia not love you?"

"Oh, yes, she does. She said so many times."

"Then what is breaking your heart?"

"I did as that rogue Orion told me to do. I have just relived all that went wrong, all the things that hurt people I cared for such as you. It was not easy."

She slid her arm through his and rested her head

against his shoulder. "I can but imagine. Did it work?"

Brant took a long moment to look inside of himself. His heart ached but also felt lighter. He could even think of Faith and feel no more than a slight twinge of regret, not the gut-clenching grief and guilt that had always had him reaching for a bottle or a woman before. He accepted, he realized. He accepted it all. There was no sudden torrent of possibilities where he might have changed fate raining through his mind anymore. The only thing he still felt guilt over, and it was a very slight one, was when Olympia had been shot. He suspected that was still too fresh in his mind to be properly accepted.

"Yes, it did. I shall have to thank the man. Perhaps next time we need a carriage, I will try to make certain we do not steal his." He smiled when she giggled.

"I am glad it worked. I suspect you feel a great deal better as well."

"That I do. Much lighter of heart. I did not understand at first but now I do. I had to let it go."

Agatha kissed his cheek. "Yes, you did. And Faith?"

He rested his cheek against her hair and sighed. "And Faith. I need to say good-bye to her. I thought I had but I had not. Not completely. I clung to her as the symbol of all the failings I felt I had."

"You are not perfect, dearest brother, but you are no failure. You just tripped a little."

He sat up and grinned at her. "A very delicate and pleasant way to say what I did. We can just ignore the part where, in tripping just a little, I fell flat on my face." He laughed along with her and then stood, helping her to her feet. "I am to bed and you should be making your way to bed as well. I need to go somewhere in the morning. I may be gone for a while."

"To Olympia's?"

"Not yet. I need my house cleansed and I need to say that good-bye to Faith. I suspect she has been waiting for it for a long time."

The graveyard beside the church was beautiful. The vicar's son took excellent care of it. Brant was pleased and knew that, very soon, one of the sons would replace the father and the last of the ones who had wronged Faith would be gone. Perhaps, he mused as he walked up to Faith's grave, Peter, who cared so well for the graveyard, would like to become his gardener.

He knelt on the grass and placed the bouquet of flowers he had brought up against the headstone. Poor Faith. She had been so young, so innocent. He could see her so easily at times, but those times grew less and less. She had been his first taste of love but he had realized on the ride here that she had not really been the love that touched his soul; not like Olympia did.

Brant had no doubt that he and Faith could have been happy together, raised a family and gone along quite smoothly, with him never realizing that something was missing. Simply being without Olympia for almost a month was as if someone had ripped out a piece of his heart. She would never be a sweet, obedient bride as Faith would have been, nor one who would always hide behind her man. Olympia was a woman a man had at his side, and his back if he needed it.

"Ah, Faith, you should have had many more years than were granted you. You did not deserve the betrayal your father dealt you, or the death you suffered. I also wronged you in the way I believed you would betray me with another man and for that I ask your forgiveness. It was like burr under my saddle for years but I have removed it. Yes, perhaps I should have asked a question or two. Yes, perhaps I should have tried to hunt you down and demand the reasons for why you left me as I would have soon seen that something was wrong. But your father was a vicar and I believed him as I now see most everyone else would have. So, I ask your forgiveness for my lapse in trust.

"I will also ask your forgiveness for not letting you go. I thought I had and Penelope said you had left, but I still clung to you. I fed my guilt with your memory. I do not know if that troubled your rest at all, but now I do set you free. Utterly. Completely. Find that rest you deserve, love."

With his finger, he lightly traced her name etched in the headstone. "I will say that, if we had wed, we would have been happy. I know it. I did love you. I would have been a faithful husband and we would have had beautiful children. Yet, I have discovered that there are many depths to love. I have a new love now and her name is Olympia. She is in my heart so deeply that I feel as if a part is missing when she is not by my side. I think, although you and she are very different, that you would approve. I would like to think of you smiling down on us, pleased that we have found each other."

"I suspect she is, m'lord."

Brant stood up and brushed off his pants before shaking Peter's hand. Faith's brother had grown and fully become the man he had seen when he had brought Faith's body home that day. The young man had kept a very watchful eye on his father to be certain the man did no more harm to his own children. It would not be long before the old man died for he had drunk himself nearly to death. It would not take many more drinks to finish the job. Brant would have removed him as vicar but he had not wanted Faith's name tainted by anything that might have emerged during such a removal.

"Do you really?" he asked as they both looked down at the grave.

"Yes, that was our Faith. Kind and generous. This was a waste. It is something none of the rest of us have ever forgiven him for no matter how the good book speaks of forgiving. It is not possible."

Brant patted the man on the shoulder. "I was recently told to cleanse my heart. I carried a lot of guilt."

"For this? This was not your fault."

"No, it was not. As were a lot of other things not my fault. It is also not yours. I think perhaps you may suffer a bit of what I did."

"And just how did you clean your heart, m'lord?"

"I relived it all, all that caused me to feel guilty, and it was hell to do so, but it works. It is much akin to working a splinter out only you work it out of your heart and not your foot."

"I shall give that a try then, m'lord, for it would be good to have a clean heart again. My father will die soon, within the week, I believe."

"Do you want to take over his place as vicar?"

"No, but my brother does. He may be too young, being barely twenty, but if there was a way to hold the place open for him . . ."

"See how the people in your congregation feel, Peter. They will let you know if they think your brother needs a bit more aging. Depending upon what they say, we will decide what to do. But you do not wish the post."

"I am willing to hold it for him until he is old enough but, no, I do not want to be a vicar. I do not deal as well with people as one must to be a good one." He looked around the graveyard. "This is what I like. The open. Working with the earth to bring out the beauty of it."

Brant grinned. "Enough to become the head gardener at Fieldgate? I know it is not the best position to offer a vicar's son."

"As soon as we know whether I must stay here a while longer or not, I will be at your door. I mean, yes, thank you, m'lord. If naught else, I can use your gardens to train myself for, perhaps something a little grander. But, yes, I would love to be your gardener."

"Head gardener."

Peter nodded and then excused himself. Brant could tell by the way the young man was racing toward the vicarage that he had the need to tell someone the good news. It was not the best position for the son of a vicar but Brant was pleased that Peter would take it, at least for a while. He had the touch, he thought as he looked around. Perhaps he would also see that the young man made the acquaintance of some of the ones now famous for the design of gardens at many a country house.

He bent and kissed the top of the headstone. "Rest in peace, my love. You deserve it."

By the time Brant got back to Fieldgate the next day, he found his home a little crowded with what appeared to be nearly a dozen women. Agatha quickly dragged the eldest of the group over to him. It took but one look for Brant to know he had a large crowd of Wherlockes in his house. He prayed they were the answer to his letter to Argus.

"This is Lady Honey Vaughn," said Agatha, who rapidly introduced the others so quickly, Brant hoped he was never pressed to recall their names. "They say Argus sent them to clean the house. I am not sure what that means except to know it does not include any use of mops or brooms."

Lady Vaughn looked up at him from her diminutive height and blinked her big brown eyes. "We have been given some very nice rooms, fed well, and will begin work soon. This is a very dirty place, m'lord," she added with a scowl that would have done any scolding mother proud.

"I know, m'lady, which is why I am in such great need of your skills as well as those of your companions."

"It is also why Argus said I should bring as many of my like as I could find. I scoffed at his insistence that I would need a small army, but I see now that he was right. And, you are right. Our Olympia could never have been happy in this place. The very fact that you asked for us to come here before she did almost excuses the way you have so sullied the energy in this place."

Brant murmured his apology and then watched as Lady Honey Vaughn led her small army up the stairs, announcing loudly that they would start in the attic. When a petite blonde said she did not see what a man could get up to up there, Lady Honey informed her that this particular man seemed to have gotten up to something everywhere else so why not up there. Brant could feel himself blushing but fought his embarrassment, even when he glanced at Agatha to find her trying vainly to smother her giggles.

"Well, at least that shall be done soon," he said and started toward his library.

Agatha followed. "It is probably best that you were not here when they first arrived. Lady Vaughn was quite, er, vocal. It took awhile for her to accept the, um, immensity of the work before her."

When Agatha flopped down in a chair near the fireplace and began to peel with laughter, his embarrassment began to ease. That did not mean he would not stop wanting to hit Argus over the head with something hard and heavy for his remarks about how an army would be needed. He had sent what Brant had asked him to and for that he would be eternally grateful.

"She is such a powerful little lady," said Agatha as she finally stopped laughing.

"She did seem to be. I do not suppose they told you how they would do it."

"They did but I am not sure I really understood. There will be some smells although she assured me they will not be unpleasant ones. Something about needing a little smoke and incense and herbs." Agatha shrugged. "She was talking so fast as she marched through the house with all the other ladies trailing after her, that I did not really think I could ask her questions."

"She did seem to be a woman who would not like to be interrupted."

Brant sat down at his desk and looked around. He was anxious for them to clean this room for he could still see Olympia's face when she had leaned against the wall by the fireplace. He would like to think that was the only memory that needed clearing away. Then again, with the amount of drink he had consumed at times, he could not claim to be certain about much of anything he had done and where he had done it.

"No. She did think that they would need two, mayhap three days to do it properly."

"Then I shall make my plans accordingly."

"And what might those plans be?" she asked but was grinning at him.

"To go and collect my bride of course. First I shall need a special license for she said, once my heart was clean, she would marry me without hesitation and I mean to make certain she does."

Chapter 20

Olympia sighed as she stared out the window of her bedchamber. It overlooked the drive up to the house, a drive she had spent far too many hours staring at over the last month. She had thought waiting two months for him to come to her would be easy but she was now struggling to hold to it. It was taking more and more of an effort to stay put and wait with each day, each hour, that passed. She missed him.

"Do you wish to go for a walk in the gardens, Mama?"

She turned and smiled at her son. "That would be lovely. Thank you." She walked up next to him and allowed him to hook his arm through hers. "I was just thinking that it was a lovely day." She frowned at him when he made a noise that was heavy with disbelief and mockery. "That was rude."

"Aye, but a lie deserves a little rudeness."

She sighed. At times she forgot what her son's gifts were. He could undoubtedly sense her unhappiness, probably even her disappointment when yet another day passed and there was no sign of Brant. It was difficult to keep any secrets from him. There was one, however, that she doubted he could sense, and it was the one that might well push her to go after Brant before that two months was over. Ilar did not have the gift that could tell him whether or not she was with child.

"Yes, it was a little lie, but mostly to save face. No woman likes to be caught out sighing with longing for a man. It is embarrassing."

"Why? You love him."

"I do but that whole sighing and longing business is such a misery. I thought myself stronger than that."

"Oh, you are. You still eat well."

"Perhaps that is simply because I did not realize that sighing and longing after a man also required a touch of decorative starvation." She smiled when he laughed.

"We are being followed you know."

Olympia glanced back to see Lurc and Dinner walking behind them. "I sometimes think that they are a little afraid that they will be left behind to fend for themselves again."

"I have no doubt that that is exactly what it is." Ilar peeked behind them and then grinned at her. "I also think that Lure believes you are his mother even though he gets his dinner from Dinner." He giggled at his own joke.

"Very amusing," she drawled but there was a hint of laughter in her tone. "I believe they also somehow know we are going into the garden and wish to come along."

"True. They do not like to go out unless someone

goes out with them. Life must have been very hard for them to be so averse to going outside. Dinner shall have to be put in the shed soon, though. I think she will come into heat in about a fortnight."

Ilar knew too much about animals and their ways for her to question him. His love and understanding of them far outreached hers. It was one reason he never really argued about his long stay in the country. She knew he would like to see the city but also knew he had no inclination to live there.

She looked around the well-tended garden and suddenly thought of the one at Fieldgate. "I wonder if Brant has been able to clean up his gardens. They looked as if, once tended, they would be beautiful."

"Did you wish to be the one to hire his staff?"

"No, although I might come to wish I had some say if I ever go to live there."

"Not if, Mother. When."

"You sound very certain of that."

"I am."

"Have you had some, well, feeling about it?" She really hoped he did not have a touch of foresight as well for he had enough to deal with as it was.

"No. But I have very good hearing and a carriage has just driven up to the door."

Her heart skipped with both hope and fear. "It might not be him."

"True, the carriage sound did not tell me so, but his voice calling for someone to tend the horses did."

She stopped and stared at him. "I did not hear that."

"You were thinking about his gardens and, as I

said, I have very good hearing. I suspect he will join us here soon. Shall I be gooseberry?"

"Only if you wish your ears boxed."

Ilar laughed with the confidence of a child who had never been struck. "I will go and visit with Agatha then."

"You heard her, too?"

"I did. *Very* good hearing."

Olympia watched her son leave, the two cats following him although Lure kept looking back as if he worried that she would stay and he would have no one to curl up with on the bed. Of course, if Brant was here for the reasons she prayed he was, Lure was going to find it a little too crowded in the bed from now on. She doubted Brant would want to share her with a cat.

The moment he stepped into the garden her heart began to race. Olympia told herself not to be silly, but that did not help. She needed him, needed him to belong wholly to her. As she watched him walk toward her, the hope that he was hers and only hers grew. There was a difference in his step, an ease that had not been there before.

Before she could even say hello, he pulled her into his arms and kissed her. Olympia sank into his embrace, as hungry for him as he was for her. When he broke off the kiss, he did not release her and she stared up into those beautiful eyes of his, eyes made all the more beautiful by the absence of shadows.

"You did it," she whispered, pleased for him and worried about what it meant for her, for the future she prayed he was going to offer her again.

"I did." He took her by the hand and led her to a

bench, slipping his arm around her shoulders when they sat down. "I admit, I thought you were all talking nonsense. It made no sense to me. Clean my heart. What the devil did that mean, I kept asking. But then Orion gave me a little advice. I did what he suggested and it worked."

"What did he suggest?"

"Relive it all. Look at it all and see that my guilt is misplaced. Toss away all the what-ifs for they are useless. It hurt like hell, to be blunt. But it worked. And then, I went to say a true and final farewell to Faith." He smiled when she took his hand in hers and kissed the back of it.

"I understand that you loved her. I can accept that. Do not think you must never speak her name or the like."

"I know. I did love her and I think we would have had a very good life together, but I did not love her as I do you. She was in my heart and will always hold a little corner of it for she was my first taste of love, but you are in my heart and soul. You are my perfect match. I would have been a good husband to Faith but I realized that life would not have been all it should have been if I had married her for she was so sweet, so ready to do whatever I said or wanted." He started to smile as Olympia began to frown at him, and then kissed the tip of her nose. "You will make me live, Olympia. You will not allow me to settle. Life will be full and fun and vigorous with you. That is what I want. I want that life as much as I want to take my next breath. So, Lady Olympia Wherlocke, Baroness of Myrtledowns, will you marry me now?"

"Oh, yes."

Instead of the kiss she expected, Olympia found her finger weighted down with a beautiful sapphire ring and Brant towing her back into the house. "What are you doing?"

"Taking you to be married. You said you would marry me without hesitation and I mean to hold you to that. I also mean to make love to you until you cannot remember your own name and I will not do that here, in your son's house, unless we are married."

She was given barely enough time to fetch a pretty bonnet before he had her, her son, Agatha, Aunt Antigone, and Enid in the carriage with Pawl sitting up beside the driver. As they pulled out she glanced out the window to see her cousin Tessa and her whole family in their carriage waiting to pull in behind them. She looked at Brant.

"You were very confident."

"Hopeful," he said. "Very hopeful."

The vicar was waiting for them and Olympia realized that she did not care if she had a fancy wedding. She was surrounded by people who cared about her, standing beside the man she loved more than life, and about to start on that future she had been dreaming about. It was, she decided, the perfect wedding. All she missed, but only briefly, was her brother to give her away. She just hoped Argus would not be too angry about missing that chance.

It was barely dark out when Brant pulled her free of her celebrating family and took her up to her bedchamber. She had been unable to fully hide her blushes for she knew they were all aware of what she was about to do and her confidence had wavered for just a moment. Reminding herself that she was now a legally married woman and Brant was her husband eased that surge of embarrassment.

"I have missed you," he whispered as he began to undo her gown. "We did not share a bed often, and I always had to creep away before anyone could catch us together, yet I found my bed very empty at night."

"As did I," she admitted as she helped him out of his coat and began to undo his waistcoat. "I also missed you in the morning, missed seeing you across the table."

"It pleases me that I was not alone in that."

And then talk ceased as they both worked as quickly as possible to shed their clothes. Olympia knew the need she had to be flesh to flesh with him was shared. The moment the last of their clothing hit the floor he picked her up and placed her in bed. They both trembled faintly when their bodies finally touched, warm skin against warm skin.

"I have missed this as well," he said as he kissed her throat, moving his hands over her body as if to renew his acquaintance with every curve and hollow.

"It may be wrong for a woman to do so, but so did I," she whispered.

"Not wrong when it is me you missed."

"Only you."

"And only you for me, Olympia. Believe me. I know how many of our class act after marriage, but I will not. I will be faithful. I want no other."

"Even when this fire between us dims?"

"Even then."

And then he kissed her and Olympia gave herself

over to the passion they shared. His every touch and kiss made the desire she felt for him grow until she clutched at him like a starving child clutched at a crust of bread. Olympia knew she would never need another, that no other could give her this.

She began to caress him wherever she could, delighting in the warmth of his skin, the strength she could feel beneath it. As he licked and nibbled at her breasts she slid her hand down and curled her fingers around his erection. The hard, silken feel of him in her hand, the way he groaned against her skin at her touch, only heightened her desire until she was almost squirming in her need to feel him inside her. She could not silence her mew of disappointment when he pulled her hand away but then purred with delight when he began to kiss his way down her body.

Olympia closed her eyes and arched into his kiss when he began to make love to her with his mouth. Every stroke of his tongue had her shaking with need, the ache inside of her growing stronger until her belly tightened to a point that was an odd mix of pleasure and pain. She grasped him by his upper arms and tugged on him, trying to pull him back into her arms.

"Now, Brant," she gasped even as her starving body arched up in demand for more of his intimate kiss. "I want you inside me. I want to be one again."

Brant groaned, unable to resist that plea. He kissed his way back up her body, lifted her legs until she wrapped them around his waist, and joined their bodies in one hard thrust. For a moment he remained still, savoring the tight heat of her and the fact that they were joined, that they were again one as she had asked. It was a joy to be with her in this way again, a joy increased by the knowledge that he could savor it whenever he wanted for the rest of his life.

"Brant," Olympia said, trying to prompt him to move with her legs. "I need . . ."

"I know," he said, and kissed her as he began to move his body.

It was not long before he could no longer move slowly, with measured strokes they could both savor. Need filled him until he could barely think straight but as he began to move with a greater greed, she met his every stroke with the same greed. He clung to the shreds of his control until he felt her body clench around his, heard her call his name as her pleasure crested, and then he sought his own.

Not sure how long he had been sprawled over Olympia's limp form, Brant moved to the side and looked down at her. He grinned. She looked like a well-pleasured woman and he was man enough to find that extremely satisfying. When she slowly opened one eye to look at him, he kissed the tip of her nose.

"You are looking very cocky, my good husband," she murmured.

"And you are looking very satisfied. My male vanity was pleased by that."

She laughed. "So, now we are wed."

"Yes, now we are wed. Marriage duly consummated."

"Your duly was very well done, if I may say so."

"You may. Are you about to start worrying about practical things?"

"I fear I might be." She hummed softly with a lazy pleasure when he began to stroke her stomach. "I do have a baron for a son when all is said and done."

"Your aunt says she is more than happy to care for the house, with Ilar coming to learn of the running of the place as he pleases. I have the feeling your cousin Tessa and her family are considering moving into the dower house so that they can help her."

Olympia blinked. "And thus all is settled. Am I the only one who has not been making arrangements as I waited for you?"

He laughed and began to nibble her ear. "Did you doubt that I would come for you?"

"Occasionally, yes. I will admit that I also occasionally thought I ought to do something in preparation for the future I was planning on but then got the oddest ideas about how that might curse it." She grinned when he laughed again.

"We are blessed, my love. Truly blessed. And it is not odd that you had doubts. I knew you, knew you were ready to begin our new life together, and knew that I was the one who was holding it up. Considering what I needed to fix, you need not feel guilty about the occasional doubt."

What she had intended to reply to that was quickly lost as he began to make love to her again. Olympia allowed him his way for a little while and then had her own way. She pushed him onto his back and began to kiss her way down his body, renewing her acquaintance with the smooth, hard strength of him. The taste of him, even the scent of his arousal only added to her desire to drive him wild with need for her. She made love to him with her mouth, taking him deep inside and savoring his somewhat incoherent words of encouragement.

Brant fought to hang on to his control, to keep his desire in check as Olympia drove him insane with her mouth. He knew he was within a heartbeat of losing the last of that control when she gently used her teeth on him and he grabbed her under her arms, pulling her back up his body. The slide of her soft flesh against his made him groan, and he quickly centered over his groin.

"Take me inside, love."

The smile she gave him as she slowly took him into her body had him nearly bellowing with delight. And then she began to ride him. Before he lost the last of his senses, he watched her, with her head thrown back, her breasts bouncing, and pleasure clear to read on her face and thought it the most beautiful sight he had ever seen. And then he fell into the abyss, hearing her cry out his name and feeling her joining him in that fall even as he sank beneath the waves of desire only she could toss him into.

A nudge woke Olympia and she lifted her head from Brant's shoulder, touching her mouth to make certain she had not gracelessly drooled all over him. "What?"

"Fieldgate," he answered, smiling as she fussed with her hair and struggled to wake up. They had spent two days and nights at Myrtledowns and most of it making love anywhere they could find a spot alone and for most of the night when they went to bed. It was no wonder she was tired.

Olympia looked out the window as they pulled up in front of the doors. It was a lovely house and she knew she would like living in it. There was only one thing she had tried very hard not to think about much. Her gift might prove a veritable curse considering how her loving husband had behaved before she had dragged him away from the house. As he helped her out of the carriage and led her to the door, she swore she would not allow any visions, any knowledge of his past that she might inadvertently catch sight of, destroy what they had found together.

She stepped into the front hall and a very elegant young man in butler finery was right there to take her things. Olympia glanced back at Ilar who studied the new butler for a moment and then smiled as he too handed the man his things. She hoped all the new hires met with the same approval as this morning, her last doubt about whether or not she carried Brant's child had faded as she had emptied her belly into a bucket. It was only sheer luck that he had not been there to see it.

As they walked to the drawing room, she began to notice something different about the house. When she had been here before there almost had been an air of sadness to the place, and the hint of what Brant had been up to during his plunge into debauchery had been everywhere as well. It was gone. She sniffed the air, certain there was a scent that had not been there before and one she should recognize. It was not until they entered the drawing room that she knew something had changed, she was just not sure what.

Olympia looked at Brant and saw that he was tense despite his smile and casual conversation with Agatha and Ilar. He waved her toward a chair but there was such an odd look on his face that she was reluctant to sit in it. Cautiously, recalling what she had seen the last time she had touched something in his home, she sat down. Nothing.

Then it hit her. That was what she sensed was different about the house. There was nothing. No sadness. No anything. It was as if the house had been built just yesterday and nothing had ever happened in it yet.

"Brant, it is gone," she said, looking at her husband and watching him relax and smile. "How is it all gone? It is as if nothing has ever happened here."

"A clean slate," he said.

"Exactly but how is that possible?"

"I wrote to your brother and told him I needed the house cleaned of the stain of my actions of the past few years. He sent one Lady Honey Vaughn and a veritable army of other women and they cleaned my house."

It took her a moment to place Lady Honey Vaughn and then she stared at Brant. "You had all the energies cleansed. Everything."

"Everything. It took three days," he added and looked embarrassed by that.

"I am not surprised," she said and met his frown with a grin even as she stood up. She recalled how he had looked as he had asked her to sit in the chair and, even though she had sensed and seen nothing, she knew he had feared she would. "I would like that chair to be gone soon, however." She winked at him when he blushed. "I saw nothing, sensed nothing, except for your wariness as you asked me to sit in it."

"Understood." Brant went to the door, called for a footman, and immediately had the chair taken up into the attic. "Better?" he asked as he returned to her side.

"Just try to hide your expressions when I sit somewhere or you may find that you need to replace more than you had planned to."

She was pleased when he laughed. His past did not trouble her. Olympia understood the darkness he had been caught up in and understood the often unacceptable ways a man of his class tried to deal with emotional turmoil. It pleased her that he had cleaned his house just for her, but what pleased her even more was that he had so accepted her gift that he had thought of how coming here, where he had misbehaved so thoroughly, might affect her. Brant would not run away when their child revealed whatever gift he or she had. He accepted her family so fully she had to blink back tears. He would probably never fully understand how deeply important that was to anyone in her family.

"So, all is well?"

"All is well." She walked to the window and looked out at his gardens. A young man was there directing several workers. "You have a new gardener."

"That is Faith's brother Peter. He loves the work. As a vicar's son it might be a little lowly for him, but he leapt at the chance. Since the congregation is more than willing to accept his younger brother as their vicar once his father finishes dying, he did not wait a day past learning that to pack and come here to work."

"If he does a good job with your gardens, you might lose him when others ask him to come and make theirs as beautiful."

"Then he will go. I somehow doubt he will rush into that or do nothing but design others' gardens. He was too pleased to come here and now has a nice cottage of his own. I will not hold him back, however." He put his arm around her shoulders. "If it bothers you that one of Faith's family is here . . ."

"No, it does not. It is perfect. It is right that you be the one to help him achieve what he wants in life. And, I think I shall go out there and see what it is he is planning."

"Are you sure you want to do that work after such a long trip?"

Olympia waved a hand in his direction as she went out the door. "I need to make certain the garden is a perfect place for our child to get a little sun."

"What?" Brant had to shake his head but her words fell into the same order in his mind, and held the same meaning. "Olympia!" He heard her laughter peel from somewhere down the hall. "Damn woman," he muttered and hurried after her.

He took one step out the door and listened to Agatha and Ilar laughing. The sweet sound of Olympia's laughter still lingered in his mind. He realized it had been a very long time since such sounds had echoed off the walls of this house. His childhood was not filled with memories of a family playing together or laughing together. It had been an unsettling mix of cold anger and a complete lack of parenting. Even the nannies and tutors had been aloof. There had been no joy in the house, only sadness and a cold anger. Olympia said it was all gone, that it was as if the house was new.

Brant looked down to see Lure and Dinner waiting patiently for him to lead them into the garden. He could hear Ilar and Agatha amiably arguing over who would get which little cake just as all young people would do. His laughing wife had just told him they would soon have a child and was going out into the garden to make certain it would be perfect for their child. He suspected it would also be arranged to endure the presence of a vast array of rescued animals.

Suddenly he grinned, put his hands in his pockets, and strolled after his wife. The house was more than cleansed. It was alive now with the happiness of his family and it was perfect.